SWIMMING WITH SWANS

A NOVEL

Austen Publishing Co.

Copyright 2003 by Carla Diane Ellis

Library of Congress Catalogue TX 1-095-396

First Trade Paperback Printing September 2004 USA
ISBN NO. 0-9761316-0-9

AUSTEN PUBLISING COMPANY
P.O. BOX 153
GLENSIDE, PENNA. 19038

DEDICATED

To

EDMUND AND MAMIE ELLIS

My Beloved Father and Mother

ACKNOWLEDGEMENTS

I would like to thank my creator, for helping me to complete this project. I would also like to thank my earthly supporters for their love and confidence. My brother John Ellis, you believed in me first. Thank you for your encouragement and a listening ear! Carla Carter, your insightful feedback made this book a reality! Kalidah Williams, your faith in me and your editorial contributions meant so much. I'd like to thank my readers for taking the time to read this book, Sherry, Marva, Debbie, Dorothy, Ken, Carla, and Kalidah. Last, but not least, I would like to thank my two sons, Irvin Williams for his faith in me and his late night service calls, and Terrence Williams, for his encouragement, advice and belief in my commitment to see this project completed.

SWIMMING WITH SWANS

BY CARLA DIANE ELLIS

A NOVEL

AUSTEN PUBLISHING CO.

SWIMMING WITH SWANS

Swans mate for life

**Humans mate until they get
Too bored, too angry, too fat, too expensive, too
imperfect**

CHAPTER 1

"Hurry up, give me my stockings. I'm going to be late!" Marie, one of the three bridesmaids, rushes over to the dresser and returns with the white lace top stockings; placing them in Lori's hand. Lori rips the clear plastic wrapper open and removes her special stockings. She received them as a gift from her mother at her bridal shower. She points her toe as she slips the stocking over her foot and up her leg. She repeats the process as she struggles to her feet, pulling them over her ample thighs. Marie pulled Lori to the middle of the floor, then she and another bridesmaid pulled the crinoline slip over Lori's head. "Be careful of my hair. It has to be perfect," Lori shouts as they continue to pull the slip down over her body.

This scene is taking place in the northwestern section of Philadelphia, at the edge of the city. It is an area that was previously populated by whites, but in the last ten years most of the residents are African-American. It is an almost suburban middle class area, with stone and brick twin and single homes. They are in April's expansive bedroom suite. It is one of the larger rooms in the house, second only to the huge family room. April invited her sister's bridal party to dress at her home, so they wouldn't be cramped into Lori's apartment or her parent's smaller bedroom.

Leeanna Amos stands in the doorway of the room in a daze, unable to participate in the frenzy of activity surrounding her elder daughter. There had been times when she'd nervously doubted that she'd ever see this day. Lori was the independent type of woman, not likely to submit to a husband. She'd turned down several proposals over the years, and watched her younger sister and many of her friends marry and start families. Lori always asserted that she'd know when the right man came along. Wayne, a tall handsome, bright eyed man with a slim physique had stolen Lori's heart. His shaven head and chocolate skin illuminated his pearly white teeth, which were revealed when he flashed that irresistible smile. After dating him for a short period of time, she eliminated two other suitors; dating Wayne exclusively.

Wayne obviously was the right man for Lori. She anxiously anticipated his proposal. At the age of thirty-two, she wasted no time planning the wedding four months after becoming engaged.

Leeanna observed April competing for her sister's attention, while she places a sparkling white gold and diamond necklace around her neck. "Don't forget my garter," Lori said loud enough for everyone to hear, as she attempts to repair the damage to her curls at the top of her head. April inserts a diamond earring into one of her sister's ears, and then the other. April was so pleased that Lori asked her to be her matron of honor. She'd prayed for Lori to find a husband. Wayne was tall, dark, and handsome with a pleasant personality. He had a gift of gab which made him an excellent car salesman. April wasn't surprised when Lori announced their engagement.

April's husband was a groomsman, her daughter was the flower girl and her son was the ring bearer. After volunteering her home for the party's use, April decided to prepare breakfast for them. She and her husband Paul awakened early to cook bacon, sausage, hot cakes, grits, eggs, Danish, coffee, tea , and juice. Lori was so grateful; she thanked them over and over. April wanted this day to be special for her sister.

The bride refreshes her lipstick and steps back from the full length mirror to assess her appearance. I'll soon be Mrs. Wayne Jackson. I can't wait to see how handsome he looks. Wayne is the man I've waited my whole life for; he's the man of my dreams. I knew he was the man for me the first time we met. I felt nervous under his stare as we were being introduced at a friend's party. He asked for my telephone number, which he used the very next day to invite me to dinner and a movie. That was the night I fell in love with him

We have always had chemistry between us, she thought.

The big white gown hangs on the door of the closet in all its glory. At last, Lori thought as she admired the beautiful satin, lace, and pearl gown. She started browsing in bridal shops shortly after meeting Wayne. She knew she would settle for nothing less than marriage from him. They dated for almost a year before becoming engaged. She'd found the gown six months earlier and ordered it the day after Wayne's proposal.

"Put the scarf over your head and face," ordered April as she removes the gown from the hanger and places it over her sister's head.

Leeanna begins to weep as she watches April zip the back of Lori's gown. April the youngest, had married seven years earlier and Lori was her maid of honor. Now April was the matron of honor and Lori's dream was coming true. Her thoughts drifted to earlier years when her daughters were playing dress up in her old dresses and high heel shoes, with crinoline slips over their heads as veils. Lori always insisted that she was the bride and April was the bridesmaid. Leeanna removes several tissues from her lavender satin purse and blots her face to avoid smearing her makeup. Lori paid professionals to give the mothers and bridal party manicures, pedicures, hairdos and makeup this morning. She didn't want to ruin things by walking down the aisle with black streaks running down her face.

She takes the veil from the hanger and gingerly places it on top of her daughter's head, pulling the curls through the top, while trying to maintain a smile.

"No crying, Mother. You'll make me cry too," Lori tearfully pleaded.

"Me too," April added, while stroking her mother's shoulder.

"You're right, I'm not going to cry," she said as she wiped her tears away. Leeanna's feet are swollen like mushrooms in her pretty lavender slippers and her back is aching from weeks of preparations. For the past two months, all of her time was filled with doing this or that for Lori's wedding. She reminded Leeanna of herself. She has my fair skin, my auburn hair, my large eyes and her father's nose and mouth. She looks like me on my wedding day.

"You look breathtaking," Leeanna compliments her daughter.

"Thank you Mother, you look beautiful too." Lori stands in front of the mirror staring at herself with a big smile on her face. Is this really me, I look so beautiful. Wait until Wayne sees me coming down the aisle, he won't believe it's me. I look like a beautiful princess, she thought.

"Can I see my wife and pretty daughters?" Frank asks as he knocks on the door. April opens the door, letting her father enter. His eyes go right to Lori, who is still standing in front of the mirror.

"You look gorgeous Lori. Is that my little rebel in a wedding gown?" He walks over to Lori and hugs her. She gives him a kiss on the cheek. "You look just like your mother when we got married."

"I was just thinking the same thing Frank," Leeanna said with a smile.

"Thank you Dad for everything! You look very handsome in that steel gray tux."

"Thanks Lori. Are we almost ready to go? It's getting late and we don't want to keep Wayne waiting too long." Frank said.

"Yes we'll be ready to leave in a few minutes Dad," April responded as she straightened her father's tie. "You're going to make those younger men look bad!" Frank smiled at the compliment.

"You do look very handsome Frank," his wife said.

"You look very nice yourself," Frank said returning the compliment. "Listen ladies, I'm going downstairs to give you girls a few minutes to do what you do. Hurry down." Frank added. He leaves the room and the women spring into action patting their hair and spraying it, putting on lipstick and tending to the bride.

April shouts over the chatter, breaking Lori's trance. "It's time to go girls, let's go. We have champagne in the limo to mellow us out and I can't wait to get a drink." She hurried the girls down the long hall, down the stairs and out the front door to the cars waiting in the driveway

Wayne paced back and forth in the small room at the back of the church. He couldn't understand the anxiety he felt in the pit of his stomach. He knew this was the right thing to do, after all, he loved Lori; he loved her from the first moment he looked into her eyes. They'd dated for a year. He would have preferred living together for a couple years before marriage, but Lori didn't believe in couples living together. Lori said it was marriage or nothing, so he proposed.

Reggie, his best man sat helplessly watching Wayne unravel. He had a look of terror on his sweaty face, as if he was going to slaughter.

"Wipe the perspiration off your face," Reggie said as he handed Wayne a hand towel. Wayne complied and returned the towel to Reggie. They were good friends from childhood. Wayne was a few years younger than Reggie. He looked up to him like a big brother. He could be himself with Reggie. They could talk about anything. Wayne was the only child of a single parent. His father died when he was eight years old. Reggie being four years older became his male role model as well as his protector. When he decided to marry Lori, he knew that Reggie would be the best man.

"Where are the rings? Do you have them?" Wayne asked nervously.

"Of course I have them," Reggie answered calmly. "Now sit down and relax, everything is under control man."

"How can you stand being with one woman for the rest of your life? It's like eating the same food everyday. Is sex still good after…how long have you been married seven or eight years?"

"Eight years" Reggie replied. "And yes, it's still good. I don't get it as often as I'd like, but when I do it's still good."

"Man, I don't think I can take that. What do you do when she won't give you sex?"

"Well," said Reggie, "sometimes we argue, sometimes I give her the silent treatment and sometimes, I don't want it anyway. You know, when you're working every day and you have children and chores; sometimes you just don't have the energy or the interest in sex. When your head hits the pillow, you fall asleep. Love is more than sex." Reggie laughed. "You'll see, everything will work out fine."

Reggie married at the age of twenty-nine after a couple of live in relationships. Carol was a special woman and he loved and appreciated her. They had two sons and a daughter. Carol worked every day and Reggie felt the children and housework was their shared responsibility. They had a good marriage and Reggie wanted the same for his little brother Wayne.

"Here have a piece of gum," Reggie said

"Thanks, my mouth is kind of dry," Wayne said as he got up and started to pace the room again.

"I wish they would hurry this shit up before I change my mind," he continues. "I don't think anything is more important than sex."

"Come on fells, it's time!"

The large stone Baptist church was located on Broad Street near Medary Avenue. This was a Saturday, so only invited guest were in attendance. The sanctuary of the church was decorated beautifully with pink and white flowers with lavender bows. One hundred and fifty guests were scattered about the room.

Wayne stood at the front of the church looking very handsome in his steel gray tux with a white brocaded vest. His skin glistened with perspiration as he shifted his weight from one foot to the other. Reggie stood behind him as they waited for the procession of bridesmaids and groomsmen to reach their positions. Finally, the flower girl entered the aisle, throwing petals as she walked. At last, Lori entered the aisle on her father's arm. She looked like an angel floating towards him.

Tears blinded Wayne's vision as he strained to see his bride's face through the veil. One look into her eyes would comfort him. Her father lifted her veil revealing her beautiful face and reaffirming his love for this woman.

I now present to you, Mr. and Mrs. Wayne Jackson. Lori turned her face upward towards her new husband and received his warm supple lips. Their eyes met and she knew that this was her prince charming. He took her hand in his and guided her swiftly up the aisle to the sound of applause. She held onto him, acknowledging to herself for the first time, that she belonged to him and he belonged to her, they were a pair.

Mr. and Mrs. Wayne Jackson, together forever!

THREE YEARS LATER

CHAPTER 2

Lori pulled the chicken out of the oven with two dishcloths and placed it on top of the counter. She turned the corn and stringbeans off. I'll surprise Wayne tonight with a hot meal, she thought. As she walked into the livingroom she heard the telephone ring.

"Hi Honey. Are you on your way home? No? What do you mean no? What time are you coming home Wayne? Why didn't you tell me this before? Why is everything the last minute with you? Why don't you plan these things in advance? You're so inconsiderate. If I'd known, maybe I could have made plans to do something. Okay. Well, I'll see you, when I see you. Oh no he didn't hang up on me!"

I'm so tired of his last minute nights out with his friends. He doesn't care if I don't want to be alone. I spent the evening preparing him a hot meal, and he's not coming home. Well, he'll certainly have leftovers tomorrow. He's so unpredictable, that's why I'm not having a baby anytime soon. He has to show me he's really ready to settle down. I'm not going to be stuck at home with a baby, while he is in the street with his friends.

When I was growing up my father used to do this shit to my mother and she used to take it, but I'm not. He'll know how to act the next time I fix him a home cooked meal, she thought. She ran up the steps of the expensive split level suburban home. They had purchased it a year after the wedding. The house needed new carpeting, new floor tiles in the kitchen, and a few rooms needed to be painted. It took them six months of active searching to find their ideal house. It was located in Cheltenham Township. It was constructed of stone, brick and wood. The three bedrooms, two baths house needed some repairs, but it had a great location and a good school system.

Wayne's contorted expression showed his displeasure with his wife's response. I'm not a child and I don't need her approval to spend a little time with my friends. Shit, I'm not henpecked, he thought. Lori wants me home every minute I'm not working. He hung up the receiver and walked back to the bar to join his friends.

"The Lakers are winning and you're going to owe me ten dollars," Reggie chided Wayne.

"I don't think so, it's just the first quarter," Wayne responded.

"Are you guys going to argue or order another beer?" asked Dave. "The Sixers are going to win this game, because Iverson is the man." "I'm with you Dave; Reggie's going to owe both of us ten dollars," Wayne chuckled. He thought about Lori's attitude. A man is entitled to a few beers and a basketball game after working all day. I need a few beers, and a few laughs with the guys to help me unwind. "We'll have three beers here," Wayne told the bartender.

Lori looked through the bedroom windows at the front lawn that needed to be reseeded. "The front lawn needs landscaping, but Wayne spends his time out with his friends," she said aloud to herself. She walked into the bathroom and started her bath water. She poured lots of bubble bath into the tub, using her hand to spread it around in the water. After undressing, she pinned her auburn curly hair up on top of her head. She noted the sadness in her eyes as she applied cold cream to her face to remove her makeup. She deposited the soiled tissues into the trash bin. She left her panties and bra beside the tub on the floor and entered the hot foamy water. She immediately felt its soothing effects. She closed her eyes to relax, but her anger would not quit.

Her class of fourth graders were unusually quarrelsome today, which left her nerves raw. She looked forward to a quiet night at home with Wayne to help her unwind. "I can't depend on him for anything," she mumbled to herself. When the water cooled, she towel dried herself, leaving the towel on the bathroom floor. She selected a nightgown from the three on the bedroom chair and retired to her bed. She missed Wayne and she was angry that he preferred being with his friends tonight. She called her sister on the telephone.

"Hi April, what are you doing tonight?"

"I just put Ashley and Anthony to bed, and I'm waiting for Paul to come back from the market. He went to get some ice cream; you know I have a sweet tooth."

"Yes, everyone knows that."

"So, what are you doing?"

"I'm just sitting here marking papers and I thought I'd check in with you," Lori responded.

"How is Wayne, what's he up to these days?"

"Oh he's asleep," she lied. "He said he was tired, so he went to bed early. You know me, I'm a night owl."

"You'd better wake that man up and get busy making some little Jacksons. What are you two waiting for?" April said while laughing.

"We don't have any money to have a baby. We're just trying to pay these bills," Lori answered.

"Girl, I'm going to let you go, Paul just came in with the goodies. We're going to snack and go upstairs to make love. I'll call you later this week, okay?"

"Okay, talk to you later," Lori responded.

Lori felt lonely. She wanted to cuddle up with her husband. April is so lucky to have Paul, she thought. Wayne wanted children and he felt they should get pregnant immediately after the wedding. Lori wanted to wait until she and Wayne adjusted to each other. She wanted to get their marriage on track before bringing babies into the world. Lori went downstairs and put the food away. She fixed herself a snack and went upstairs to grade her briefcase full of papers. After several hours, she heard the front door close. She looked at the clock and noted it was 12:15 AM. She dropped the papers on the floor, turned off the lamp and threw the covers over her head as she heard her husband's footsteps on the stairs.

Lori awakened early. She had a restless night's sleep. She was still angry with Wayne for going out with his friends last night. She quickly showered and dressed in the dimly lit room. She didn't want Wayne to wake up and try to talk to her this morning. She kneeled beside the bed and gathered the student's papers she'd tossed on the floor last night. She looked over at Wayne sound asleep, looking so innocent. She would not allow herself to forgive him so easily this time. Lori tipped quietly down the steps and went to the kitchen. It was 7:15 AM and she usually didn't leave until 8:00 AM, but this morning she was leaving early. She ate a cold bowl of cereal and drank a glass of juice before leaving for work. She slammed the front door as she left the house, hoping to wake Wayne.

Wayne sat up at the sound of the front door slamming shut. "Lori, Lori, Baby are you here?" he shouted. He received no response. Oh, she's still mad, that's why she's slamming the door. He smiled to himself, I'll call her later; maybe I'll take her out tonight. Wayne turned over and went back to sleep. He could sleep at least an hour longer, he thought.

Later in the afternoon, Wayne thought about his wife. He called her on the telephone. "Hi Baby. I missed you this morning. Did you have a good day? Are those brats driving my wife crazy? Well, don't let them get the best of you. Did you eat dinner yet? I sold three cars today and I socked it to them. I made twenty-six hundred dollars. Yeah, it will be in my paycheck next week, that is what's left after taxes of course. Get dressed, I'm taking us out for dinner and a drink, then we can make wild passionate love all night. Pick you up in thirty minutes!"

"I'll be ready," Lori answered. She hangs up the phone and gathers the students' test papers that were covering the livingroom floor and placed them in her briefcase. Her footsteps echoed in the empty diningroom as she walked into the kitchen. She placed a cup and saucer into the already full sink. I'll wash these dishes tonight when I get back, she told herself. She raced up the steps to wash the important places and to change her clothes. "What to wear, what to wear," she repeated.

She awakened the next morning to the blare of the alarm clock. Lori tried to reach the clock to turn off the alarm, but Wayne was asleep on her breast. She looked at his angelic face with its chiseled features. She hated to arouse him, but the noise from the clock was quite annoying. She rolled him over and slammed the off button on the clock. Wayne moaned and rolled back as she slipped out of bed. Wayne is a handsome, chocolate man, she thought. He knows how to please a woman. He certainly had me climbing the walls last night. She looked at his broad muscular back, his sexy ass and his muscular arms; sweet thoughts raced through her mind, as she fought the temptation to climb back into bed with her husband for a quickie. We certainly would have made a baby last night if I wasn't on these birth control pills, she thought, as she popped one into her mouth and followed it with water. She stepped into the hot shower, lathering and caressing her body until she was satisfied.

Selling cars is getting harder and harder, Wayne
thought. I spent three hours with that cheap ass woman.
She was looking for something for nothing; just wasting
my time. I haven't sold a car all week and it's Thurs-
day. I may need to get a salaried job if this continues. I
make good money, but it comes in spurts. Lori doesn't
understand that with commission jobs, the money is
never the same. Sometimes you make a lot, sometimes
you make a little. She makes the same money every
week. She gets angry when I bring home a little paycheck, but when I bring home a big paycheck, she goes
shopping for shit that can wait.

     The sweat moistened his back and forehead as
he walked across the car lot to the showroom to return
car keys. He cleared his desk and prepared to leave. He
spied an elderly couple entering the showroom. "Showtime," he said. He hustled over to the pair with his hand
extended and a big smile.
     "Hi, my name is Wayne. How may I assist you
today?"
     "We're looking for a small used car for my
wife," answered the husband, "but nothing too expensive."
Wayne spent an hour and a half trying to sell a car, only
to be told they'd get back to him. He left the showroom
feeling tired and dejected. When he arrived home, Lori
was impatiently waiting for him.

     "Wayne, hurry and change your shirt. We are
already running late. You know Daddy will be angry if

we show up late again. He says if Paul and April can get there on time with two children, then we should be able to get ourselves there on time."

"Lori, I don't give a damn what your father says. He bosses you, your mother, your sister, and Paul, but he is not my boss. I'm just getting off work and I'm tired. I'm going to take a shower and change my clothes, and I need to relax a little before I'll be ready to deal with your family," Wayne retorted.

"You don't have to do all of that when you go out with your friends, you get off work and keep going."

"Look, I told you what I'm going to do. If you are in such a hurry, then you can go without me. I don't know why you're always accepting invitations without discussing it with me first. I've told you over and over not to do it, but you won't listen to me. You don't care what I want. You're busy trying to satisfy your family," Wayne shouted. He stomped upstairs to the bedroom and slammed the door.

Lori slumped in the big brown chair in the livingroom. Tears ran down her cheeks, staining her makeup. She wiped her bronze face with the back of her hand. I don't understand how someone can change so completely. We were happy the first two years of this marriage, but now he acts like he doesn't care. When we were dating, he pretended to love my family, but now every time we're suppose to go to my parents' house, he doesn't want to go. It's one excuse after another. When he does go, we're always late because of him wasting time or coming home late. Lori had taken extra pains to look beautiful for him tonight. The red linen dress he loved was now wrinkled and her taupe heels were thrown across the room. Lori called her mother on the telephone.

"Hi Mom, I'm sorry, but we're not able to come to dinner tonight. My stomach is a little upset. I think it's something I ate earlier today, she lied. No, I'm not pregnant. I'll be fine. Yes, I'll take something for it and lay down. Yes, I'll tell Wayne that you sent your love. Okay, tell Dad I said I'm sorry."
Lori walked upstairs unbuttoning her dress. She threw it on the chair and climbed into bed. The glare of the television shown in her eyes, causing her to turn her back towards Wayne. She covered her head with the quilt as her tears stained the pillow.

Wayne was still angry that Lori had accepted her parents' invitation without talking to him first. She didn't even tell him until the last minute. I had a lousy day and I come home to her rushing me. When I come home after a bad day at work, I don't want to socialize. I want to take a shower and relax. I'd like to come home to a hot meal and an understanding wife. Now, she's laying on her side of the bed crying as if I've done something wrong. I hate to make her cry. It always makes me feel bad.

"Lori, I'm sorry Baby. I just had a lousy day and I took it out on you. Don't cry. I love you. I'm sorry," Wayne said with remorse. Lori turned over as Wayne leaned over to look into her eyes. "I really am sorry, Lori." He hugged her close to him. "Are you hungry?"

"Yes, I'm hungry."

"Let's order some cheesesteaks and fries," Wayne suggested. She smiled through her tears

Leeanna stirred the spaghetti sauce, turning the fire down low. She turned off the linguine, pouring it into a colander and running hot water over it. She returned it to the pot and tossed it with seasoning and a little oil. She put the garlic bread in the oven on a low temperature. She enjoyed fixing lunch for her daughters and grandchildren, Ashley and Anthony. They are growing in leaps and bounds and I'm looking forward to having one or two more grandchildren before I'm too old to enjoy them. She poured the grape juice, ginger-ale, tea and sugar into the large crystal pitcher and stirred. Those children love my punch, she thought, as she places it into the refrigerator to cool. She removed the garlic bread from the oven and turned it off. She looked around her kitchen and wished it was newer and larger, but she didn't see that happening in the near future. She wiped the counter and washed the dishes and utensils in the sink.

Leeanna went upstairs to her bedroom to change clothes. The sleeveless floral housedress left bare the bruises on her upper arms and she didn't want her girls to get upset. This is going to be a pleasant afternoon, she told herself. She slipped into a pair of size 14 jeans and a long sleeved light blue blouse. She practiced smiling in the mirror as she combed her mixed gray cropped hair, there were still traces of auburn scattered here and there. My children and my grandchildren are the joys of my life and we're going to have a good time today, she resolved to herself again. She winced as she bent over to tie her sneakers. Her arms and back were still sore and bruised from Frank's drunken temper tantrum two days earlier.

The doorbell chimed. Leeanna slowly walked down the stairs to greet her family. Ashley raced in first looking just like her father. Her pretty maple colored face beaming with triumph.

"Nana, I beat Anthony up the steps to ring the bell first. I'm eight years old and I'm bigger than Anthony." She wrapped her arms around her Nana's waist. Next, comes Anthony with a frown on his face that showed his displeasure with his defeat.

"I'm big too, I'm six years old," whined Anthony as he pressed his head against Nana's stomach. Leeanna hugged and kissed each of her grandchildren and waited at the door for April and Lori to enter. Lori pecked her mother on the cheek as she entered carrying a bag.

"I brought an apple pie for dessert in case you didn't have anything. I'll put it on the kitchen counter," Lori said.

April entered and locked the door as she scolded her children for once again running to the door of her parents' house.

"I've told you kids to stop running up these steps every time we come over here. One day, one of you are going to fall and get hurt. The next time I'm going to spank your behinds."

"Oh, they're just being children April, don't be so hard on them. They're just anxious to see their Nana. You should bring them to see me more often."

"We're just being kids," Anthony repeated looking pleadingly at his mother. She looked down at his repentant face and laughed, everyone else's laughter followed.

"I hope you are hungry, because I have spaghetti, salad, garlic bread and your favorite punch. Let's wash our hands and eat. There are paper towels on the counter," Leeanna offered.

"Mom, you look like you're tired. Have you been sleeping well?" April asked.

"You know as you get older, you don't sleep as long. I'll sleep two hours and wake up for one hour. I go back to sleep for a couple of hours and wake up again. When I don't get enough sleep, then I walk around tired all day; but life goes on," Leeanna sighed.

"You should have called us and cancelled lunch, you need your rest. We could understand that," April said.

"Oh no, and miss having lunch with my girls and my grands. Never! I can rest after you leave. I enjoy my family too much to let sleep interfere with our monthly lunch dates," Leeanna affirmed.

"Nana, can I have seconds of spaghetti?" Anthony asked.

"Me too," Ashley added.

"You sure can Honey," Leeanna agreed.

"Mom everything is delicious, I really enjoyed it," complimented Lori.

"Especially since you didn't have to cook it," laughed April.

"You've got that right," chuckled Lori. "I love my Mama's cooking."

"You should ask her to give you the recipe, so you can make use of those beautiful shiny pots and pans hanging in your kitchen," April teased.

"Oh, so now you're Julia Childs? Why are your children eating like they're not used to such good food?

Ashley, Anthony, does your mother's spaghetti taste as good as Nana's?" questioned Lori.

"No," the children said in unison.

"There, you see, you could use Mom's recipes too," Lori joked.

"That spaghetti is nothing special," Leeanna said. "I've eaten spaghetti at April's house and it was very good."

"Don't waste your time telling her I can cook Mom. She knows I can cook, that's why she calls me asking how to make this or that when she feels like being nice to Wayne," April retorted.

"Lori, don't you cook for your husband? You know you can't keep a man if you don't feed him. If you don't feed him, someone else will," Leeanna cautioned her daughter.

"Mom, I feed Wayne, besides Wayne knows how to cook as good as I do. His hands aren't broken," Lori said.

"You know a man likes for his wife to make him a home cooked meal. It makes him feel important," Leeanna added.

"I show Wayne love in other ways," laughed Lori.

"I told you not to waste your time Mom, that girl will not listen. She's just lazy," April teased.

"Okay, okay, you two are double teaming me. I know how to take care of my man. He must like it, he's still with me," laughed Lori. "Let's get out of the house and go to the mall."

"You two go ahead to the mall, I'll stay here and enjoy my grandchildren," Leeanna said.

"Okay Mom, we won't be long. Do you need anything?" Lori asked.

"No, I don't think so. I'm tired of spending my money," Leeanna confessed. "You two go on and enjoy yourselves. Make sure you're back before dinnertime."

"Can't we go with you?" Ashley asked.

"No, stay here and keep Nana company," April ordered.

"We'll have some fun! We're going to eat pie and ice cream, and we're going to play Uno," Leeanna said.

"Okay, we're staying with Nana," Ashley and Anthony agreed

Lori calls Wayne at work.

"Hi Wayne, how is your day going? I'm trying to wash a few loads of clothes. I called to ask you to bring some Chinese food when you come home. I want shrimp egg foo young and you get what you want, so we can share. No, I don't feel like cooking. I'm trying to wash clothes and clean the bathrooms. You can cook if you feel like it. Well, I'm tired too, so bring the Chinese food. Okay? I love you. See you soon."

I hate to wash clothes and sheets, she thought. If my menses hadn't stained the sheets on the bed, I would have put off washing until next week. I won't let Wayne think I'm a pig. She threw the pile of clothes from the bathroom floor into the laundry basket, stopping to pick up clothes scattered about the bedroom floor She carried them to the washroom and sorted them by color. Lori removed the sheets from the washer and put them into the dryer. She put a load of sorted clothes into the washer and carried the dried clothes upstairs and deposited them on the bed. Wayne refused her offer to wash his clothes, because she didn't fold them immediately after removing them from the dryer. Good, let him wash his own clothes, she thought. I certainly don't care. That's less for me to do.

Lori knew she wasn't the best home-maker, but she worked everyday, so she did what she could. Men want women to cook, clean, have babies and work, and not necessarily in that order. They want a maid and a sex slave that pays half of the bills. She surveyed the disarray in the bedroom and decided to ignore it. I work just like Wayne does, and I can only do so much. He doesn't spend his days off cooking and cleaning. He's usually in bed sleeping most of the day or out with his friends. When people come to your house, they never look at the man if the house is dirty; they always look at the woman. Wayne's lucky I'm doing anything in this house, after all it's Saturday. I could be out shopping instead of washing sheets and clothes. Maybe, if I put on some music it will give me some energy to finish this shit. She placed the sheets on top of the dryer and deposited another load in the dryer. Lori sat on the bed and started folding the clothes as she hummed to the music.

Daddy has Mom trained. If dinner isn't on the table everyday at 5:30 PM, then he throws a fit. April is just like her, she tries to be Miss Perfect Homemaker, but at least Paul helps with the children and the housework. April looks older than she is. She doesn't wear enough makeup and she's still wearing last year's clothes. She wouldn't even buy herself a new outfit when we went to the mall. They're always on a budget. Maybe, because Paul is an accountant, but he owns half of the business, so they're not paupers. They have a beautiful English Tudor home and it's furnished nicely, but they won't spend a penny unless it's planned.

They both have to agree. Better her than me, if I waited until Wayne agreed to me spending money I'd be naked, she thought as she laughed to herself.

She's off today, and she knows that Saturday is my hardest day at work. Why can't she cook a decent meal for me? She has the nerve to ask me to pick up food and bring it home to her. She's out of her damn mind. Wayne stopped at the diner on his way home and ordered a smothered pork chop platter: pork chops, mashed potatoes, mixed vegetables, and rolls. A brother has to look out for himself sometimes, he thought as he ate the tasty hot food. The plate was empty after he used his roll to sop up the last of the gravy. Feeling satisfied, he then went to the Chinese restaurant to pick up the egg foo young for Lori. She can eat this shit by herself; I'm tired of Chinese food. She thinks I should give her a medal for washing clothes. That's a laugh!

"Baby, the food is on the table. I only got the egg foo young, because I ate late and I'm not hungry," Wayne said.

"I thought you would get something so we could share. What are you going to do if you get hungry later? What are you going to eat?" Lori whined.

"Don't worry about me. I told you I ate late, I'm not hungry! You just worry about yourself, don't worry about me," Wayne snapped. He went upstairs, removed his shoes and pants and stretched out on the bed. He turned on the television and settled for a movie. He belched and the taste of the smothered pork chops returned to his throat. He smiled to himself as he succumbed to the fatigue of the day.

"Wayne, Wayne, wake up Wayne! Why are you laying in bed knocked out? I want to go to the movies! I've been stuck in this house all day and I want to go to the movies!" Lori said sarcastically.

"I'm tired! I'm not going anywhere. We can watch a movie at home. Go to the video store and rent one. Let me sleep for a little while and I'll watch a movie with you later," Wayne pleaded.

"I don't want to rent a movie. I want to go to the theatre. Get up Wayne! Let's go to the movies!" she shouted. Although Wayne was tired, he relented and went to the movie theatre with Lori.

Wayne, Wayne," she whispered as she elbowed him in the side. "He's no company at all," she whined. "He didn't say a word on the way to the movies and now he has the nerve to sit here and go to sleep! He's become impossible!" Lori complained. She finally gave in and let her husband sleep uninterrupted, except for the occasional jab in the ribs when he began to snore. The lights in the theatre and Lori's jab awakened Wayne from a sound sleep.

"Let's go Wayne," Lori snapped.

"What's wrong with you? I told you I was tired, but you insisted upon coming to the movies anyway. You've gotten what you wanted and you're still not satisfied. There is no pleasing you. Fuck it, the next time I just won't go," Wayne threatened.
Lori walked rapidly towards the car with a frown on her face. Her displeasure with Wayne was apparent.

"She's always mad about something!" Wayne mumbled to himself. Lori always wanted to have her way. He usually gave in to her, he didn't mind most of the time. He knew that women were more emotional than men, so most of the times he would do what he could to appease her. I can't help it if I fell asleep. I told her I was tired. What am I suppose to do? She's being unreasonable, Wayne thought. She's mad, too bad, let her get over it.

They rode home in silence. The silence continued after they arrived home. Lori showered before getting into bed and turning her back towards Wayne.

"I'm sorry Baby," Wayne murmured as he began to massage her back. He could feel the release of the tension leaving her body as he caressed her. "You know I love you."

"I love you too," she whispered.
His hands and mouth explored her fragrant body and she surrendered to his advances.

"Oh Wayne, I love you!" Lori shouted.

CHAPTER 3

Leeanna removed her shoes, placing her feet on the sofa while she sipped the grape cranberry juice. She was tired and needed to relax before preparing dinner. She pondered what to cook with the ground turkey she'd left in the refrigerator to thaw. Perhaps mashed potatoes and broccoli, that's quick, she thought. Going to work everyday was no longer fun, it had become a burden. Her irregular sleep pattern left her feeling tired too often.

Leeanna had been a housewife at the beginning of her marriage. She and Frank agreed that she should stay home to raise the children and take care of the house. She'd volunteered at the children's school, participating in numerous fundraisers. She was also active in the community organizations, but as soon as the children were older, she opted to go to work. She was tired of penny pinching to maintain the meager budget that

Frank's salary dictated. He was resistant to the idea at first, but he eventually gave in. She had to assure him that she would continue to cook, clean, and supervise the girls.

Leeanna was so excited when she started her first job. She didn't make much money, but it gave her a sense of independence. She finally had her own money to buy little things for herself and her daughters. Designer clothes for the girls, new drapes, new lamps and a big screen television for the livingroom, were some of the purchases that made her feel proud. Now she mostly shopped for herself and saved money for a new kitchen. She lived up to her promise to Frank. She kept her house clean and usually served dinner on time, even when she didn't feel well. Her father insisted that her mother serve dinner at 5:00 PM six days a week. On Sundays, because he was a minister, he wanted dinner at 3:00PM. Her mother was an easy going person, very gentle to her children and obedient to her husband. Her father was a caring person, but he felt that women existed to serve men, and he demanded obedience from his children. At dinner time, he wanted them seated at the table waiting for him with clean faces and hands. "I'd better get up and start this man's dinner," she said aloud to herself.

She mixed the ingredients for a turkey meatloaf and placed it into the oven. She mixed the potato flakes for the mashed potatoes and turned the broccoli off. Now, she could go upstairs to the bedroom to change her clothes.

She removed her clothing and placed them on hangers in the closet. Her closet was organized by color, articles of clothing, and occasion. Since she secured her own credit cards and the children were grown, she bought clothes for special occasions that never came, but she'd be prepared just in case. Dresses and suits hung in the closet still bearing store tags. Her shoes were also organized by color and occasion like her clothes. She loved lingerie best of all. She had a drawer that held many of her first purchases from Victoria's Secret and other specialty shops. She often opened the drawer when she was alone to admire the lingerie. She would remove the lingerie and gaze at it. She sprayed them with perfume and sniffed the pretty panties, slips and nightgowns that she's secreted away under flannel and cotton pieces. She thought them too beautiful for her aging body. They were there to lift her spirits and to help her recall memories of times gone by.

In the earlier days, Frank would buy her beautiful lingerie as gifts and ask her to model them for him. He would marvel at her beauty and caress her, telling her how much he loved her. That stopped after the birth of their second daughter. He began to take her for granted and spend evenings away from home. She thought he might have had an affair, but she could never prove it. His interest in having sex with her began to diminish. She tried to peak his interest again by putting the children to bed early, so they could have time alone, but after a few drinks; Frank often fell asleep before she finished. She tried to show her love for him by taking good care of the children and the house, but their

lovemaking was never the same. Whenever she complained of his lack of attentiveness towards her, he
would make her feel guilty by saying, "I work hard everyday to support you and the children while you sit
around watching television all day." When she went to
work she had less energy and she busied herself with
other things. She resolved herself to accept things the
way they were, after all, Frank was a decent man, and
you never get everything you want in a marriage, she
thought.

Frank made sure they all knew that he was the
man of the house. He made the decisions. He allowed
her some input, but he made the decisions and everyone
had to live by his rules. Now that the girls were gone,
living their lives, she sometimes felt isolated; almost
trapped. The reason for the marriage had shifted from
the two of them to the children, raising the children.
The children were now adults, living away from home,
and their union no longer had a focus; only two people
with little in common existing in the same house.
Leeanna felt like his maid. She felt insignificant to him.
Everything she enjoyed, he thought foolish or frivolous.
He loved football, now that's important to him. What is
more foolish than a bunch of men chasing a ball and
causing permanent injury to one another? Leeanna put
on her housedress and went downstairs to make gravy
for the meatloaf.
        "Hi Lee, I'm home. What's for dinner?" Frank
asked.

Frank wasn't given a college education by his
parents. He served four years in the Air Force, taking

classes whenever he could. His father had a barbershop and his mother was a housewife. They were poor and couldn't afford to send their children to college. Being the oldest of four children, he knew he had to make his own opportunities in life. He was the first person in his family to go to college and he knew he had to stay focused on his goal to attain a degree. He had a year of college to complete at night school when he was discharged. He earned a degree in physical education, and a master's degree in administration. He married his minister's daughter while he taught school and attended graduate school. Frank Amos became a principal twenty-five years ago. He was known throughout the district as a no-nonsense principal, and because of that, he was burdened with discipline problems from other schools. He thought it unfair, but he had to take orders as well as give them.

For the most part, his teachers were more than competent, but some of them were there to collect a paycheck. They were the ones that created the problems in the school. Their students were the ones that filled the discipline room and roamed the halls getting into trouble. He'd had his success stories with some of the kids, but some of them were beyond hope, and he bided his time until he could expel them. It was much more difficult to rid the school of certain teachers. Unions, unions, unions, he thought.

Frank relaxed in his recliner in the livingroom in front of the big screen television. Dinner was good, he thought. I've always been a meat and potatoes kind of man. Just feed me the basics. I don't like all of that fancy stuff. He watched the six o'clock news, as he sipped a drink with little interest. He was really waiting to see the weather and the sports segments. He could hear Leeanna cleaning the kitchen. It was a familiar sound. He remembered playing on the kitchen floor as a child and listening to his mother clean the kitchen. The sound made him feel secure. Frank liked a routine. He awakened at 5:30 AM every morning, showered and dressed, and then he went to his home office to complete school paperwork. He ate breakfast at 7:00AM and left for school at 7:30 AM. Every evening he ate dinner at 5:30 PM and watched the six o'clock news, while Lee cleaned the kitchen. He had a few drinks after dinner to relax, occasionally nodding off, and going upstairs to bed at 9:00 PM.

It was good having the girls out of the house. At last, he had some privacy. He could walk around the house nude, lay something down and come back and find it still there, he could take leftovers for lunch and he enjoyed controlling the remote control. Lee watched the television in the kitchen or the bedroom most of the time, unless something special was coming on, then he would let her watch the big screen television in the livingroom. After all, she did buy it with the money from her little job at Dr. Phillips office. Since the girls left home, he could have his space and Lee could have her space.

"Frank, do you want anything before I go upstairs?" Lee asked.

"Yes, I'd like a piece of that lemon cake and a cup of tea."

Lee didn't respond, she went off to fill his request. She tried to meet Frank's needs when he came home from work. She knew he had a lot of pressure at work, and she wanted to make his time at home stress free. She wanted him to return to work the next day feeling renewed. She knew that behind every good man was a good woman, and she strived to be that good woman. It would be nice if he would bring me a cup of tea or a piece of cake, every now and then, she thought as she returned to the livingroom.

"Put your dishes in the sink when you finish, okay?" Lee said as she placed the tea and cake on the table beside Frank's throne. Yes, he was the king of this house and she was his trapped servant. Frank's home was his haven away from the children, the teachers, the unions, the administrators and the constant meetings and interruptions. He was dedicated to his job and he gave it his all. He had little left when he came home for his wife. He just wanted to have a drink and vegetate.

The sun shining in Wayne's eyes awakened him at 10:30 AM. Reluctantly he got out of bed and took a shower. Feeling refreshed, he went downstairs to the kitchen and poured the remaining coffee into a cup. He sat at the glass top table sipping and planning his day. I have to take shirts to the laundry, buy shoe polish, pay the cable bill and visit my mother, he thought. He looked over at the sink and it was full of dishes again. He filled the sink with sudsy water and washed them. He wiped down the refrigerator and counter tops and cleaned the glass top table with Windex. I can't live in a dirty house. My mother kept our house clean, and she made me help. I had chores to do in the house, and I did them or faced the consequences. Lori's mother waited on everybody in her house and she sure as hell didn't teach Lori to cook or clean. If I knew then what I know now, I wouldn't have been in a hurry to get married, he thought. He swept the floor and mopped it. Now, it looks like someone lives here. He cooked himself some turkey bacon, eggs and grits. He washed his dishes and went upstairs to get dressed. The bedroom looks like shit, but I'm not going to clean it. Lori throws her clothes around like she has a maid. I'm out of here, before Lori gets home

Wayne, Wayne are you here? Baby are you home? She listened for the sound of movement. Silence. Oh well, he's in the streets again! I thought we could go food shopping. She looked in the kitchen and noted how clean and sparkling it looked. Well, at least he cleaned the kitchen, she thought. It's a shame he didn't notice how empty the refrigerator is, and it's going to stay that way until he goes shopping with me. I'm not carrying those heavy bags of groceries by myself. I'll just wait for him.

Wayne stopped over Reggie's house on his way home.

"Wayne would you like a beer or something else to drink?" Reggie asked.

"Yeah man, I'd like a beer. Are you going to drink one with me?"

"Sure man, my wife and kids are asleep and I'm just sitting here relaxing and watching television; a beer would hit the spot," Reggie responded. "Isn't today your day off?"

"Yeah, I usually have Wednesdays and Sundays off. I had some running around to do and I went to visit my Moms," Wayne said.

"How is your Mom? She's good people."

"Oh, she's doing good. She's still complaining that I don't come to see her enough, but it's hard. I work fifty to fifty-five hours a week, so I don't have much time for myself. Lori tries to monopolize the little time I do have. I need time to take care of my personal things just like she does. She only works thirty to thirty-five hours a week, so she has lots of time to herself. Man, you can never satisfy a woman, no matter what you do, so you're better off satisfying yourself," Wayne declared.

"What are you talking about Wayne?"

"There's this girl I sold a car to about a month ago; not a bad looking woman, in fact, she's sort of cute and she has a nice body."

"Okay, so where are you going with this Wayne?" Reggie asked as he sipped his beer.

"Anyway, she keeps calling me at work, telling me how much she appreciates my help and how much she likes her new car."

"It sounds like more than that is going on," Reggie chuckled. "Come clean man, I know you've been all up in that thing."

"No, I haven't slept with her, but we have gone out to lunch a couple of times and dinner once. She's been paying for it. She wants me man. I think she wants my body," Wayne laughed.

"Well, you'd better be careful; after all you are a married man. Some of these women out here are crazy. Man, they'll make your life a living hell. Make sure you're thinking with the right head. That little one will get you in big trouble," Reggie stressed.

"To be truthful man, I did hit that thing twice, but it's nothing serious. I've told her that I'm married and I don't plan on leaving my wife. I only see her when I can."

"Well, like I said man, just be careful. I don't get involved in relationships outside of my marriage. A one night stand is one thing, but a relationship can create problems at home. I love my wife and kids too much to jeopardize my family."

"If I had what you have I'd feel the same way, but you know Lori, she won't even get off the pill so we can start a family. I'm not trying to break up my marriage, but she frustrates me. She just steps out of her clothes and leaves them laying around. She doesn't like housework, but then again, who does? Her mother's house is always neat, and so is her sister's house. Lori just is not into cleaning up….if I really wanted to run around man, I could. I mean there are plenty of opportunities when you work with the public." Silence.

"Well man, I'd better get on home, I know Lori is wondering where I am." Wayne rises and walks towards the door.
Reggie clears the coffee table of the beer cans that were covering it earlier. He joins Wayne at the front door.

"Stop by anytime. I enjoyed your company."

"Okay, see you soon," Wayne says as he exited the house.

April towel dried Ashley and gave her the pajamas. "Go to your room and get into bed," she ordered. She peeped into Anthony's room and smiled when she saw him trying to stay awake as he watched TV. April turned off his light and the television. Anthony turned over on his pillow and she kissed him on the back of his curly head. She partially closed his door so the light from the hall could filter into his room. He was afraid of the dark. She then opened the door to Ashley's room and kissed her on the cheek. She lowered the volume of her television. "Ashley you can watch television for thirty minutes, then it's lights out. Do you understand?" April asked

"Yes, Mommy."

"Goodnight Sweetheart."

"Goodnight Mommy."

April went downstairs and joined Paul in the kitchen as he washed and rinsed the dishes. She took a towel from the counter and began drying and stacking the plates.

"Thanks Sweetie," Paul said. Now that we're finished the dishes, let's play some cards."

"Sounds good to me and I'm going to get a slice of that delicious chocolate cake you made. Do you want a slice?" April asked.

"Sure, I'll take a slice. Do you want a cup of tea?" Paul asked.

"Yes, I do, but make mine herbal tea. "

"Alright, I'll fix the snack, you go and get the cards," Paul suggested.

"This reminds me of when we were in college," said April. "You always wanted to play cards, but you hate to lose. I think you like to play with me because, you usually win.

"That's true, plus you're not a sore loser. Gerald, my roommate at college was such a bad loser, we'd almost fight over a game of cards," Paul laughed. "I was glad to get away from him. I think spending so much time in your dorm room is what made me fall in love with you. You were so cute with your bangs and ponytail," Paul teased April as he reached across the table and kissed her on the forehead.
April blushed at the compliment. "You're so silly Paul. You fell in love with me because I had lots of snacks in my room and you were always hungry."

"Growing boys eat a lot," said Paul. "You were my best friend."

"Only after you and Gerald fell out," April chided.

"Gerald didn't have any snacks," Paul laughed. "You're still my best friend," he said as he looked into her eyes.

"And you're my best friend too Honey."

"Forget the cards, let's go to bed and play some more serious games. I feel like hearing you call my name." He pulled her up from the kitchen chair, kissing her, darting his tongue in and out of her mouth. He caressed her buttocks, pulling her closer to him. She responded by taking his hand and leading him to the livingroom towards the sofa. She frantically tugged at his trousers as he unbuttoned her dress.

I just love to shop, Lori thought. It relaxes me. When I'm shopping I don't think about anything, but what I'm looking at then and there. Lori sifted through the sales rack. She was known for finding great bargains. She loved to take new purchases home. They made her feel happy. Shopping filled a void in her life. There has to be something on this sales rack that I can use. Linen pants, I love linen. It wrinkles, but it is so comfortable and it looks great. The pants came in an assortment of colors. I think I'll get red and black. After looking at some light weight tops, she selected a red one. I'd better get out of here before I buy something else, she thought. She paid for her purchases with a charge card.

On the way out of the store she spied an adorable jean dress. She tried on a size 6 and 8. The size 6 was snug, but the size 8 was too large. The credit card was turned down because it was maxed out, so she used the cash Wayne gave her for food. She gave the cashier three twenty dollar bills. I'll replace the money before Wayne finds out, she thought. She stood at the counter smiling as the dress was being wrapped.

Lori dropped the shopping bags on the bedroom floor. She removed her shoes and skirt. She emptied one bag on the bed to inspect her new finds. When she checked the tags on the linen trousers, she realized they were originally $158, reduced to $89. While trying on the slacks, she saw they were too long, but otherwise the fit was perfect. She was glad she had bought two pairs of pants. The red top matched the red pants perfectly, like a set. She beamed as she looked at herself in the mirror wearing the red outfit. She made a mental note to buy red flats shoes to match.

The second bag contained the jean dress. She tried it on and thought it was short, but sexy. "These are keepers," she said aloud as she cut the tags from the items. Sometimes, after a shopping spree, she would suffer buyer's remorse and return everything she bought the following day. Sometimes it took a week before she came to her senses and returned them. She hid the tags and receipts inside her pocketbook. She placed the clothes on hangers and put them in her closet. "I can't let Wayne see that I have been shopping again," she said to herself. She folded the bags and hid them at the bottom of her closet.

Lori went to the bathroom to wash the makeup off her face, so Wayne would think she'd stayed home all day. It was almost time for him to come home, so she called the pizza parlor and ordered a pepperoni pizza and a salad. She took the glasses and bowls downstairs to the kitchen and placed them in the sink with the other dishes. She rushed through the empty diningroom to retrieve the coffee mugs from breakfast. She hurriedly washed the dishes, wiped down the counters and windexed the glass table. She returned to the livingroom sofa to relax and grade some papers from school. Lori paid the pizza delivery man and tipped him three dollars. She placed the hot pizza on the glass table and refrigerated the salad. She prepared herself a plate of food, poured a glass of Coke and returned to the livingroom to eat and wait for Wayne. She marked her students' papers while waiting for Wayne. She fell asleep while waiting for Wayne.

Wayne opened the door and saw his wife asleep on the sofa. Damn, why didn't she go upstairs to bed? He quietly shut the front door and walked into the kitchen. He put the cold pizza into the almost empty refrigerator. He tiptoed up the stairs to avoid awakening his wife. He hurriedly undressed and got into bed. Safe, he thought.

"Oh, it's cold," Lori said as she rubbed her hands up and down her forearms to generate a little warmth. She walked into the kitchen, noticing the pizza missing from the table. "Wayne is home and he didn't wake me up," she mumbled. She went upstairs and looked at Wayne sleeping so peacefully. She reached over and pinched his arm. "Wayne, why didn't you wake me up?" she said. Wayne moaned and turned over, away from his wife. Safe, he thought.

CHAPTER 4

"Do you want anything while I'm out?" Paul asked April.

"No Sweetheart, I can't think of a thing. You just enjoy your walk. I'm going to finish bathing the kids."

Paul liked to walk at least three times a week. It helped to clear his head and maintain his slim physique. He is six feet tall with broad shoulders, small waist, and narrow hips. He still looked much as he did when he married nine years earlier. They married two months after graduating college. April was four months pregnant. She was the first woman he'd ever loved. Although he was attracted to men, he decided he wanted a traditional family with a woman. He felt the world didn't need to know his sexual preference, it's private, it's personal. He and April loved each other and they had a passionate sex life. Her pregnancy just expedited the inevitable.

He and April were friends for a year before they realized they were in love. She was so sweet and understanding, willing to listen to a troubled friend. Paul walked past the mini mall at a brisk pace. He walked towards the park. As he entered the blackness of the park, he could feel his heart racing. He sat on the bench, looking nonchalant, as he crossed his legs. A slim figure approached him slowly and sat down beside him. They looked at each other, their eyes meeting and holding the stare; his heart pounding with the excitement of meeting someone new. They sat in silence, only communicating with their eyes and their body posture. Paul rose from his seat and slowly walked into the darkness behind the large oak tree. The slim stranger followed him.

As Paul exited the park, he thought about his wife. When I met April, my life was coming apart at the seams. Gerald was giving me a hard time at the dorm. He wanted to party all of the time and I was on academic probation, which meant that I had to improve my grades or risk expulsion. I didn't want to go back home to my father and brother. I was never going to live there again. Gerald was fine initially as a roommate, until we started having sex with each other. It was those green eyes that attracted me to him. One night we were partying, and drank one too many beers, and it happened. I'd felt attractions to men before, but I'd never acted upon them. The sex blew my mind. I thought I was going crazy. I became jealous of him, and I followed him everywhere he went. I didn't trust him with anyone. This behavior was so unlike me, I didn't recognize myself.

Gerald soon had enough and ended the relationship after a year and a half and I became depressed.

April worked in the registrar's office part-time
and so did I. We became friends and I poured my heart
out to her. After a mourning period; April and I started
dating. Our love grew out of friendship. At first April
thought I was gay, but when she found out that Gerald
was my first male lover, she thought it was just a phase,
and so did I. For the first few years of our marriage,
during the births of our children, everything seemed
fine, and then I started to feel the attraction towards
men again. I didn't know how to handle it. I loved my
wife and my children so much; I didn't want to risk losing them. They keep me sane in this crazy world. Paul
returned from his walk invigorated. He'd stopped by
the store and bought April some yogurt. He knew she
liked to carry yogurt to work for lunch and she enjoyed
the treats he brought home to her from his walks.

Lori often used the telephone for company. She called friends, co-workers, and family. Wayne worked late three nights a week, which often left Lori feeling lonely. She didn't feel that she saw her husband nearly enough. Lori's shopping filled the void she felt in her life. She went shopping several times a week, which challenged their budget and angered Wayne. She promised to curtail the shopping sprees when her credit cards were maxed out. Every time she'd try to pay the credit cards down, she'd give in to her urges to shop. She loved matching fabrics, composing outfits and most of all, looking for bargains.

Her closets were packed beyond capacity. Lori would also buy things for the house, new lamps, comforter sets, picture frames, paintings, drapes, etc.. Her motto was, you can find something to buy in any store. Initially, Lori would bring her purchases home and share them with Wayne. He marveled at her good taste and her savvy at finding bargains. After finding themselves over budget too many times, Wayne insisted that Lori stop shopping.

Shopping was Lori's hobby and she had problems trying to stop. She changed her shopping habits from overt to covert. She hid her purchases in closets, the garage, the basement, under beds, and even in the trunk of her car. Sometimes she rode around for weeks with shoes, dresses, lamps, etc. in her trunk until she could sneak them into the house. When Wayne wasn't home, Lori would place her new items on closet doors or on the floor, so she could admire them. She would make resolves to stop shopping, only to break them.

Lori went to visit her mother after school. She needed to borrow some money from her mother, but it made her feel uncomfortable.

"Hi Mom."

"Hello Sweetheart."

Lori hugs and kisses her mother. Come on in the kitchen and eat a snack, I know you're hungry after working all day," Leeanna said to her daughter. "How is Wayne?"

"He's working as usual. I've never seen a person work so much and still not make any money. He works all of the time, but if he doesn't sell a car, then he doesn't make any money. He needs to find another job. I can't take it anymore," complained Lori.

"Oh Lori, Wayne makes money. He may have slow periods, but he is a smart man, he's not working for nothing.

"You're right; he does make good money sometimes, but when he doesn't it drives me crazy. I'm trying to decide who will get paid and who won't get paid. Some of the bills are behind and I don't know what we are going to do," Lori whined.

"Well Lori, I have a little something put away for a rainy day and it's yours if you want it," Leeanna offered.

"Oh Mom, I'd really appreciate it, but I don't know when I can pay you back."

"Don't worry about that, I'm not."

"Will Dad mind? I don't want him to get upset."

"What your father doesn't know, won't hurt him, besides it's my money and he doesn't even know I have it," Leeanna confided to Lori.

"Well, that's a relief, Lori confessed.

"I'll go to the bank tomorrow on my lunch and bring the money to you at school. Okay?"

"Okay, thanks Mom. You're a lifesaver."

"Don't mention this to your father," Leeanna warned.

"Wayne, you haven't made more than two hundred dollars all month and the bill money is short again. Maybe you should try to find a regular job. My Mom is going to loan us some money tomorrow, but I really hate to take it. She doesn't make that much and I feel ashamed taking money from her," Lori confessed.

"If you would stop spending money like we're rich, then you wouldn't have to take money from your mother. Keep your ass out of the stores and you'll have more than enough to pay the bills," Wayne said defensively. "I made $65,000 last year and I'm on track to make more this year. If you can't budget the money, then don't blame me," he shouted. "I'm not having this conversation with you again, Lori. It's always the same old shit with you. When we have money, you spend it, and when we don't have money it's my fault." Wayne slammed the door as he left the house.

Wayne called Shelly on his cell phone after driving around aimlessly for fifteen minutes. "Hey Girl, what's up? I have a little time and I thought I'd come over your house to see that beautiful face of yours. Yeah, I love that big ass of yours too. Put on something sexy, I'll be there in twenty minutes," Wayne said. He spent the night with Shelly.

          Wayne showered, shaved and changed his clothes. He'd waited until Lori left for work. He didn't feel like arguing with her before he went to work. He was already frustrated that business was slow. Everybody at work was depressed. I have to go to work and call all of my old customers to try to get them to come in and buy a car. I made over one hundred calls, to no avail. All of the salesmen and managers are walking around telling jokes that aren't funny. Everyone laughs to pretend they aren't depressed. Damn, I hate going in there when we aren't busy.

As Paul walked towards the park at a brisk pace, he took note of the clear sky full of stars. It's a perfect night for adventure, he thought. He could feel the blood rushing through his body as he entered the darkness, stopping at the bench under the light. A lone man was already positioned on the bench. Paul sat, leaning his head back to marvel at the big dipper, which was very clear tonight. He could feel the intensity of the stranger's stare. He slowly sat upright and looked at him. He was quite handsome, almost feminine, with blond hair and shocking blue eyes. Blue eyes rose from the bench and disappeared into the blackness behind the big oak tree. Paul was aroused by the man's feminine beauty. He tried to hide his excitement by leisurely following the man. He dropped to his knees in front of Paul and began to undo his pants as Paul stared straight ahead into the darkness. Paul enjoyed the sex.

Paul broke away from the stranger's embrace and adjusted his clothing. He hurried through the park to the street. He crossed the street to the mini mall. He gathered several snacks that he thought April would like. These gifts helped to quiet his feelings of guilt. He preferred taking her healthy snacks from Trader Joe's. The mini crackers are delicious and so are the sweet potato chips, he thought. As he approached the cashier, he noticed someone following him. He turned and looked into shocking blue eyes. He panicked and walked around the store again. Maybe it's a coincidence, he thought as he waited for the stranger to leave the store. He didn't leave; he stood at a distance and watched Paul. As Paul approached the cashier again, the stranger came up behind him and said "Fancy meeting you here."

Paul ignored him and got out of line and walked down another aisle. The stranger followed close behind him.

"Why are you evading me? I thought you liked me. I certainly enjoyed you," the stranger said.

Paul turned to confront his pursuer. "What do you want? You're breaking the rules."

"I'm sorry," he apologized. "I only wanted to let you know that I think you are special. I wanted to know if we could get together and maybe... go out for a drink or something."

"Absolutely not! Stay away from me and don't try to follow me again! You've broken the rules," Paul said adamantly. He took his purchases to the register and left the store. He was paranoid as he walked towards home. He walked around in circles, using evasive tactics to avoid his admirer. He could ruin everything, he thought. He stealthily made his way home, locking the door and peering out through the livingroom window. He couldn't risk losing April and the children. They were his only family; nothing was worth that. He'd lost contact with his father and brother years ago.

"Honey, is that you?" April shouted down the stairs.

"Yes, yes it's me. I picked up some treats from Trader Joe's."

"Oh, I was beginning to worry; you were gone longer than usual."

"It was such a lovely night, I lost track of time," he said as he entered the bedroom where April laid watching television. "I'm a little sweaty; I'm going to take a shower." He threw her a bag of yogurt covered raisins. "Don't eat them all before I come out of the shower," he chuckled.

"You'd better hurry if you want some," April giggled.

He started the shower and stripped out of the soiled sweatsuit. He let out a sigh and fell back against the wall. He was caught off guard by the moan that emanated from his throat. He reached for a towel and covered his face, as the moans became loud sobs. He slid down the wall to a sitting position on the floor and cried into the towel.

"Why am I so weak?" he asked himself. "Why am I so weak?"

CHAPTER 5

Lori stirred the spaghetti sauce with the wooden spoon, tasting it to see if it tasted like Mama's sauce. Mmmmmm, it was very close. She added the sweet Italian sausage to the sauce. That should make it taste better. She turned off the linguine and drained it. She prepared the garlic bread to put in the oven when Wayne came home. He would be quite pleased with himself, of that she was sure. Wayne begged her to have a baby for three years, and now, he was finally getting his wish. She didn't stop taking the birth control pill on purpose, she forgot to take them for two days and Bam, just like that, and she was pregnant. She waited to see if she would miss another month of her period before telling him. She didn't want to give him any false hopes, if she wasn't pregnant.

"I'm not sure that I'm ready for this," she said to herself. I'm not sure that Wayne is ready for this either. I know he wants a baby, but talking and doing are different things. Getting up two or three times a night won't be easy. Oh well, it's too late to worry about that now. I'm pregnant; I'm two months pregnant with Wayne's baby.

Lori placed the baby bottle into the gift bag and put pink and blue tissue paper on top. She would give it to him at the right moment. She could just imagine his face lighting up with pleasure. She had a salad and wine cooling in the refrigerator. Wayne would be surprised that she'd cooked him a meal. She planned to wait until after dinner to give him the gift bag. She'd even bought an instant camera to commemorate the occasion. These pictures would be the first in the baby's book.

I was upset when I first realized I was pregnant. I even considered getting an abortion. After giving it some thought, I realized I was being selfish. At thirty-five, I wasn't getting any younger, and Wayne really wanted to start a family, so here we are getting ready to become parents in seven months. Wayne has been staying home more for the past few months. He hasn't been hanging out with his friends. He's been attentive, calling home at least twice a day.

"Hi Baby, what's that I smell? I hope it's food, because I'm starving."
Lori walked towards Wayne and kissed him. "I made you some of my Mama's spaghetti. I even put Italian sausage in the sauce," she bragged.
"That's great Lori," he said. He washes his hands in the kitchen sink and sits down to the table. "Bring it on!" Wayne orders.

Lori heated the garlic bread while she fixed Wayne's plate. He ate two plates full of the spaghetti. He wanted to encourage her to cook more often. She sat at the table smiling as she watched her husband eat. Wayne enjoyed the food and the attention. When he finished eating, Lori excitedly grabbed his hand and led him into the livingroom. "Sit on the sofa Wayne; I have something to give to you." She reached behind the sofa and pulled out the gift bag.

"What's this Lori? What, is this my birthday, our anniversary or what?"
"Open the bag Wayne!"
Wayne pulled out the pink and blue paper from the bag. He reached inside the bag and pulled out a baby rattle. A smile slowly spread across his face. He reached into the bag again and pulled out the baby bottle, while Lori snapped several pictures.

"Does this mean what I think it means?" Wayne asked apprehensively. He reached for her hand, as he looked into her eyes. "Are we pregnant Baby?" Wayne inquired. Lori shook her head up and down as tears glistened from her eyes.

"Yes Wayne, we're pregnant. I'm two months along."

"That's wonderful news. I'm so glad we're finally going to be a family." He embraced his pregnant wife, giving her tender lingering kisses. Wayne was an only child and he wanted to have three children. He didn't want his children to grow up lonely like he did. He wanted them to enjoy the companionship of sisters or brothers. This baby would be the first of three, he hoped. This baby would make them a family. This baby would make him a father and Lori a mother, he thought. Wayne looked at Lori and thought she looked more beautiful than ever before, she had that glow that only pregnancy brings. She looked happy and radiant.

Wayne was very tender while making love to Lori that night. He didn't want to risk injuring the baby. Lori felt special, as she fell asleep in his arms. Wayne was restless, he couldn't get to sleep; he had a lot on his mind.

Wayne was tired after working all day. Business had picked up and he was making mad money now. He'd insisted that Lori cut up all but two of their credit cards, and he was trying to pay the others off. "We have a little money in the bank now, and I want to keep it that way," he said to himself. He'd spent most of the night worrying about Lori's pregnancy. He was ready to be a father, but now wasn't a good time.

Wayne received a call from Shelly. "Hello, yeah it's me. Who else did you expect to answer my cell phone? I told you to stop calling me. I don't want to hear that shit. I gave you money to get an abortion four months ago, even though I knew it wasn't mine. Yeah, that's right. Now you're trying to tell me that you didn't get the abortion. Where's my $600. That's right, my damn money. No, I'm not giving you another cent. Call your baby's daddy and get some money from him. Look, I know you're screwing at least three other guys. I told you I was married and it was just a sex thing. No, nothing has changed. Well, don't call me again. You,

your baby and your baby's daddy have a good life." He
hung up the phone while she was still talking.

     Lori's two months pregnant and this crazy girl is
six months pregnant, and she's trying to blame it on me.
I guess I'm the only brother with a job. I made the mistake of giving her money in the first place. Now, she
thinks she's going to milk me. No way; Wayne is not
going out like that! This woman is making it impossible
for me to enjoy Lori's pregnancy. Fuck Shelly. Lori and
I will have the prettiest Jackson baby you ever did see.
Wayne calls Lori on the phone. "Hi Baby, how are you
feeling? I didn't hurt you did I? I love you. Dinner was
delicious! I hope you and little Wayne didn't eat all of
the sausages out of the spaghetti sauce," he joked.
"Heat it up for me Baby, I'm on my way home."
Wayne was so happy that Lori was finally pregnant. He
wanted the kind of family that he never had. Wayne's
childhood was lonely. His mother never remarried after
his father's death, so there was just the two of them. His
relationship with her wasn't as close as he would have
liked, because she was never home, but he loved her for
all of the sacrifices she made for him. She was a good
mother, but sometimes he wished she'd remarried, so
he could have had a father figure, some siblings and
more time with her. He knew Lori would be a good
mother to their children, in spite of her rebellious nature. He loved her high spirit even though she aggravated him sometimes. Every now and then she would
let her guard down and reveal the warm and fuzzy Lori,
he thought as he smiled to himself. The Lori that she
didn't reveal to the world; the Lori that made passionate
love to him and then fell asleep in his arms.

Shelly slammed the phone onto the cradle. She was so angry with Wayne for not being supportive. He knows this is his baby. He's just like all the other bums out here; they will screw you morning, noon and night, but as soon as you get pregnant, they'll say it's not mine, or you were sleeping with three other guys. I'm sick of this shit. I asked Wayne for money to buy some maternity clothes, so I can go to work and he doesn't want to give it to me. I can't go to work in clothes that are too small for me, and I can't take food out of my two sons' mouths to buy new clothes. I need help! He's not going to get away with ignoring me.

She walked barefoot through the two bedroom apartment, stepping on an action figure and hurting her foot. "These damn kids and their toys," she screamed. "James and Wilson, get your asses in here and pick up these toys before I throw them into the trash." She continued to the kitchen and poured a glass of Cola. She pulled a big bag of barbeque potato chips from the top of the refrigerator and sat down at the table to have a snack.

I thought Wayne was a quality guy. He's so handsome, dresses nice, always has money and works everyday. At first, he used to wine and dine me, taking me to quality restaurants now and then. When the newness wore off, all he wanted to do was come over here to get laid. I didn't mind that since he is a good lover and his dick is as large as his feet. Then, I missed my period and everything changed. Now, he acts like he doesn't know me. She finished her snack and hobbled back through the apartment to the livingroom to the sofa. "James and Wilson, didn't I tell you to pick up these damn toys? Get in here right now," she shouted as her two sons came running into the room. I'm already raising these two boys by myself and it's not easy. Now, I'll have three kids to raise alone, she thought. I know Wayne said he was married, but if he loved his wife so much, then why was he over here fucking me? True, he wasn't the only one, but I know exactly when I got pregnant, and it was while I was fucking Wayne.

I know I told Wayne that I was getting an abortion, but I thought about it, and I decided against it. I've already had three abortions in two years. I thought it was too dangerous, besides, every woman needs a daughter and I have two sons. This is my body, and I'll make the decisions that affect my body. That man had better bring me some money or I'll take this big belly right up to his job. I'll put his business in the street.

When I first met Wayne at the dealership, I thought he was really cute. I was wearing a pair of tight jeans and a low cut tee shirt. He couldn't stop looking at me. When we were walking around looking at cars, he kept walking behind me, checking out my ass. When we were sitting down in his office, he kept standing over me looking down my tee shirt at my breast. He was all smiles. He sold me a used car. I kept calling him, telling him how much I liked it and what a great salesman he was. They always respond to flattery, and he has a big ego. I knew it wouldn't take much to get him interested. Men are weak. Four or five phone calls from me, and he was over here in my bed. He couldn't get enough of me and I enjoyed every minute of it. Now he's acting like he's not interested, but I know he is. He's just mad that I didn't get the abortion.

Lori called her mother to give her the good news. "Oh Lori, I'm so happy for you and Wayne! You're two months pregnant? How wonderful! Another grandchild, your father will be happy to hear this. I know Wayne is thrilled. What do you want, a boy or a girl? Doesn't matter, well that's true, as long as its healthy. What about Wayne, what does he want? I knew he would want a son, but he'll be happy if it's a girl. Don't worry about it. It's not as if you have a choice; as long as it's healthy. Make sure you eat right and don't take any medicine unless the doctor orders it for you. Well Honey, I have to go and make your father's dinner, you know how he gets if it's late. Congratulations! I love you. Bye," said Leeanna.

Imagine that, another grand in the family. I hope it's a boy. Frank would enjoy having another boy in the family. He was so disappointed that we didn't have a son. It's a little late, but at least he'll have grandsons. My father would have loved Anthony; like Frank, he didn't have a son. He was disappointed when my sisters and I gave birth to girls. There are a few great grandsons, but too late for my father to enjoy them. My mother enjoyed her granddaughters, Leeanna thought with a smile; especially Lori. She was the first grandchild and both my parents spoiled her rotten. Frank spoiled her too, until she got big enough to talk back to him.

Leeanna put the chicken on to boil. She cut onions and green peppers into the pot. She went upstairs, changed clothes and returned to the kitchen. She took the canned biscuits from the refrigerator and placed them on the counter to reach room temperature. After the chicken was done, she dropped the biscuits into the boiling water to make dumplings. She stirred the pot to keep them from sticking. She opened a can of celery soup and dumped it into the pot. She added seasoning and stirred.

"Dinner is delicious," Frank said. "I'd like some more dumplings." Lee complied. They talked sporadically to each other about their children, their grandchildren, and trivia from Frank's job and the weather. Leeanna saved the best for last.
"Lori is pregnant, she's two months." She looked at him for a reaction.
"Well it's about time." He said sarcastically. "I'd almost given up on her.I guess Wayne had almost given up on her too. That girl is so lazy and selfish, she'll probably try to make Wayne give birth for her," he laughed
"She's getting a little better. She's been calling me for recipes lately."
"Really," Frank said as he raised his brow. He got up from the table and walked towards the livingroom. He continued, "She kept her room like a pigs sty when she was growing up. She refused to learn to cook and she always left the sink dirty when she

washed the dishes. I punished that girl so much, until I got tired of punishing her. Let's see what kind of mother she makes." Frank prepared himself a drink, sat in his recliner and turned on the television.

Leeanna knew the conversation was over. Frank was on his throne. He'd had his say and he really didn't care what she thought. Leeanna removed the plates from the table and started her routine of cleaning the kitchen. Why couldn't he just say he was happy for her? He always had something negative to say, especially about Lori. He thought April was wonderful, but Lori didn't see things his way. He would spank her, punish her and yell at her, but Mr. Educator couldn't change Lori. She had a mind of her own. It's ironic that she went to college and became a teacher like Frank. April became a counselor, listening to the problems of others and trying to keep the peace.

Lori didn't give into his whims. April tried to keep the peace like me She always tried to please her father, Leeanna thought as she prepared to go upstairs to watch television.

"Frank do you want anything before I go upstairs?" She asked

"Yes, I'd like a glass of water." Leeanna brought him the water.

"Do you have any grapes in there?" Frank asked.

"Yes we have grapes, do you want some?"

"Yes, bring me a bunch will you?" Leeanna didn't respond. She brought his Majesty the grapes. Leeanna went upstairs and called April.

"Hi April, how was your day? Good. I'm glad to hear that you had a good day. How is Paul doing? I guess he's out walking. Yes, it is good exercise. It keeps him slim and trim. Are the children sleeping? I know they keep you busy. I have some good news to tell you. You would never guess, so I'm just going to tell you. Lori is two months pregnant. Yes, at last. You know Wayne has been trying to get her to have a baby for ages. Can you imagine Lori as a mother? That means that she will have to grow up. I Know. I'm very happy for her and Wayne. Don't tell her I told you, let her tell you herself. Well, I'm going to let you go. I know you probably have one million things to do before you go to sleep. Give my love to Paul and kiss my grands for me. I love you. Goodbye."

So, I'm going to be a grandfather again, he thought as he sat in his chair. He usually didn't go upstairs until he was ready for bed. His shoes sat in front of the sofa, his pants were neatly stretched across the sofa and his jacket and tie hung on the back of the chair in the corner. He always gathered his clothing when he was ready to go upstairs to bed. He hung them in the closet carefully, so they wouldn't wrinkle. His shoes stayed in the livingroom until the next morning. He spent evenings in his recliner with only his socks, boxer shorts and white work shirt unbuttoned. He was tired when he arrived home from work, after spending the day walking up and down stairs, supervising students and staff. He tried to remain visible at school. It kept everyone on their toes and less problems developed.

Leeanna seems to be happy about the pregnancy, he thought. We'll see how happy she is when Lori is over here every other day asking her to baby-sit. April didn't burden us with her children. She and her husband hired babysitters when they wanted to go out. I'll have to lay down some laws for Lori or her baby will become our baby. Lee has enough work to do around here without Lori putting her responsibilities on her mother. I have to admit, Lori is more like me, and April is like her mother. Lori is strong willed and independent, she's always resisted taking on a woman's role. Nature will show her that she is a woman and so will the baby. Frank smiled as he thought of his first child. I spoiled her rotten when she was little; I helped to make her the selfish person she has become. She acts just like a man. She wants, what she wants, when she wants it.

Wayne has been trying to get Lori to have a baby for the past three years. Now, why should a man have to beg his wife to have a baby? That's a part of marriage. She knew he wanted children when she married him, he thought as he poured himself a drink. I've heard him talking to Paul about his children. Wayne loves kids. Whenever he's around Ashley and Anthony; he's always playing games with them and giving them attention. I think Wayne will make a good father. There's something about Wayne that I like. He's an alright kind of guy. He certainly has a lot of patience with Lori. He's a hard working guy and seems to be taking care of Lori. I haven't seen him for a while. The last few times we invited them over here, he's been working. You can't blame a man for working. Well, I'm happy that Wayne is finally going to be a father, that Lori has finally decided to give him a child.

"Paul, Paul, guess what? Lori and Wayne are pregnant," April said excitedly.

"I don't believe it," Paul responded "I'll have to see it to believe it."

"Oh she's pregnant alright, Mom just told me."

"I was beginning to wonder if there was a problem, you know she is getting older and her biological clock is ticking." Paul said

"Me too, I just heard on television that women are born with a specific number of eggs. Eggs are released each time a women has a period. I thought maybe, she'd used up all of her eggs. Well, I'm glad she had one left," April laughed.

"So am I. Now Ashley and Anthony can have a little cousin. You'll probably have to tell her everything. She won't know what to do with a baby. I guess the baby will be over here as much as it will be home," Paul chided April.

"I don't think so," said April. "I'll buy her a book."

"You go upstairs and lay down; I'll get the kids ready for bed tonight. You look tired," said Paul. "Yes, I don't know why I'm so tired. I think I may be catching a cold." April retired to the bedroom. April was so excited about Lori's pregnancy. She knew Lori would make a great Mom. She was always attentive to Ashley and Anthony. Lori tried to portray a hard exterior, but she was really more like a marshmallow. Lori felt that she had to protect Mom and I from Dad's angry outburst. She would tell Dad to stop screaming at Mom. She would take the blame when I'd break something or get in trouble. Dad would spank her, but she wouldn't back down; she was our protector. Now she can relax and enjoy her husband and her baby.

Dad's tirades always frightened me. I'd run and hide. I just wanted everything to be quiet and peaceful. Dad didn't hit Mom, but his voice was so big, it was scary, and sometimes he would knock things to the floor. It was very intimidating. Mom would say, you girls go to your room and close the door. Dad and I are talking. I would run to my room and get under the bed. Lori would stand there looking at him, saying, stop it Dad, you're scaring us. Mom would pick her up and carry her to her room and close the door. She didn't like for us to see Dad acting like that. We could look forward to these outbursts every few months. That's what I love about Paul; he's so even tempered and loving. He's a good provider and a good companion. He's my best friend. He promised me before we were married that he would never terrorize his family like my Dad.

He never has. He rarely raises his voice, unless it's in laughter, April thought. Paul and the children played several games of Mancala.

"Let's run to the market to get some root beer soda and vanilla ice cream."

"Yea Daddy, are you going to make root beer floats?" asked Ashley.

"I certainly will," Paul answered.

"Let's go Daddy," urged Anthony as he tied his sneakers.

"Okay, but let's ask Mommy if she wants something from the store."

"April," he yelled up the steps, "Do you want anything from the store?"

"Yes Honey, I'd like some grape juice and some vitamin C."

"We'll be back shortly," he shouted.

The children raced ahead of Paul as he pushed the shopping cart through the supermarket. They had placed several boxes of cereal in the cart. Paul remembered, they needed maple syrup for breakfast in the morning. Anthony chased Ashley down the aisle as she ran to get a loaf of bread.

"Let me get it," Anthony shouted. "I want to get it."

They disappeared out of the aisle. Paul moved swiftly to keep the children in sight. As he turned out of the

aisle, he collided with another shopper's cart. Paul
looked up, saying I'm sorry……he looked into deep
blue eyes.

"Hello there, I haven't seen you in quite some
time."

Paul stared at the man in front of him, momentarily for-
getting about Ashley and Anthony. He unlocked his
cart, attempting to maneuver around the stranger.

"Ashley, Anthony, wait right there for me. I'm
coming."

"You have two lovely children. You are a lucky
man," said blue eyes as he stood admiring Paul.

"You'll have to excuse me, I don't have time to
talk," Paul said nervously as he turned his cart around.

"Listen, I can understand that. I see you are
busy, but please let me give you my card. Give me a
call," said blue eyes.

Paul read the card aloud with a look of surprise, "Eric
Benz Esquire."

"Yes, that's me. If you ever need a lawyer, I'm
your man," he laughed "I'd still like to get together for
that drink," said Eric Benz Esquire.

"I'm not interested in having a drink with you. I
don't know you," Paul said firmly.

"We can remedy that over a drink," Benz flirted.

"I'm not interested in getting to know you or in
developing a relationship with you. My needs are being
met," Paul told him.

"I thought something more personal and exclusive would be more to your liking. You obviously are
an intelligent man, you have too much class for such
superficial involvements like Living on the Down
Low," Benz said trying to convince Paul.

"I'm satisfied with the relationships that I have. When you are Living on the Down Low, and participate in the park activities, it's supposed to be anonymous. Everyone that comes there, comes for that reason, otherwise they would go to the clubs or gyms to meet boyfriends. You don't seem to understand," Paul said in a frustrated manner as he walked away.

"Oh, I understand alright, I just found you to be very attractive and I wanted more," Benz flirted.

"Well the feelings aren't mutual, and I'm through with this conversation. Stay away from me!" Paul said with conviction while looking him in the eye to let him know that he meant it. Paul rushed away from blue eyes, stopping to get the vitamin C. He went to the cashier, hurriedly placing his purchases on the conveyor belt.

"Why are we rushing Daddy?" Ashley asked. "I want to get some cookies."

"Not today, we have to get home to Mommy. She'll get lonely," Paul said.

"Okay," complied Ashley.

Paul hustled the children into the black Volvo. He wanted to exit the parking lot before Eric Benz Esquire left the market. Who knows, he might try to trace me through my registration tag. I don't trust that man. He's strange, Paul thought.

"Daddy, your hands are shaking. Why are your hands shaking? Are you alright?"
Ashley inquired with concern.

"Daddy's fine Ashley, I'm just a little tired."
As Paul drove home, he cursed himself for being lulled into a false sense of security, for allowing Benz to catch him off guard and make him feel threatened. Benz ob-

viously is openly gay. He wasn't a regular at the park and his presence there was an indication that word of the DL park activities was spreading outside of the circle. He knew that there would be others like Benz frequenting the park; others that had nothing to lose. There would be others threatening to expose his bisexuality. He'd have to be cautious.

When Paul's sexual attraction towards men rekindled, he wasn't sure what to do. He found himself admiring men as he walked down the street. Although he dressed conservatively, in a business suit and had a masculine demeanor, he noticed some men trying to make eye contact with him. Their flirting flustered him, making him feel vulnerable, so he quickly walked away to escape their gaze. It was at a cocktail party, that a muscular man with a thick mustache approached him and asked if he was DL. Paul's expression betrayed his ignorance. At that point he asked Paul if he was Living on the Down Low? Paul told him, he didn't know what he meant, but he knew that his inner desires had been discovered. Malik slipped a key into Paul's hand with a piece of paper containing a nearby address. He left the party and Paul followed a short time later. He met the stranger at his apartment and had sex with the second man in his life. It satisfied the sexual yearnings he'd been experiencing.

Paul opened up to the stranger, revealing his dilemma. He told him he was married and very much in love with his wife, and they had two children. He said he wasn't interested in a relationship, but he did enjoy having sex with men from time to time. Malik told Paul that he dated women and men, and there were lots of men that did the same. He informed Paul of a gym in Center City that catered to men Living on the Down Low, that were in committed relationships with women. He told Paul about websites, private clubs and suburban parks that catered to a more exclusive group of men. Paul thanked him for the information and once or twice a week, he checked out some of the DL places. He found the gyms and clubs didn't offer him the anonymity that was so important to him. There were too many men that patronized those larger places, and he didn't want to risk running into neighbors or clients. He wasn't interested in on going relationships, so he preferred a transient clientele. The parks offered him the cover of darkness and only one or two participants at a time. These men were on the Down Low like him, and they adhered to an unspoken, strict code of conduct. These encounters didn't take long and he could fit them in without raising April's suspicions.

"What do you think of Morgan for a girl and Taylor for a boy?" Wayne asked Lori as she lay in his arms watching television.

"Not for my baby, I like Madison for a girl and Wayne Jr. for a boy," Lori responded.

"I don't want a junior. I never liked my name. My mom named me after her dead brother, so I never complained, but I would have preferred a name like Brian or Dean."

"I like Ryan, Aaron, Tyler or Blaine," Lori suggested.

"I like Blaine for a boy and Blair for a girl. Blaine Wayne Jackson, how do you like that?" Wayne asked

"It's okay. How about Bentley for a boy, Terren for a girl?" she asked.

"We don't have to make a decision now, there's plenty of time. I'll pick up one of those baby name books," Wayne said.

"That's a good idea."

"I'm going to make a couple of turkey burgers. Do you want one?" Wayne asked

"Yes, I'd like mustard and ketchup."

Wayne went to the kitchen to make the burgers. Lori spread out on the sofa. She was enjoying the attention that Wayne was showing her. He's a good man, she thought. Ever since I told Wayne about the pregnancy, he's been so sweet! He's babied me, waited on me, cooked for me and rubbed my feet. I could get used to this, she thought.

"Do you want chips with your burger?"

"Yes, I'm hungry; you know I'm feeding two."

"What do the two of you want to drink?" he teased.

"We'll have a Coke," she said.

"I don't know if caffeine is good for you. How about a gingerale?" he suggested.

"Okay, gingerale it is."

Wayne brought her a tray and sat it on the coffee table.

"Wayne what do you think of Micah, Whitney or Kalidah?" she asked.

"They're cute names for a girl," Wayne responded Lori sat on the sofa eating and thinking of more names.

"I like Justin or Edmund or something like that. After all we're going to have a son," Wayne giggled.

"Why do you want a son, Wayne?"

"I want a son to play basketball with, to watch football with. Sports are something we can share and it would cement our relationship. I never had a father to share those interests with. Reggie was like an older brother to me; he taught me how to play basketball, football, and baseball. I want to be the kind of father to my son that I didn't have," Wayne said.

"That's so sweet Wayne. That makes me want a son too. I hope you get your son," Lori responded.

"If not this time, then maybe the next time," Wayne laughed.

"Have you ever heard of Daddy's little girl? If we have a girl, then she will be Daddy's little girl, and Mommy's daughter," Lori teased Wayne.

Lori rang the bell of the lovely English Tudor house. She immediately heard the footsteps of her niece and nephew running towards the door. She admired the beautiful tulips that were waving in the wind. The flower beds on both sides of the door were filled with colorful flowers. The freshly cut grass looked like a green velvet rug. Lori knew that April loved to work in her garden. She had a gardener, that cared for the grass, but April planted and cared for these beautiful flowers.

"Hi Aunt Lori, come in; Mommy will be right down," Ashley announced.

"Give me a big hug you two." The children hugged their aunt and ran back upstairs to continue their play; almost colliding with their mother on her way down the stairs.

"Hello stranger, this is quite a surprise," April said.

"I know," Lori said. I should visit more often. Don't make me feel guilty. I came to share some good news with you, that is, if Mommy hasn't told you already."

"What are you talking about?" April lied. "Come into the kitchen." Although April was the younger sister, she'd always acted like the big sister. She mediated family disagreements and tried to convince Lori to avoid confrontations. April tried to keep everyone happy. Lori was the protector.

"I have grape juice, soda, milk and tea. What's your pleasure?"

"I'll have grape juice."

"Are you hungry? I have lunchmeat, apple pie, cookies or chips," April offered.

"I'll have a slice of apple pie." April sliced the pie and returned it to the refrigerator. She sat across from Lori with a broad smile on her face.

"Now tell me the good news. I can use some good news."

"I'm pregnant," Lori blurted out.

"You're pregnant! Now that's good news! How far along are you?"

"I'm just two months." Lori answered excitedly.

"Is Wayne happy about it?"

"You know Wayne, he's thrilled. He's been trying to get me barefoot and pregnant for a long time," Lori laughed.

"Well my big sister is finally going to be a mother. That's wonderful. I know Ashley and Anthony will be happy to know that a little cousin is on the way'" April said excitedly.

"Let's not tell them, until I start to show. It will make it more real to them," Lori requested.

"Whatever you say Mommy," April laughed. "Can I get you anything else to eat, since you're eating for two?"

"No this is plenty. I don't want to get too fat, too fast," Lori replied.

"I'll have to dig out the kid's baby things. I think I have a cradle, a high chair, a playpen, a crib, a chest and maybe a few other things, if you're interested in second hand furnishings," April offered.

"Second hand anything sounds good to me," Lori said gratefully.

"I'll have Paul pull them out and we'll see what kind of condition they're in."

"Great! If we have to paint a few things, that will be fine. I just hope I look like you, after I have this baby. I don't want to blow up and stay that way."

"Don't worry about that, you'll get your figure back," April responded.

"I guess you're right, maybe I will have another piece of apple pie. After all, Little Wayne hasn't eaten in three hours."

"Would Little Wayne like some ice cream on top of the pie?" April teased.

Lori looked down at her stomach. "Little Wayne said yes, he'd love some ice cream."

CHAPTER 6

Lori had the glow of an expectant mother. Her cheeks were rosy and her hair had sheen. As she stood in front of the mirror in the nude, she noticed her body was beginning to expand in preparation for the baby. Her breasts were fuller and her nipples were sensitive. Her waist now included a small bulge. Yesterday she was unable to button her pants. She had to wear a blouse outside of her pants. She turned to the side and massaged her stomach.

"Little Wayne is growing," she said happily.

Lori loved the attention that Wayne was showing her since learning of her pregnancy. Motherhood has its rewards, she thought. Mom and April have been calling to remind me to eat properly. A friend at work gave me three pairs of pants with elastic waists, and they're so comfortable. She put the black pair on with a red tee shirt. She brushed her hair and went to the kitchen. She had a salad, sandwich and milk. I have to eat for the baby she thought.

Wayne was very busy trying to sell two clients at once. The showroom was crowded and all of the salesmen were running from customer to customer. Wayne entered his office to look for a set of keys to a car he wanted to test drive.

"How are you today?" she said. Wayne was startled. He hadn't noticed anyone in the room. "What are you doing here?" he asked cautiously.

"I thought I'd pay you a visit, since you don't want to talk on the phone," Shelly said sarcastically.

"Look, I'm quite busy as you can see and I don't have time to talk."

"Well, you'll just have to make time, because I'm not going anywhere until you do."

"What do you really want Shelly?" Wayne asked. He noticed that her body was filling the entire chair. She didn't look very much like the sexy chick that used to make him horny just by talking on the telephone.

"I need some money and some support from you," she responded.

"What kind of money are we talking about?" he asked softly. He didn't want to draw attention to his situation. No one needed to know, she could be a customer, he thought.

"I need a couple hundred dollars to buy a few things to wear to work. As you can see, I'm too big with your baby to wear any of my clothes." Shelly's voice was beginning to crack as tears welled up in her eyes.

"Look, I have to get back to my customers. All I have is one hundred dollars." He reached into his pocket and peeled a one hundred dollar bill from the roll of money inside his pocket. "Take this and I'll bring you some more in a couple of days; after I get paid. I have to go. I'll talk to you later." Wayne quickly walked out of the office, straight through the building to the back door. He stood outside taking deep breaths, trying to release the anxiety he felt.

I don't believe that crazy ass girl had the nerve to come to my job. I almost shit myself when I saw her, but I played it cool. You can't let street girls like Shelly think that she's intimidating you. I think I handled it well. He cautiously reentered the building, peeping into his office to see if she was gone. She was gone! This girl is going to be a problem. I have to get focused. I have to go out here and sell some cars. "Showtime" he said as he returned to his customers.

Shelly left the car dealership with a smile on her face. I got him good. I almost scared him to death. I don't think he saw me when he came into his office. He looked like he was in shock. I only got one hundred dollars, but that's more than I had. I'll wear the maternity clothes my sister gave me. This one hundred dollars is going to pay my cable bill. Wayne had better bring me some more money or he'll be sorry. The next time I'm going to his house. I hate to get ugly, but these guys don't think they have to be responsible for their

SWIMMING WITH SWANS 85

actions. I didn't make this baby by myself and I'm not going to take care of it by myself.

I had my first child at age twenty-two. I was in love and thought I had met the right man for me. I moved into his apartment and things were pretty good until our second child was three years old. That's when I came home from work early to find him in bed with my next door neighbor. He didn't even try to hide when I walked in on them. He just laid there naked, looking at me as if I was intruding. I went to the kitchen and got the broom and beat both of them until I got tired, then I packed me and my sons clothes and left. I never had anything else to do with him. I took him to court for child support, and whenever he doesn't pay, I take him back to court again. He doesn't even come to get the boys that often. He's supposed to keep them for the summer, but he never does. Well, now I'm older and wiser, and Wayne is not going to get away with not living up to his responsibilities.

Wayne rang the doorbell of the large colonial twin house in Glenside. It was the perfect family home for Reggie and his family, with a wrap around porch and a huge backyard. He anxiously waited for a response. Shelly's visit to his job left him feeling stressed out. Talking to Reggie always seemed to make him feel better.

Reggie answered the door appearing surprised to see his friend. "Hi Wayne, come on in man. It's good to see you. What's a married family man like you doing out at ten-thirty at night during the week?" he joked.

"I was riding by your house and I noticed the light in the livingroom. I know you're the only night owl in this house," Wayne teased.

"Come on in the kitchen, I'm finishing up the dinner dishes. Would you like a soda?" Reggie offered.

"Sure, do you have gingerale?"

"Yeah." Reggie gave Wayne a canned soda. "So, what's going on?"

"Man, I know it's getting late, but I just had to talk to you. I won't stay long. You remember the girl I told you I was seeing a while ago?"

"Yeah."

"I didn't want to tell you before, because I was hoping it would go away, but she's pregnant and she's trying to say it's mine," Wayne confessed.

"Oh man!" Reggie exclaimed.

"Look, I know it's not mine. She was fucking a few other guys while I was sleeping with her. I knew about them, but I didn't care. It was just a booty call. I used protection every time I had sex with her. I don't ride bareback with anyone but my wife."

"Then how can she say it's yours, if you used condoms?" Reggie inquired.

"She's trying to act like she wasn't screwing anyone else, but I know for a fact that she was," Wayne asserted.

"Does Lori know?"

"No, she doesn't and I'm trying to keep it that way, but this girl is acting crazy."

"What is she doing?"

"She's blowing up my cell phone and she had the nerve to come to my job today. Can you believe it?"

"What does she want?" Reggie quizzed Wayne.

"Money, money, money," Wayne answered sarcastically. "That's what it's all about."

"Why does she need money, the baby's not even here yet?"

"I made the mistake of giving her $600.00 to get an abortion, even though I knew it wasn't mine. I just didn't want any shit."

"Well, why didn't she get the abortion? You gave her the money. What's her excuse?"

"She changed her mind and spent the money. Now, every time I hear from her, she's demanding money!" Wayne explained.

"You may have to give it to her to keep her quiet until she has the baby, then you can get a DNA test done. They can take the blood from the umbilical cord or swab the baby's mouth," Reggie explained.

"I guess you're right. I have to keep her quiet, before she starts some shit that can snowball. Do you know what I mean?"

"Yeah, I know exactly what you mean."

"And guess what else, Lori is two months pregnant," Wayne announced.

"Oh no!" Reggie exclaimed. "No wonder you're so stressed out. You're dealing with two pregnant women at the same time. Just keep them apart until you can get the DNA test done."

"That may be easier said than done," Wayne complained.

"I know you want the baby with your wife, we talked about that."

"Sure I do, but Shelly's making it difficult to even enjoy Lori's pregnancy. She keeps me upset."

"Calm down, Little Brother. Don't let her see your fear, If you do, then she's going to take you to the cleaners!" Reggie warned Wayne.

"I know, I'm trying to stay cool, but this shit is getting to me."

"Don't let it get you down. Just stay on top of it. That's all you can do until Shelly's baby is born."

"I think I'm the only potential father with a job. That's why she's saying it's mine,"

"Yeah that happens more than you know," Reggie agreed. "That's why it's dangerous to start relationships with these crazy ass women out here. As soon as something goes wrong, then they want to make you pay for all mankind," Reggie continued. He felt sorry for Wayne, but he did warn him about this when he first started messing with this girl.

"Look man, I appreciate you listening to my woes. I had to talk to someone," Wayne said. He tilted his head back as he drained the last of the soda from the can. "I'm going to leave and let you go to bed man. Thanks a lot," Wayne said as he walked towards the door. "I'll let you know what happens," he said as he stood on the porch of Reggie's home. "Yeah, keep me up on it, and don't worry, everything will be alright. Goodnight." Reggie knew this was just the beginning of Wayne's woes.

Shelly calls Wayne on his cell phone. "Hi Shelly. I'm busy right now and I don't have time to talk. Yeah, I know I said I'd bring you some money, but I haven't had any money. When I get some, you'll get some. I'm not screwing you around. I just haven't had any money. I don't draw a paycheck, I work on commission. If I don't sell a car, I don't get any money. I can't give you what I don't have. Well, fuck you too."

Five days after she talked to Wayne on the phone, Shelly comes to the dealership again. Wayne was outside on the car lot with some customers when he saw a pregnant woman wobbling towards him. He was showing a woman and her sister a Honda CRV. He excused himself and walked towards Shelly to head her off.

Hi Shelly, what is it now?" He placed his hand over her shoulder and spun her around, walking her back towards her car.

"You know what I want. Why do I have to beg you for money when you know you should give it to me without asking? I need money! Doctor visits cost money. I have to eat a balanced diet, and eating for two is twice as expensive." They stood in front of her car arguing.

"I don't have much money Shelly," he said defensively.

"Don't give me that bullshit Wayne. I don't want to act ugly on your job," she said as her voice began to rise. "This is your baby and I need some fucking money."

Wayne reached into his pocket and pulled out two, one hundred dollar bills. "Here take this Shelly and don't come to my job again. This isn't a joke. The people here know that I am married, and it doesn't look right for you to keep popping up here on my job. If you come here again, you won't get anything else from me." Wayne turned and quickly walked away from her. She's getting on my last nerve, Wayne thought to himself.

Shelly looked at Wayne's back as he walked away from her. "You're still one fine ass brother," she said softly to herself. She shouted to him "Thanks Wayne, you're so sweet." Not bad for ten minutes of my time. Two hundred dollars, not bad at all, she thought. Shelly still found Wayne attractive. She still cared for him and she wanted him to show some interest in her. She wanted to lay in his arms and have him massage her stomach with lotion. She wanted him to talk to their baby in her stomach. She wanted him to be happy about the baby. She wanted him to rub her back where it ached. She wanted him to get up at night and make her an egg sandwich when she woke up hungry.

She wanted him to assure her that everything would be alright. She wanted him to live up to his responsibilities.

Shelly missed Wayne. She missed his smile. She missed his jokes. She missed his kisses. She missed his lovemaking. He'll be back after I have this baby and I'm back in my clothes looking good. He'll be back, she smiled to herself, as she drove towards the mall, but until then, I'll make sure he gives me money for his baby, she thought.

Wayne called Reggie. "Hi Reggie, do you mind if I stop by your house on my way home? Great, I'll see you soon." When he arrived at Reggie's house, Reggie could sense that something was wrong.

"Come in and have a seat on the couch man. You look like you've had a bad day. Can I get you a beer?" Reggie offered.

"Yeah, I'd like a beer. Reggie, I appreciate your support man. Shelly came to my job again today, but I caught her before she got to the showroom and turned her around."

"Good! That's what you have to do, minimize the damage," Reggie advised.

"She's so pregnant, she wobbles when she walks. I was talking to some customers and I looked up and there she was wobbling across the car lot. I left my customers and rushed over to her and turned her fat ass around."

"Did she call before she came, or did she just show up?" Reggie asked.

"She just showed up!"

"Did you tell her not to do that again?" Reggie question Wayne. He could see his discomfort with the whole situation, so he tried to take things slow. "Well, what did she want this time?"

"Money, she always wants money. I feel like I'm being blackmailed," Wayne stated as he drank beer from the can.

"It is a form of blackmail," Reggie agreed. He noticed that Wayne had finished his beer. "Can I get you another beer man?"

"Yeah, I could use another one."

"What do you think she'll do next?"

"I don't know what she'll do, she's very unpredictable. She might do anything at anytime. She's one of those women that answer to no one."

"Oh man," Reggie exclaimed. "Did you give her some money?"

"Yeah, how else was I going to get rid of her? I gave her two hundred dollars."

"I know that made her happy." Reggie said.

"I guess so, but it won't last long. She'll be back next week wanting more."

"Try to be nice to her, maybe that will pacify her for a while. You know, women respond to kindness, especially in her condition," Reggie suggested.

"That's not easy man, I get so angry every time I see her and I think about my $600, that she kept instead of getting the abortion. I don't even like her as a person. She's too demanding."

"I would try to keep her calm until she has the baby, then you can do something about her demands."

"You're right, I'll have to try to appease her until I can get the DNA test, then I can prove I'm not her baby's father."

"But don't forget, you were screwing her, so there is a possibility that it is yours. Condoms aren't one hundred percent," Reggie warned Wayne.

"No, I used a condom every time I slept with her, and none of them were leaking. It's definitely not mine. You'll see, it's not mine," Wayne protested.

CHAPTER 7

"Dinner was good Lee. Could you bring me a Johnnie Walker on the rocks?" Frank asked as he sat at the kitchen table.

"I'm glad you enjoyed it," said Leeanna. She placed the drink and a napkin on the table in front of Frank. She prepared herself a cup of tea. They sat at the table lost in their own thoughts. Frank fixed himself a second and a third drink while Lee put the food away and made some macaroni salad for the next day. Lee asked Frank, "Would you like something else to eat?"

"No, if I wanted something to eat, I would ask for it," Frank answered in an irritated tone.

"You don't have to get nasty about it," Lee responded sarcastically.

"Don't start anything with me today Lee, because I'm not in the mood for your foolishness. Those union people have aggravated me enough. I don't need to come home to more aggravation," Frank shouted. He jumped up from the table quickly, knocking the chair over.

"Now was that necessary Frank? Do you always have to make a big deal about everything? Always making a mountain out of a molehill," she continued. "You need to grow up!"

Frank turned towards his wife and stared at her. He pointed his finger in her face, threatening her. "You don't want to start any shit with me today. I guarantee you, you won't like the outcome."

Lee returned his stare. They were locked into the moment. "No one is bothering you. I asked you a simple question. All you had to say is yes or no."

"Oh, now you're going to put words in my mouth. I don't need you to tell me what to say in my own house. That's enough; I don't want to hear another word Lee, not another word!"

Lee glared at Frank. Who does he think he is, talking to me like I'm a child? "Get out of the kitchen Frank. I'm trying to finish cleaning the kitchen," she ordered.

Frank rushed over to her and grabbed her by the throat with both hands. "Do you know that I can snap your damn neck like a twig? I can take your breath away, just like this," he said as he applied pressure to her neck. "When I tell you to shut up, then I mean what I say, I mean exactly that. Do you understand me?" he asked while glaring at her.

"Get off me Frank!" Their eyes were glued to each other. "Get off me Frank!" she shouted as she pushed him away from her.

He released his grip. "Stop playing with me Lee before you end up getting hurt."

Lee rushed towards the steps, holding her throat with a look of hate in her eyes. "Fuck you Frank," she screamed as she ran upstairs to the bathroom, slamming the door and locking it. "That man is crazy. He gets crazier everyday," she said aloud to herself as she looked in the mirror at her bruised neck. "He's just a bully, attacking a woman for no good reason." She sat on the toilet seat and cried.

Frank could hear his wife sobbing in the bathroom upstairs. He felt bad for letting things get out of control. I should have ignored her, but she knows I'm under a lot of stress. She always pushes me too far, he thought, as he fixed himself another drink. Lee knows me better than anyone and she knows when I've had enough, but she keeps pushing me until I lose my temper. He sat in the recliner staring, but not seeing the television. He closed his eyes as he heard her soft footsteps on the stairs, entering the kitchen. Then, he heard the familiar sound of Lee cleaning the kitchen. He sighed as he drifted off to sleep.

April and Paul returned home from a lovely night out in Center City. Paul took her to Warm Daddy's, an elegant restaurant that his partner in the accounting firm told him about.

"Paul the restaurant was beautiful and the food was delicious," April said.

"Yes, I enjoyed it. The service was excellent. We'll have to go again."

"I'd like that," she reached over and kissed Paul on the cheek. "Thank you for being so thoughtful."

Paul parked the car in the driveway. "April go inside and send the babysitter out. I'll take her home while you fix us a drink."

April waited for Paul. She wanted to discuss her mother with him. She didn't mention it earlier because she didn't want to ruin their evening. When he returned, they sat on the livingroom sofa drinking Brandy.

"Paul, I went to see my mother earlier today and I was very alarmed at what I saw," April said.

"What did you see, Honey."

"I saw bruises on my mother's neck. Of course, she said it was nothing, but I'm concerned. Do you think my father is capable of doing that to my mother?"

"I don't know April, you should have asked your mother. It's hard for me to guess. You never know what a person is capable of doing under the right circumstances," Paul responded.

"I love my Dad, but he can be very controlling. I'd hate to think that he is abusing my mother, while I did nothing; after all, I am a counselor. I work with abused women all of the time. They are often in denial."

"I don't know that it's up to you to do something about it. I think your mother is the one that has to do something; she has been married to him for over thirty years."

"What can she do if he's physically abusing her; maybe she's afraid of him."

"She doesn't act like she's scared of him. I mean......I know she caters to him, but I don't think she does it out of fear," Paul stated.

"I would feel so bad if I went over there and found her with a black eye or something worse," April said.

"Maybe you should have a talk with her and explain the dangers of letting Frank get away with abusing her. Frank is a large man and he could seriously hurt her without meaning to do it," Paul suggested.

"My Dad is a high school principal and he deals with issues of his male students abusing their girl-friends, he knows exactly what he's doing," April protested.

"Why don't you get your sister involved and the two of you take your mother to lunch or something and discuss the situation."

"Yes, that sounds like a good idea. I think I will tell Lori."

April calls Lori. "Hi Lori, can you stop over my house after school tomorrow? I'd like to ask your opinion about something. Great, see you tomorrow."

"Come in, come in and have a seat, Lori. The children are visiting with a friend because I wanted us to have some privacy."

"Now, you have made me curious. What is all of this about?" Lori asked with concern.

"I visited Mom yesterday and I saw something that upset me very much," April confessed.

"What did you see?" Lori asked impatiently.

"Mom had some bruises on her neck, and she couldn't explain how they got there."

"What! You mean to tell me that our mother has bruises on her neck? That bastard!"

"Don't jump to conclusions before we get the whole story. We need to talk to Mom," April advised her older sister.

"What whole story? He choked her, it's that simple. He choked her."

"We can't be sure of that until we talk to Mom," April stated calmly.

"You know, I'm not surprised. Dad's been throwing temper tantrums for years. Whenever he doesn't get his way or if dinner is late, then he screams all over the house or he starts breaking things. I don't know how Mom puts up with his behavior," Lori said while pacing the floor.

"Lori I counsel clients everyday and I know it's not good to jump to conclusions. Let's invite Mom to lunch and have a conversation with her about those bruises."

"Okay, but she's just going to take up for him like she always does; that much I know," Lori said disappointedly.

"Let's just wait and see what she has to say," April repeated.

Lori drove into the city to pick up April and Leeanna. They drove down the Parkway under the cascading trees on both sides of the highway. A parade of flags from countries around the world swung in the breeze along the Boulevard.

"I love to come to Center City this route because it is so beautiful," Leeanna exclaimed. "Philadelphia is sprucing up to attract tourism."

"You're right Mom, they've built a new convention center and plenty of hotels," Lori added.

"You should see Delaware Avenue, there are all kinds of clubs and restaurants there to accommodate the tourist," April said. "Some of them are quite beautiful and unusual."

"Everything looks beautiful and it's the perfect Saturday afternoon to spend with my favorite daughters," Leeanna laughed. "Thank you for getting me out of the house, otherwise I'd spend my day doing housework. When you work all week, you have to spend the weekend catching up on all the things you don't get done during the week."

"You're right about that," April agreed. "I've been looking forward to this all week. Anything that I haven't done won't get done this week. It's good to be out, just us ladies."

Traffic was heavy, so Lori didn't have too much to say. Her mind drifted from time to time to the conversation in the car. She'd nod in agreement while clutching the steering wheel. They finally arrived at the waterfront restaurant and parked the car. The restaurant was decorated sparingly, with mahogany stained wood flooring. There were dark wooden tables and chairs with red cushions. Red roses in crystal vases adorned the tables and pewter ornaments hung on the walls. Waiters in black tie stood at attention around rooms in the three story building and water with hues of green could be seen running under the glass steps.

Lori made small talk during the meal about her pregnancy. Leeanna joined in, telling her daughters about her pregnant experiences with them. April reminded them of her difficult pregnancies. Lori noted how lovely her mother looked in her burgundy suit, which was accented by a multicolored scarf around her neck. She was trying to pick the right moment to mention the problem to her mother without spoiling their lunch. As they sat waiting for their desserts to arrive, April asked her mother, "how is your neck feeling?" Leeanna was taken by surprise. "What do you mean April?"

"I mean, do you still have those bruises on your neck?" April asked.

"No, they're starting to clear up. You know I bruise easily, pale skin doesn't hide very much," Leeanna responded.

"What bruises are you talking about?" Lori asked.

"Oh it's nothing, nothing to worry about," Leeanna answered.

"Mom has some bruises on her neck and I was curious to know if they had gone away," April stated.

"Take your scarf off and let me see," Lori asked.

"No, I'm not undressing in public," Leeanna said defiantly.

"How did you get bruises on your neck, Mom?" Lori inquired.

"Look, I don't want to talk about this now. We're having a lovely time, and I don't want to ruin it," Leeanna pleaded.

"Well, I want to talk about it now", Lori insisted. "Did Dad put those bruises on your neck Mom?" Leeanna looked down at her hands, refusing to make eye contact with her daughters.

"Mom, please talk to us. We're worried about you. Please!" April pleaded.

"Okay, what do you want to know?"

"Did Dad put those bruises on your neck?" Lori asked again.

"Yes, he did," Leeanna confessed. "But he didn't mean it."

"Does he hit you, Mom?" April inquired.

"No, he's never hit me. He grabs me when he's been drinking too much and he gets frustrated. I don't think he realizes his own strength until it's too late. When he sees the bruises, I can tell he feels bad."

"He's a grown man, he knows his strength and he knows what he's doing. He's trying to intimidate you. That's what he's doing," Lori declared angrily.

"It usually starts with an argument about nothing. He says something, I say something, and the next thing you know, we're arguing like kids. You'd think one of us would have the sense and maturity to walk away, but we keep at it until he gets frustrated that he can't shut me up. He strikes out. I should stay away from him when I see him drinking too much."

"Mom, it has to stop, it's that simple, it has to stop. Don't blame yourself. He knows there is no excuse for him putting his hands on you. It has to stop!" Lori commanded.

"It sounds like Dad could use some anger management therapy, and he needs to stop drinking," April suggested.

"I agree with you girls, but I can't make him go. I can't make him do anything."
The waiter arrives with the desserts. No one touches them.

"Mom, I think you need to talk to him when he isn't drinking and you're not upset. Make him aware that there is a problem and something must be done about it before someone gets seriously hurt," April instructed her mother.

"I'll talk to him, if you want me to Mom. I'll tell him that his behavior is unacceptable and he needs some help," Lori volunteered.

"No, Lori, you two are too much alike. That will just cause another problem. You girls are right. I'll talk to him, but in my own time. I don't want you to worry about me because your father would never hurt me."

"He already has hurt you." Lori said in disbelief of her mother's denial.

"Don't wait too long to talk to him Mom, this is important," April advised.

"I won't," Leeanna promised.

They rode home with sporadic superficial chit chat. Lori had nothing to say. She knew her mother would avoid talking to her father about the abuse. Lori dropped April off at her home last. April kissed her big sister and said, "Well, at least we tried; now it's up to her."

Paul enjoyed his evening walks. After working all day, sitting in the office reading files, meeting with clients or his partner, it was a relief to get out in the air and move around. The DL sexual adventures were an added release. They helped him to relax. After the negative experience with Benz, Paul continued to walk, but not in his neighborhood. He drove his car to a park several miles away. He missed his sexual adventures, but he had to be cautious. He didn't want to risk running into Benz. Maybe if they had met in another place, in another time, maybe they could have gone for a drink. He certainly found him attractive enough, especially his eyes, they were so clear, almost a transparent blue. Paul knew the dangers of falling in love with a man. He made the decision long ago to have a traditional family, and he loved being a family man. Everyone else had to take a back seat to his wife and children. God had blessed them with two children that were perfect in every way. He had the kind of family life he'd always wished for when he was growing up. Paul didn't like the stigmatism that comes with living an open gay lifestyle.

Paul grew up in a small town in South Jersey. He and his older brother grew up in a large house near the shore. His father was a doctor and his mother was a housewife. Paul's brother was the kind of son that his father wanted. He played baseball and football. The whole family went to every game his brother played. His father expected Paul to follow in his brother's footsteps, but he wasn't athletically inclined. He was too skinny for football and he didn't have any talent at playing baseball. He ran track, but he was only fair at it.

He played basketball, but he wasn't a starter. He sat warming the bench with the other scrubs, which humiliated his father. Paul excelled in academics, earning straight A's and an occasional B. His father ignored him and his mother tried to compensate by overprotecting him. She protected him from his father's and his brother's wrath, but she couldn't protect him from the cruel comments of the children in school.

Paul's mother was black and his father was white and his biracial heritage made him the recipient of many unkind words. His maple colored skin and course hair made it difficult for him to hide in a crowd of white students. His brother had his father's hair texture and skin color, which made it easier for him to fit in. No one teased him, and if they did, he would dive into them with his fists, but Paul was the zebra. He didn't have any friends, just his mother. She died during his last year of high school, which left him feeling alone. He'd learned to cook and clean from his mother, so he took on her chores until he left for college. He couldn't wait to leave for college and leave all of his critics behind. Paul was grateful that April came into his life. She became his family. She was the kindest person he knew.

It's a lovely evening to walk, Paul thought. Tonight I'll return to the park. Benz should have disappeared by now. He walked down the street, past the mini mall and crossed the street to the darkness of the park. He noticed a lone figure sitting on the bench as he approached. He scrutinized the man until he was sure it wasn't Benz. Paul sat on the opposite end of the bench, slowly turning his eyes towards the stranger. Their eyes locked in an embrace. Paul's heart raced in anticipation of a DL sexual encounter with the stranger. He rose from the bench and slowly and provocatively walked towards the big oak tree. The stranger followed. The sex was great!

I missed having sex in the park, Paul thought as he left the park feeling satisfied. He crossed the street to the mini mall. Eric Benz Esquire is the reason I've had to deprive myself of this pleasure. I've been coming here and DL places like it for the past five years, and never had this kind of problem; hopefully, he will not reappear. The men that engage in our DL kind of adventures know that it's just a sexual encounter; they're not looking for a love connection. If you meet the same person more than once, you never show any sign of recognition, and you certainly don't follow them, trying to get a date or solicit a relationship. He has no class!

Paul bought vanilla and chocolate ice cream to take home to April. He was radiant as he briskly walked home to his family. He knew April and the children were waiting for him.

"Daddy, Daddy, do you want to play Uno?" Ashley asked.

"Sure Ashley, I'll play Uno with you after I take a shower. Why don't you fix Mommy a bowl of ice cream, and fix you and Anthony some too," Paul replied.

"Okay Dad," Ashley said. She filled three bowls with ice cream. She took them to the family room. The three of them sat watching television and eating ice cream as they waited for Paul to cleanse himself, and join them to play Uno as a family.

Shelly calls Wayne on his cell phone. "Hi Wayne, how are you doing? You know I really miss you. Why don't you stop by this evening and I'll make you some pepper steak? We can watch a movie. My kids are with their father and I'm feeling a little lonely. What are you so busy doing? You weren't too busy before you planted your seed in me. Come on Wayne, I really would like to see you," Shelly pleaded. "Well, to hell with you Wayne, don't come then," she slammed the phone down on the receiver.

He acts like I have the plague or something. He won't come anywhere near me. Every time I see him, he's rushing away. He used to be all over me, now that I'm pregnant; he acts like he doesn't know me. One monkey don't stop no show. I should call someone else. I'm tired of being mistreated by these sorry ass brothers. My sons' father thinks he can treat me like dirt, and now Wayne thinks he can treat me like dirt. There's nothing worse than being pregnant and alone. She stretched out on the couch with her swollen feet and legs elevated. She flipped through the channels, searching for a good movie to distract her from her discomfort. She settled for a movie she'd already seen. The baby's kick startled her awake from an uncomfortable twilight.

Shelly sat up feeling miserable. She stumbled to the kitchen, returning to the sofa with a cold glass of soda, and a large bag of pretzels. She sat on the couch feeling lonely and unhappy. If I'm going to be miserable, then I'm not going to be miserable by myself. She picked up the telephone and dialed 411. "I'd like the

home telephone number for Wayne Jackson. He lives at
823 Hewlett Avenue, in Cheltenham Township."
Wayne doesn't know I have his address. I saw it on his
driver's license when he was asleep in my bed and I
went through his pockets. "Yes, I have a pen." She
wrote down the phone number, then dialed it. I'll make
his ass miserable too, she thought.

"Hello, I'd like to speak to Wayne. Yes, Wayne
Jackson. Do you know when he'll be home? Are you
his wife? You don't know me, but I know of you. My
name is Shelly and I'm seven months pregnant by your
husband. Yes, I've been fucking him for about a year.
You don't believe me. Just ask him about Shelly and
tell that bastard that I need some more money. Tell him
that he doesn't want me to come to his job again. That's
right; he doesn't want me to embarrass his ass. Tell him
I said......that bitch hung up on me, but that's alright, I
won't be the only one that can't sleep tonight."

I don't believe it; some women will go to any lengths to try to steal someone else's husband. Shelly, who the hell is Shelly? Lori thought. Wayne wouldn't do something like that. He loves me. We're three months pregnant. He's finally going to be a father. Tears ran down her cheeks. Why am I crying, I know it's a damn lie. Wayne couldn't do that to me, but what if it's true? No, I won't allow myself to think this way. I'll wait for Wayne. He'll clear this whole thing up. It's probably someone unhappy with a car he sold them.

She sat on the sofa rocking back and forth. She remembered, in high school, girls would tell girlfriends all kinds of lies to break up relationships. They wanted their boyfriends. The tears streamed down her face as she waited for Wayne. But, why would this woman say that she'd been sleeping with my husband for a year? Maybe, Wayne wasn't working or with Reggie every time he was late. Maybe, he was with Shelly or some other woman. Maybe, Wayne was unfaithful. No, I don't believe that. I'll just wait for Wayne. She jumped up and ran to the toilet to vomit. She threw up everything she'd eaten for dinner. She flushed the toilet and blew her nose. She brushed her teeth and washed her face.

Lori went to her bedroom and laid across the bed. She felt nauseous, she felt dizzy. Who the hell is Shelly and where is Wayne? Lori laid on the bed and tried to think who Shelly could be. How did she get this number? Why would she call here with such a dreadful lie? If she's been sleeping with Wayne for a year, then why would she call here; she should know his cell phone number. She obviously wasn't looking for Wayne, she was looking for me. Why would someone tell such an ugly lie? Wayne might not even know this woman. Maybe, she's someone that doesn't like me; maybe she's the parent of a child I failed. She could be anyone. Lori got up and went downstairs to fix herself a sandwich. I can't allow myself to get upset because some crazy woman felt like pulling a prank on me or Wayne. She sat at the kitchen table and bit into the sandwich. She tried to chew it, but she couldn't swallow. Her throat felt full, like it was blocked. Lori placed the sandwich into a freezer bag. She drank a glass of milk and put the sandwich into the refrigerator. She went to sit on the sofa to wait for Wayne.

Where could he be? He is thirty-five minutes late. Maybe he's with Shelly. Maybe Wayne is sleeping with other women. No, it can't be true. Should I ask him about Shelly or should I just observe Wayne's actions and see if he's missing and unaccounted for? Yes, I'll just wait and see if he knows that she called. I'll act normal. I don't want to make myself sick. My stomach is already upset. Wayne should be here any minute.

Wayne came home two hours later carrying a bag. "Hi Honey, I picked up some fruit for you from the truck on Mermaid Lane. You should start eating more fruit. It will make you and the baby healthier."
Lori sat on the sofa staring in space. She couldn't bring herself to look at him. Wayne continued to the kitchen to put the fruit away. Returning to the livingroom he said, "I bought a couple of cantaloupes, some tokay

grapes, oranges and apples; you can snack on them and take some to work with you. That will help you to stop eating so much junk food." He admired his wife's beauty as he approached the sofa. He kissed her forehead and sat beside her. "Is there something wrong? You don't look well. Have you been vomiting again? Are you sick?" Wayne asked his wife with concern.

In a barely audible voice Lori asked, "Who is Shelly? Who is she Wayne? His startled expression betrayed his guilt.

"How should I know? Why are you asking me that?"

"Some girl named Shelly called here looking for you."

"I don't know a Shelly."

"She said she is seven months pregnant with your child. Is that true Wayne?" Lori asked while staring at him to watch his reaction.

"Look, I don't know anyone named Shelly. Someone is playing a vicious joke on you." He lied.

"She said she's been screwing you for a year."

"That's a lie. I don't know her."

Lori noticed the perspiration on Wayne's forehead, and the way he kept looking down at his hands. "Wayne"

"Yes"

"Have you been cheating on me with Shelly?"

"No, I haven't."

"Are you sure?"

"Yes, I'm sure."

"Who is Shelly? Why would she call our house?"

"I don't know, it's a joke."

"How did she get our telephone number?"

"I don't know. Our telephone number is listed. You can't let people upset you like this. I don't know a Shelly."

"Are you sure, Wayne?"

"Yes, I'm sure Baby." He reached over to hug her, but she pulled away from him.

"Don't touch me!" she said angrily.

"You know I love you! I have too much to lose to mess around with a floozy. Don't let a prank call come between us," he pleaded.

Tears ran down Lori's cheeks. She felt insecure. She was unsure of Wayne's fidelity. Wayne was nervous; she could hear the quiver in his voice. "I'm not letting a phone call come between us, but I think you know this Shelly. If you didn't know her, then why did she call here? How does she know our phone number?"

"You know our number is listed. Let's not let this ruin our evening. Let's drop it. I don't want to talk about it anymore," he asserted.

"Okay, let's talk about something else. I have to go to the bathroom." Lori went upstairs to her bedroom and star sixty-nined the telephone to get Shelly's telephone number. She wrote it down on a piece of paper and put it in her wallet. She returned downstairs to find Wayne watching television.

That woman is out of her mind. What did she hope to accomplish by calling my wife, Wayne thought.

"Come over here and sit down. This movie looks pretty good," he said with a smile. He kissed his wife and held her in his arms as they watched the movie. What am I going to do now? She's gone too far this time. Now that Lori has talked to Shelly, she's not going to just forget it as if it never happened. Why now, when everything is going so well? Leave it to Shelly to try to mess up my life, because her life is messed up. That girl is out of her mind. If Lori really finds out about her, then she'll never get another dime from me, Wayne thought.

Reggie opened the door with his ever present smile. "Hi Wayne, who died?"

"You don't want to know man."

"Come on in and tell me about it. Can I get you something to eat or drink?" Reggie asked.

"No thanks. How's your wife and kids?"

"They're fine. Carol took the kids to a birthday party, so I'm doing the Saturday chores. I'd rather clean than fight with all of those children," Reggie laughed. "How is Lori doing?"

"She was fine until last night. Shelly called my house and told Lori everything. She said I've been screwing her for a year and she's seven months pregnant with my baby. Do you believe that crazy ass woman?" Wayne said as he paced back and forth in Reggie's livingroom.

"No she didn't, no she didn't. What did she hope to gain by telling your wife that shit?"

"She did it just to be mean, that's why. She called me last night trying to get me to come over to her house to screw her. I turned her down, so she got mad and called my wife. She's evil like that. What would make her think I'd ever fuck her again? I'll never, ever touch her again," Wayne declared.

"I told you to be careful with that girl, something just didn't feel right. She was too aggressive. She doesn't have anything to lose. First she wanted money, now she wants you. Be careful with her man, I have a feeling that you haven't heard the last of her," Reggie warned Wayne.

"The last of her, she's going to harass me for the rest of my life if she can prove that I'm her baby's daddy. She'll ruin my life."

"She's trying to do that now Wayne, anytime she can call your wife and tell her that shit."

"You're right about that! Man, I don't know what I'm going to do!"

"What did Lori say? Did she believe her?"

"I don't think so. I tried to smooth it over and change the subject to get her mind off of Shelly. You know Lori is a curious person, I don't think she's going to let it drop that easily."

"Did she ask you if you knew Shelly?"

"Yeah, I told her no, I didn't know her."

"Did she believe you?"

"I don't know, I hope so. She kept asking me who is Shelly? I kept saying I don't know."

"You're in a bad position. You're at the mercy of a crazy woman."

"I know. I just hope she doesn't try anything else. Lori was very upset, and I don't know how she'll react to something else happening," Wayne stated.

"I know you're walking on egg shells around your house."

"Yeah man, I'm in hot water. That kind of phone call would raise anyone's suspicions. You know Lori is an intelligent woman. She's not going to take this lying down, I just don't know what she'll do either."

"Oh man," Reggie exclaimed. "I wouldn't want to be in your shoes."

"I messed up this time man, I really messed up," Wayne lamented.

"No one is perfect, we all have our faults. Don't be so hard on yourself," Reggie consoled Wayne.

"I'm scared that Lori will find out that I've been cheating on her. I don't know what made me think Lori wouldn't find out about Shelly. I knew that girl was hard to control, but I thought she was too street smart to let herself get pregnant, and if she did, then she would know what to do about it," Wayne confided to Reggie. "I'm surprised that she wants another child. She already has two kids, and she's always complaining about the hard time she's having raising them," Wayne added.

"Yeah, that's strange," Reggie said.

"And she's always complaining about how expensive kids are," Wayne remembered.

"She obviously wants you. Maybe she thinks this baby will make you leave your wife and come to live with her," Reggie said.

"Do you think that's it?"

"Sure, that's why she's busy calling Lori, trying to break up your marriage," Reggie theorized.

"Never man, I would never move in with that crazy girl. Our contact was just a fun thing, a distraction," Wayne confided.

"Well, she thinks it's more than that. She wants to hook up with you."

"She can forget that. If that's what's on her mind, then she can forget it. Don't even say that man. I'm getting mad just thinking about it. I just don't want my wife to find out about this shit," Wayne moaned.

"I know, I'd feel the same way."

"What do you suggest I do?"

"I don't know Wayne."

"You're a happily married man, what would you do?"

"Well Wayne, I'd be good, but not too good. Be nice, but not too nice. When you're not working, stay home, but go out every now and then. Call her often and let her think she knows where you are and what you're doing. If you have a new piece on the side, get rid of her. And no matter what you do, keep your cell phone away from her. Leave it in the car when you're in the house, keep it on your body when she's in the car. Be humble and act dumb. Let her think she knows more than you do. If she didn't see it, then you didn't do it. That's what I would do."

"I hear you!" Wayne said as he high fived Reggie. "Thanks man, I really appreciate your support. I guess I'd better get back home," Wayne said as he headed for the door feeling better than he did when he came.

CHAPTER 8

Lori felt nauseous, she hated morning sickness. She kept a box of crackers beside the bed to ward off these feelings, but sometimes nothing helped. She jumped out of bed and ran to the bathroom to vomit. A green bile was all she eliminated, but she felt like there was more. She felt listless, like a rag. She crawled back to bed on her hands and knees with perspiration running down her neck, face and back. She laid on the bed hyperventilating, with her heart beating rapidly.

"Wayne, Wayne, wake up. I'm sick," Lori moaned. "I threw up and I feel weak."

Wayne turned over to look at her. She looked a little green. He jumped out of bed and wet a wash cloth in cold water and placed it across her forehead. He repeated this four more times.

"I feel terrible," Lori groaned.

"What should I do? Do you want to go to the hospital?" Wayne asked her. "I know, maybe I'll make you something to eat, your stomach is probably empty.

He cooked her some bacon, eggs, grits, toast and tea. He brought a tray upstairs and fed her. She fell asleep after eating. She slept for three hours and awakened feeling like a new person. Wayne stayed by her side until she felt better.

"How are you feeling, Sweetheart?"

"Much better, thank you; I think you should go to work now," Lori suggested.

"I can take the day off work and stay here with you," Wayne offered.

"No, that won't be necessary, you go to work. I'm feeling much better."

"Okay, if you're sure."

"Yes, I'm sure, and thanks for taking such good care of me. I don't know what I would have done without you. I love you."

"I love you too. I'll call later to check on you, but if you need me before then, give me a call and I'll come back home."

"You're sweet Wayne."

Shelly laid in her bed among rumpled covers and flat pillows. She felt miserable. The doctor told her to stay home on bed rest. She tried to get comfortable. She placed a pillow under her stomach. I'm as big as a house, she thought. I'll be glad when this is over. I'm looking forward to losing this weight. I can just see my stomach flat again and me in my fine clothes again. I'll have to get this weight off as soon as possible so I can wear my clothes. I can't afford to buy new ones.

She fluffed her pillows again, trying to get comfortable. She'd gone to the African Braid shop and had micro braids put in her hair. They were bulky and tight and felt uncomfortable, but they looked good and required little care. They cost a fortune, but they last three to six months. She can keep these until after the baby is born and she can get to a hairdresser, she thought.

They say that I'm having a girl, which is just what I wanted. I couldn't take having another boy, they're too rough. I'll buy my little girl lots of pink frilly dresses with Wayne's money, she thought as she smiled to herself. I'll dress her like a little doll. I know she'll be pretty, whether she looks like me or her father. Wayne doesn't have any children, so when she's born, he'll sing a different tune. That stuck up wife of his thinks she's too good to have a baby for him. That's her loss, if she's not careful, me and my baby girl will take him right away from her.

I had to stop working yesterday because my feet and legs were swelling too much. The doctor says to stay off my feet, but I still have to take care of the boys.

Their father isn't much help. He'll take them for a day or two, but not for six weeks. I'll have to call Wayne and ask him to help me financially, until the baby is born. He'll have to give me money for the baby, so he might as well get used to it. He's going to be mad about me calling his wife, but he made me mad. He's lucky I didn't come to his house.

Shelly dials Wayne's cell phone number. "Hi Wayne, this is Shelly. We need to talk. I think you should come over here so we can talk in person. Okay, then I'll tell you on the phone. I had to stop working yesterday because my feet and legs were swelling, so I'm going to need some money to help pay my rent and other bills. No, my paid maternity leave doesn't start until after I have the baby, and that's not for six weeks. What do I need? How much can you give me? Yeah, well, I need about $800. I know it's a lot, but that's what I need. You can get back to me tomorrow and let me know what you can do."

He didn't mention me calling his house. I wonder if she told him. What's going on over there? I wonder. His wife was very upset when I talked to her, so I know she let him have it when he came home; unless she's smarter than I think she is. She might be waiting until she can catch him in a lie or even catch him in the act. Wayne had better be careful. Little Miss Stuck Up is watching him. Maybe she didn't tell him, because she's one of those women that doesn't care. Maybe she's going to hold on to him, no matter what. I made the first move, and I'll make the second move if Wayne doesn't come up with that money. I wonder what she's up to, I wonder if she's planning something.

Wayne sat in the dealership office fuming with anger. He hung up the telephone mad with Shelly for asking him for more money. Damn, where am I going to get $800 from? I can't take it from my family's budget without raising Lori's suspicions. I knew this woman would make my life hell, that's why I told her to get an abortion. Now I'm trapped, at least until the baby is born. I'll have to get out here and sell a couple of cars. Damn, I hate that slut, Wayne declared in his mind. He counted on a piece of paper the commissions he would get in his paycheck at the end of the week. He abruptly left his desk and walked around the car lot looking for customers. Shelly's constant demands for money frustrated him, making him restless and uneasy. He needed to think of ways to make extra money, or he'd have to tell her that he didn't have it. He could give her $400, and that's it. She'd have to get the rest from somewhere else. He couldn't afford to support her and her two kids. She's trying to play me, but it won't work. She has to be able to understand that I just don't have it!

Wayne had been staying home with Lori. He wanted to build up her confidence in him. He wanted her to trust him enough not to believe what Shelly might tell her. He sometimes caught her looking at him out of the side of her eyes, as if she didn't trust him. He loved his wife and he didn't want to lose her because of his error in judgment. He wished that it would all just go away, but he knew that wasn't going to happen. The best thing he could do is to keep Shelly away form Lori.

Lori sat at the kitchen table fingering the paper with Shelly's telephone number. I wonder why she called me telling me lies about Wayne. What have I done to her? What has Wayne done to her? She'd looked at the paper a hundred times in the last two weeks; trying to get the courage to make the call. Just do it, she told herself. Clear it up once and for all. She dialed the number and quickly hung up the phone. She hesitated, took a deep breath and dialed again. This time a voice said "Hello."

"Hello, my name is …..my name is Lori Jackson, I'm Wayne Jackson's wife."

"Yeah."

"You called my house a while back and told me some things I found to be very disturbing."

"Yeah."

"Have you been in a relationship with my husband?"

"Yeah."

"Are you pregnant by my husband?"

"Yeah, I told you I'm pregnant by your husband. In fact I'll be having his baby in four weeks."

"Oh really, did you know Wayne was married when you met him?"

"Yeah, he told me he was married."

"So, why did you go out with him, if he told you he was married?"

"What? Why did I go out with him, you mean why did he go out with me? He's the one that's married, not me. Now, that sounds like a question you should ask your husband."

"How do I know you are telling the truth? You could be anybody calling here."

"I wouldn't waste my time, if I wasn't telling the truth."

"What proof do you have that you've been seeing Wayne? He says he doesn't know you."

"Of course, he's going to tell you that."

"Well, I believe my husband."

"If you believed your husband, then why are you on my phone?"

"I just wanted to know why you would call here lying on my husband?"

"I'll tell you something you don't want to hear," Shelly said with a cynical laugh. "You bought Wayne a lot of plaid underwear last Christmas, didn't you?"

"What...... yes, I did," she answered hesitantly.

"Wayne has a light birthmark on his penis, doesn't he?"

"Yes," Lori answered tearfully.

"I told you, I don't have time to waste calling your house to lie on Wayne. I just thought you might want to know the truth," Shelly said confidently.

"Well, that may prove that you slept with him, but that doesn't mean that you're carrying his baby," Lori said angrily.

"He knows it's his and that's all that matters."

"Wayne obviously has dropped you like a hot potato or you wouldn't be calling my house. You didn't call here before. You called here looking for me, you weren't looking for Wayne. He doesn't want you, so you're trying to break up his home, but if he's been sleeping with you, then you can have him. He's all yours, that is if he wants you!" She slammed the telephone down as tears flowed from her eyes. "I knew he was lying, I knew it!"

"How could I have trusted Wayne? How could he betray me like this? I loved him. How could he do this to me? I'm having his baby, and he's having a baby with someone else," she shouted to the empty house. The tears continued to flow like water. "He lied! He lied to me!" She cried as she pounded the kitchen counter. After her tears were spent, she went into the livingroom and laid on the sofa to think. That's why Wayne is away from home so much. I wonder how many nights he really had to work late and how many nights was he with Shelly?

Wayne's betrayal was more than Lori could take. She loved him so much, but she would not tolerate his infidelity. She knew her husband was a virile man, so she tried to meet his sexual needs; even when she didn't feel like it. What good did it do, he still went out and slept with Shelly. I wonder if there were others, she thought.

"He and Shelly can live happily ever after with their baby, because he's out of here!" she shouted. She pulled three trash bags from the box in the kitchen cabinet and ran upstairs to the bedroom closet that housed Wayne's clothes and began throwing his suits, shirts, shoes, sneakers, and ties into the bags. She walked to the dresser and emptied his drawers into the bags. She then, looked around the room and put everything she saw of Wayne's into the bags. "He's out of here" she said softly as the tears streamed down her face. She dragged the bags down the steps, not caring if something in them broke. The sweat and tears blinded her as she dragged the last bag to the front door. Breathlessly, she made her way to the sofa and sat down with her arms folded across her chest. The crying is over, she thought, now I'm mad. Lori sat in the silent house with her leg crossed, dangling her shaking foot with her lips protruding replaying the conversation with Shelly over and over in her head.

Wayne entered the dark house with a bewildered expression on his face; he wondered where Lori could be. Light from the street lamp illuminated the livingroom. He saw her sitting on the sofa with a stern expression on her face. He approached her cautiously with concern. "What's wrong Baby, are you sick?" Wayne asked while surveying her appearance. Lori didn't respond. He turned on the lamp on the end table. "Why are you sitting in the dark?" He looked at her as he removed his jacket and shoes and walked to the sofa to join her.

She looked up at him as he stood over her and said, "Put back on your shoes and jacket and get out! You're not needed here anymore. Go to your other family!"

Wayne's mouth flew open as his eyes opened wider, revealing his shocked expression. "What are you talking about Lori?" He asked as his pulse increased, "I only have one family; you."

"You know exactly what I'm talking about, how long did you think you could get away with your infidelity?"

"What happened Lori?" he asked as his expression changed to one of concern.

"Don't try to look so innocent, you know what I'm talking about. I called your girlfriend Shelly and she told me everything that's been going on."

"I told you, I don't know a Shelly."

"You told me a lot of things, but they were all lies," Lori said angrily.

"You've got it all wrong Baby," he said while reaching for her hand. "You can't believe what that woman said. I don't know why she's lying to you, but I'm going to find out why. You don't need to upset yourself like this in your condition!"

"In my condition, my condition, what about Shelly's condition? She's going to have your baby soon."

Wayne tries to touch Lori's hand. "Don't touch me Wayne!"

"What's that woman's number? I'll call her and clear this up right now. Where's her phone number?"

"You're a good liar, but it's too late for that. She's proven to me that she's been sleeping with you for quite some time."

"How did she prove that I've been sleeping with her, when I don't even know her?"

"Then, how did she know about the light birthmark on your penis, or that I bought you plaid underwear last Christmas, unless she has been intimate with you?" Lori shouted.

Silence!

"Your clothes are in those trash bags by the door. I want you to get your clothes and leave right now," she said as she stood face to face with Wayne. "You obviously, don't respect me enough to tell the truth, even when you're caught; you're still lying," Lori screamed.

"We can work this out Baby, please, let's work this out," he said as he tried to kiss her. "I love you and only you! Alright, I'll tell you, we did something a couple of times, but I used protection. It's not my baby Lori!"

"I don't give a damn if it is yours or not, you've been screwing that woman while you were screwing me. Now, I want you out of this house right now or I'm calling the police," she screamed between tears.

"Okay, okay, calm down; I'll leave for now, but I'll be back. I'm not going to lose you like this. I'm not giving up on our marriage. I love you and only you."

"Just leave!"

Wayne gathered his bags and struggled out of the house to his car.

Lori fell back on the sofa and sobbed.

Lori closed the door and locked it after the locksmith left. She had all of the locks rekeyed, so she wouldn't receive any surprise visits from Wayne. He will lie until the end. This marriage is over, Wayne is in my past, she thought. Wayne called the house repeatedly, but Lori stopped answering the phone. She screened her calls with caller I.D. and an answering machine. Wayne came to her school on several occasions and Lori not only refused to talk to him, she threatened to call the police and say he was stalking her. He came to the house and tried to enter with his key, but Lori had changed the locks. He banged on the door on several occasions and Lori ignored him. His attempts became less and less frequent as he became discouraged. Twice, he stood in the backyard yelling "I love you Lori, over and over, but she still ignored him; she had been betrayed, and she was heartbroken.

Lori loved Wayne, but she could not live with his disrespect. How could she ever trust him again? She pledged to put this marriage behind her, and to move on with her life. The baby that Wayne said he wanted so badly was growing and thriving in her body. Could she give birth to this baby and raise it alone? She felt that raising a child with Wayne would just prolong the agony; their lives would still be intertwined. A baby would allow Wayne the power to continue to manipulate her life. No, I want a clean break from Wayne; I want to start with a clean slate. Maybe, an abortion would be the solution. Lori had considered an abortion before telling Wayne about the pregnancy, but after thinking about it; she decided against it. She thought she was being selfish. Little did she know that Wayne was fathering another child by another woman, she thought. Let Shelly have Wayne's children, I'm going to move on with my life, without Wayne or his baby. Lori looked in the phone book for the nearest abortion clinic. She called and made an appointment for a consultation visit. "I'll need to get this over with as soon as possible," she said to herself.

Lori decided against telling anyone in her family about the abortion. She knew they would be against it., but this is my life and I'm going to do what I want to do. I know they will try to talk me out of it, even April. Carrying this baby, having a part of Wayne inside of me is too painful. It's a constant reminder of our love. This baby would make Wayne a constant in my life and I can't live like that. After going to the abortion clinic and signing all of the necessary papers, Lori went home and cried all night. She cried for the loss of the baby, she cried for the loss of their family, and she cried for the loss of their shared dreams.

Lori arrived alone at the abortion clinic three days later in a taxi. The nurse reminded her that she would need someone to sign her out of the clinic and to escort her home. She assured the nurse that someone would be there to get her. Hours later Lori called April and asked her for a ride home, telling her sister that her car was in the repair shop. She gave her sister the address, but she didn't tell her it was an abortion clinic.

April checked the address twice. Why would Lori be at an abortion clinic? she wondered as she entered the building. This must be a mistake. Maybe I wrote down the wrong address. "Hello, I'm looking for Lori Jackson, I'm her sister April Wilson, is she here?"

"I'll let Mrs. Jackson know that her ride is here. Will you please sign this release form?" the Nurse at the desk asked.

April signed the form feeling bewildered. April's eyes filled with tears as she watched her sister enter the reception area looking pale and weak. Her hair was in disarray and she walked slowly with a slight bent; as if she was in some discomfort. April rushed to her sister's side to assist her. She helped Lori to her car.

"Lori, what is wrong? Please tell me that you didn't just have an abortion," April pleaded.

"Yes, I did, but I don't want to talk about it right now," Lori said as tears ran down her face.

April shook her head in disbelief as they rode to Lori's house in silence. She was very concerned about her sister. She knew that something was terribly wrong, but what? April helped Lori upstairs to her bed. The house was a mess. April went to the kitchen to make Lori something to eat. The sink was full of dirty dishes and the table was cluttered with more. April collected the dishes from around the house and washed them all. She wiped down the stove and cleaned the glass top table. She prepared her sister some soup, tea and toast on a tray and carried it upstairs to her.

"Lori, I know something is terribly wrong, please tell me what it is? I want to know; maybe I can be of some help to you."

"No one can help me April. Wayne has another woman pregnant and my marriage is over."

"Are you sure? How do you know?" April asked.

"This woman called my house and told me," Lori cried.

"Women lie. They'll say anything to get your man."

"She wasn't lying," Lori answered softly.

"Sometimes men cheat, but you two love each other, you might be able to get beyond this and save your marriage."

"How can I save my marriage, when my husband is starting a family with another woman?"

"How do you know she's pregnant?"

"Wayne's girlfriend is seven months pregnant."

"Really, are you sure?"

"Yes," Lori sobbed uncontrollably. "How can I have a baby under these circumstances? Let his girlfriend, Shelly have his baby and make him a father."

"Did Wayne admit it? Did he say it was his baby?"

"No, he didn't say it was his baby, but he admitted sleeping with her."

'Oh Lori, I'm so sorry, I didn't know. Where is Wayne?"

"I put him out two weeks ago."

"Oh Lori!"

"I couldn't stand to look at him. I feel so betrayed, as if our lives together was all a lie. I just wanted him out of the house."

"So, you decided to get an abortion?"

"Yes, I didn't want to be tied to him for the rest of my life with a baby, after what he's done."

"Why didn't you come to me or Mom, before you made such a permanent decision?"

"Well, I was already three and a half months pregnant, and I didn't want to wait until it was too late to do something about it. I didn't want to be talked out of getting the abortion," Lori stated.

"It's too late to change things. What's done is done. I guess you did what you felt you had to do, but we are family, we want to share your problems. You've been here by yourself for two weeks with those kinds of issues on the table. We love you Lori," April told her sister as tears stained her make up.

"I know you do, but I'm a big girl; I have to handle my own problems."

"That may be true, but you don't have to handle them alone. Sometimes you just need a sounding board; someone to listen."

"I was ashamed to let you know what Wayne did, that my marriage had failed."

"You don't have any shame in this, that's his shame. He broke his vows! Well I'm not leaving you in this house alone. You're going home with me. I'll take care of you."

"I don't want to be any trouble, and I don't want anyone else to know that I had an abortion. Mom and Dad would never forgive me."

"I won't tell them, your secret is safe with me," April pledged.

"I can't go to your house; I don't want Paul or the children to know."

"I'll tell Paul that you had a miscarriage, and the children didn't know you were pregnant. We can tell Mom and Dad the same thing," April suggested. April rises from the bed and begins going through Lori's drawers and closet, gathering clothes to take to her house. "I'm not leaving you alone; you're going home with me."

"Okay, but don't tell them about Wayne yet, I don't want to talk about it," Lori said.

April puts a coat over her sister's pajamas and takes her back down the steps to her car and drives Lori to her house.

Wayne knocked on the door of his house. He knocked and knocked and knocked. He rang the door bell repeatedly. No answer. He knew Lori was at home, he'd seen her car through the garage window. She has some nerve locking me out of my own house, he thought. The least she could do is to hear my side of the story before she just gives up on our marriage; after all, we have a child on the way. She refuses to answer the door and the telephone, so how are we suppose to communicate? He stood in the driveway looking up at the bedroom window. I don't want to upset her any more than she is already. I guess she needs more time, he thought as a lone tear traveled down his left cheek. I want my wife back! Wayne slowly backed his car out of the driveway. He hated leaving his home, leaving his wife, leaving his family. I hope and pray that her anger won't last too long, I need Lori. He slowly drove to Reggie's house.

Reggie opened the front door of his house. He could tell that Wayne was very upset.

"Come on in man, are you okay?"

"Reggie, I've really screwed up man. I've ruined my marriage. Lori is heartbroken. I love her. I just don't know what I'm going to do." Wayne started to cry, but he stopped himself. He took the back of his hand and wiped his eyes. Reggie threw his arms around Wayne and patted him on the back. He walked him into the privacy of the family room at the back of the house; he didn't want his wife and children upstairs to over-hear Wayne's sorrows.

"Wayne, take a deep breath and tell me what happened?" Reggie asked.

"Lori called Shelly and Shelly convinced her that I was sleeping with her and that she's pregnant with my baby. Lori believes her."

"Then, what happened?"

"Lori threw me out of the house."

"She did?"

"Yeah, she had all of my things packed in trash bags when I came home from work,"

"She did?"

"Man, I love Lori. I don't want to lose my wife and my baby she's carrying." Wayne wiped his eyes again as he talked with his head down.

"I can understand that."

"She won't answer the phone when I call. I went over there and the locks have been changed and when I knocked, she wouldn't answer the door."

"Sounds like she's very upset."

"I know she's upset, and she has every right to be upset, but I just want to talk to her, to explain my side of the story."

"It sounds like she means business," Reggie said softly.

"I know, that's what I'm afraid of. I think I've lost her for good." Tears ran down Wayne's face. Reggie gave him some tissues.

"You never know man, women are funny, one minute they're mad and the next minute they're forgiv-ing you; they're unpredictable. She's pregnant with your child, so at some point, you two are going to have contact. You'll just have to be patient. You can't rush her man."

"It's hard because I really love her."

"She loves you too, she can't just turn her love for you off, but she's hurt. That love is being smothered by the pain she's feeling. Give her some time and maybe that love will return," Reggie suggested.

"I hope so, I can't live without Lori."

"Be patient man. Where are you staying?"

"I'm staying with my Moms."

"Does she know the deal?"

"No, I told her we had an argument and I didn't want to discuss it."

"What would we do without our mothers?"

"You've got that right, you can always go home," Wayne said.

"What about Shelly? Have you heard from her?"

"She's been blowing my cell phone up, even calling my job, but I won't talk to her. She messed up my marriage, and she'll never get another cent from me. I don't want to hear anything from her until she has that baby."

"I'm sorry Wayne, if there's anything I can do to help, just let me know," Reggie offered.

"I know."

"You might have to get a lawyer to make Shelly give you that DNA test that you want."

"You're right, especially since I didn't give her that $800 she wanted. I know she knows that I'm not her baby's father."

"Well, you'd better get a lawyer to help you with that. Let me get you a drink man."

"Okay, make it straight." Wayne emptied his glass and Reggie poured him another.

"You're a young man Wayne; you may have to start over with someone new if Lori can't find it in her heart to forgive you. You know, Life is too short to spend it grieving over someone that doesn't want you."

"I had it all and I didn't realize it. I don't want anyone but Lori. I know I did wrong, but I want my wife back. I don't care how long it takes. I want her back."

"I hope that happens for you man. I'll keep you in my prayers." Reggie put on some jazz and sat the bottle of whiskey on the table. They drank and talked till the wee hours of the morning.

CHAPTER 9

"April thanks for coming by to visit me. I appreciate the hospitality that you, Paul and the children showed me while I was staying at your house. It really made me feel much better to know that the people you love, also love you. I could feel the love in your home. Thanks again, for nursing me back to health, physically and emotionally," Lori said with gratitude.

"I'm glad I could help. You're my one and only sister and nothing is too good for you. I know you'd do the same for me if I needed it," April responded.

"Staying with you and Paul and the kids made me realize that I want what you have. I want a loving husband that is also my best friend, and two wonderful children like yours," Lori complimented April.

"Everything that glitters isn't gold. We have problems like everyone else, and my children drive me crazy sometimes. On occasion, I've envied you; not having the responsibilities that children bring," April confessed. "Have you thought about what you're going to do? Are you interested in counseling to save your marriage? I can recommend one if you'd like."

"No, I don't think I could ever forgive Wayne. That's why I got the abortion, because I don't want to see him or talk to him. Counseling is definitely out of the question. Counseling won't make that baby disappear or make Wayne a faithful husband. This marriage is over."

"What are your plans?"

"For one thing, I know I'll have to sell or rent this house."

"Why don't you try to keep it? You have to live somewhere?"

"Because, I can't afford it on just my salary."

"Rent it out, that will give you time to decide what you want to do in the long term."

"I have to find somewhere to stay until I can rent it out. It needs a little work and I need to save some money to get another place to live; an apartment or condo or something," Lori stated.

"You can stay with me, we enjoyed your company," April offered.

"No, I don't want to wear my welcome out, besides you and Paul need your space. Thanks anyway."

"Maybe Mom and Dad will let you stay there, after all, your old room is still empty," April suggested.

"That's a good idea. I'll ask Mom when I talk to her."

"Yes, I think that will work," April said.

Frank and Leeanna Amos live in a large stone twin house in West Mount Airy. The house is hedged in by red and white azalea bushes. A large pink flowering dogwood tree adds contrast to this grey stone, well maintained house. There are working fireplaces in both the livingroom and family room; there are matching bay windows in the livingroom and diningroom. It is a three bedrooms and two and a half baths house with an attic and a basement finished in knotty pine. The large eat in kitchen is where Leeanna spends most of her time preparing food for Frank or cleaning it after meals. She would like the oak cabinets replaced with dark cherry wood cabinets. She's been saving money for two years to make her dream a reality. She asked Frank to help her pay for the remodeling, but he said, there's nothing wrong with the oak cabinets and if she wanted to change them, she'd have to pay for them.

Frank and Leeanna raised their daughters in this lovely house. They finished paying off the mortgage two years ago. He made a home office in April's old room and Leeanna kept Lori's room as a guest room. When their grandchildren came to spend the night or out of town guest arrived, they had a nice spacious room to sleep in. Leeanna had the room painted and bought new drapes and bedding, but when Lori moved in with them; she felt like she was living in the same old room. She felt like a failure, returning to her parents' home, but she enjoyed the companionship and love of her mother.

"Mom, thanks for allowing me to move back home. I hope my being here doesn't create a problem between you and Dad," Lori said as she sat at the kitchen table drinking tea.

"Oh no, your father loves you girls. If he had his way, you'd both still be upstairs in your old rooms," she said while laughing.

"I'll try to stay out of the way as much as possible, and I won't over stay my welcome," Lori promised.

"What are you talking about? This is your home. When you have no place else to go, you can always come home."

"It could be as short a time as three months or as long as six months, just until I save some money to pay off some bills and get me a place to live."

"That's fine, stay as long as you like. You're home," Leeanna added. "I'm so sorry you lost your baby. It was a loss to us all. We were looking forward to a new grandchild. Just know that your father and I feel a sense of loss too."

"I know you do Mom, it was devastating."

"Yes it is, but you're young and there will be more children."

"I hope so."

"You and Wayne love each other, and it may take some time, but I'm sure you will work out your differences."

"I don't think so."

"Just give it some time."

"I'm going on with my life and Wayne should go on with his. I know you think marriage is forever; sometimes it's not."

"Just have faith in your love Lori."

"That's over Mom. I wasn't enough for my husband; he thinks he's entitled to a harem."

"People make mistakes Lori, we can't all be as perfect as you," Leeanna said

"I don't want to hear it Mom, I'm moving on with my life," Lori said firmly. "I'll wash these dishes; you can relax more since I'm here."

"You're not here to do my work. I can do these dishes, you go and relax."

"I'm younger than you, a few dishes won't hurt me, besides, I don't want you waiting on me. Dad is more than enough. I want to help out around here. If I can make life a little easier for you while I'm here, that would make me very happy."

Frank sat at the table eating dinner with Lori and Lee. The table conversation was different. Lori often talked about her students, and Lee talked about the doctor she worked for, which surprised Frank since she rarely discussed Dr. Phillips. Frank didn't have much to say, because Lori and Lee often had a two way conversation, which excluded him. Things were different with Lori back home. Lori and Lee were always complimenting each other. They seemed to really enjoy each other's company, constantly chattering and giggling.

Frank sat in the livingroom watching television with his shoes and jacket off. He couldn't remove his pants with a grown daughter walking around the house. Lori helped Lee wash the dishes and then came into the livingroom to watch the big screen television. They always want to watch something that doesn't interest me, so I tell them to watch whatever they want, and I go upstairs to the bedroom to watch television. I can hear them laughing and enjoying themselves. I don't like watching the smaller screen TV, I've become accustomed to watching the 36 inch screen.

When I call downstairs for Lee to bring me a snack, Lori brings it up. I hope she's not here for very long. April and her children are over here a few times a week now, visiting Lee and Lori. This house is full most evenings now. No privacy! My favorite chair has become Lori's chair whenever I'm not sitting in it. If they aren't watching television, then they're blasting music. Lori's computer plays music like a stereo. Lori is always moving things around or dropping her clothes all over the place. Lee doesn't have the time to pick up after her, she's not a child anymore. I love my daughters, but it took twenty-five years to get Lori out of the house the first time, I wonder how many years it will take to get her out this time; it's been three months already. My home is my refuge. I can't take all of this activity, all of the time.

"Two of my teachers were fighting in the hallway in front of the children. Of course, I wrote them up for disciplinary action, wouldn't you? Now, the union is trying to give me a hard time, as if they have a right to fight in front of their students. Any adult, not to mention a teacher that fights in front of children deserves to lose their job on the spot," he told Lee as they prepared for bed. He laid on his side of the bed, leaning on three pillows. "I gave them a two weeks suspension without pay, with the intent to dismiss. I've had five meetings with the union over this already, and another is scheduled for tomorrow. It's disgusting."

"Try not to worry about work when you come home. You have to leave it at school," Lee advised her husband.

"I know, but it's just ridiculous, the union will defend them no matter what they do."

"I know things don't always work out the way they should, but maybe you can get the union to agree to transfer them to another school," Lee suggested

"No, that's too good for them. They'll go to another school and do the same thing," Frank said.

"Try not to think about it before you go to sleep, you might dream about it."

"If I do, then maybe I'll be successful at getting rid of them in my dreams," Frank laughed.

"Oh Frank."

"How is Lori doing? Do you think she'll go back to her husband?" Frank asked.

"She seems to be coping, but she won't even consider talking to Wayne. It's probably still too painful for her to consider building bridges," Lee concluded.

"She's not a child anymore. She has to understand that these things happen. She can't run away from her problems. This is real life. She has to accept the imperfections in her husband, like he has to accept the imperfections in her," Frank declared.

"You know your daughter, she's as stubborn as you," Lee said as she crawled into bed.

"Don't blame me; you're the one that's babying her."

"Maybe you should have a talk with her, I haven't had any luck. You try," Lee said as she rolled over and turned the lamp on her night table off,

"Maybe I will," Frank agreed. Maybe that will get her back to her own house and out of mine, he thought to himself.

Lori and Frank sat at the table eating in silence. They were both absorbed in their own thoughts. Leeanna faked a headache, saying she was going to lay down and she would eat something later. Let Frank talk to her, maybe he can convince her to go home to her husband because I sure can't, Leeanna thought.

"Dinner is very good Lori."

"I didn't cook it, Mom did."

"I saw you helping her."

"Yes, a little. Thanks Dad."

"So, how are things going?"

"Everything is going as well as can be expected; I guess."

"And how is that?"

"What do you mean?"

"How is Wayne?"

"I wouldn't know."

"Have you seen or talked to him?'

"No, I haven't."

"How do you expect to work out your problems? You have to communicate to do that."

"I'm through communicating with Wayne."

"You need to at the very least, hear Wayne's side of the story. He is your husband. Remember your vows, Lori."

"He didn't remember his vows. I don't want to hear anything he has to say."

"Two wrongs don't make a right. You should try to take the higher ground."

"Not me Dad, I'm through."

"That's not what marriage is about. You have every right to be angry and hurt, but you should try to mend your marriage. Remember, you said for better or for worse," Frank lectured.

"Wayne betrayed me. I could never trust him again," Lori said.

Have you tried; you'll never know what you can do until you try. Your vows said until death do us part, not until I get mad."

"My marriage is over. I'm sorry to disappoint you, but it really is over." She rose from the table, scraped her plate and put it in the sink. "I'll wash the dishes later; I'm going to check on Mom."

I tried, but she's as stubborn as ever. I guess she'll be here for a while. Some men are very weak when it comes to the flesh. Wayne is no different than many men. He seems to love Lori and he certainly puts up with her selfish ways. You can't just walk out the door of one relationship and find the perfect love waiting for you with someone new. Lori needs to grow up, after all, men will be men.

A few days later, Lori makes dinner for her parents.

"Lori, you didn't have to make dinner. I would have cooked. Your father, he doesn't like change," Leeanna said.

"I know, but you work everyday and I'm sure you're tired when you come home too. I feel guilty sitting at the table eating the food you've cooked everyday," Lori confessed.

"No, I don't want you to feel that way. I promised your father when I went to work that I would cook and keep the house clean. He pays all of the bills. I use my money to buy extras or spend it on myself. I don't mind living up to my promise," Leeanna said.

"You're still old-fashion Mom; women don't live like that anymore. People order out and go out to restaurants to eat. Some men will even share the cooking with their wives. You're taking a lot upon yourself. It wouldn't kill that old man to go out to dinner once or twice a week. You two could afford it."

"You know your father likes to come home and relax. He's under a great deal of pressure at work. He doesn't want to go out to eat; he likes my cooking too much."

"What would he do if you weren't around to cook for him? He wouldn't starve; he'd learn to eat someone else's cooking. I'll guarantee you that."

"I guess you're right, but old habits die hard."

"You should lay around and relax like Dad does, you're getting older too. You wait on Dr. Phillips all day and then you come home and wait on Dad all night. Who waits on you? Some days I see you come home looking like you're going to fall on your face."

"It doesn't kill me to cook my husband and me a decent meal, and we only have a few dishes to wash; after that I go upstairs to rest. I'm fine. I've done it so long, until it's automatic." She said with a smile and a wink of her eye.

"That's because you divorce yourself from your own feelings and needs, until you have met all of Dad's needs. How much longer do you think you can continue to do this before your body starts to breakdown?" Lori challenged her mother.

"You're so dramatic Lori."

"I'll bet Dad doesn't even say please or thank you. I know I've never heard him use those words with you; he uses them when he's not in this house. He's a very polished professional out in the world."

"Your father has supported me financially for almost forty years. I don't ask him to please pay the bills or say thank you for the electricity. He should say those things, but it isn't the end of the world if he doesn't; we're beyond that."

"You should never be beyond common courtesies; everyone wants to be treated with respect. Please and thank you, just show appreciation and respect. We all need that; recognition for our efforts." Lori told her Mother

"Oh Lori, please. Let me see what you've cooked." She walks over to the stove, lifts the lid and looks into the pot. "That looks good."

"I made spaghetti and salad," Lori said softly.

"That's good; did you make it like I showed you?" Leeanna asked wearily.

"Yes, I did Mom," Lori answered impatiently.

"Good! I'm going upstairs to change my clothes and put my feet up until your father comes home."

"Okay Mom," Lori responded. She's so old-fashioned, until she doesn't want to hear about anything new that challenges her belief system. She feels that a man is supposed to financially support a woman and a woman's job is to serve a man. He's the king of the castle and she's supposed to do the cooking, washing, ironing and cleaning. They were the roles of marriage when men worked and women stayed at home with the kids. They were the roles when she got married. Things change, today some women are the bread winners of the family and some men perform all of the domestic duties. Some couples share the financial responsibilities and the household chores, although I must admit, there are plenty two income families where the wife shares the financial responsibilities and still does all of the household chores. At least Mom's money is her own, but she still needs to make Dad take her out to eat a couple of times a week. He can afford it, but she won't. I don't think she'll ever change. Oh well, it's her choice, she thought.

Wayne's repeated failed attempts to contact Lori left him feeling distraught. When she changed the locks on the doors to his home, he felt that she was taking advantage of the situation; after all he helped to pay the mortgage. He told Lori he was leaving temporarily and he would return when she was feeling better. She never gave him the opportunity, before she changed the locks.

Wayne parked near Lori's school in different cars from the dealership to watch her from a distance and to pick the right time to approach her. Lori had rented out the house and moved in with her parents. At least she didn't try to sell it. She couldn't sell it anyway without his consent. She hasn't asked for a divorce, which is a good sign; it leaves room for hope. Today as Lori walked towards her car, Wayne impulsively got out of his car and approached her.

"Hi Lori, you're looking well," he said apprehensively.

"Hi Wayne, what do you want?" Lori said defensively.

"I thought we needed to talk, we left so many things unsaid."

"Like what? I've heard all I need to hear from you."

"That's not fair Lori, we're married, we need to talk," Wayne repeated.

"Wayne, you cheated on me with that woman. She's carrying your child, what else is there to say?"

"I made a mistake Baby, but I'm sorry. I realize now how important you are to me. I would never do something like that again; I would never be unfaithful to you again," Wayne pleaded as he blocked her path.

"You didn't make a mistake; you deceived me and had a relationship with Shelly. This wasn't a one night stand Wayne, this was a year long relationship with another woman, and after you left her you came home and got in bed with me. That's not a mistake Wayne, that's betrayal," Lori said angrily.

"You're right Lori, and I'm wrong. I can't deny it, but I never loved her, and I'm not her baby's father; I promise you that!" Wayne begged.

"I have nothing to say to you Wayne. Now get out of my way and stay out of my life," Lori said as she pushed past him and got in her car and drove off.

"Man, I was weak! I had my chance and I blew it!" he said to himself as he stood on the sidewalk watching her drive away.

Wayne had lost weight. He didn't have much of an appetite for food or women. His mother cooked for him everyday, but he ate very little. She tried to ask him about the separation but he refused to talk to her. His car sales declined, he was no longer pleasant; he appeared to be depressed. He ignored the women that flirted with him at the dealership and on the street. His beautiful smile was rarely seen.

Wayne had never dated a college educated woman and he had a great deal of respect for Lori's degree. He went to college to satisfy Reggie and his mother, but his heart wasn't in it and he dropped out after failing most of his class finals. Wayne decided that he wanted to be a salesman and he quickly secured a job selling men's clothing. After selling many things over the years, he found his niche selling cars. He couldn't believe his good luck when he met Lori. She was pretty, intelligent and independent. He prayed that Lori would give their marriage a second chance.

CHAPTER 10

"I saw Wayne today when I went to his dealership to look at some cars," Paul said.

"How is he?" asked April.

"He's really heartbroken over Lori, he looks bad."

"Is that what he told you?" April inquired with sarcasm.

"He didn't have to, I could see it."

"He should be happy with his new family."

"He asked me if Lori was going to have their baby soon. I told him that Lori had a miscarriage right after they separated. He appeared to be in shock. Didn't anyone tell him about the baby?" Paul asked.

"Not that I know of."

"Someone should have told him", Paul said incredulously.

"Like who Paul? I certainly wasn't going to tell him anything after the way he treated my sister."

"If I'd known that he didn't know, I would have called him."

"I'm sorry Paul, but I don't have any sympathy for Wayne. At the time I was concerned about Lori, no one was thinking about him. His girlfriend should have had his baby by now," April said nonchalantly. "If it makes you feel better to buy a car from Wayne, then it's fine with me, but I really don't care what he thinks or how he feels. I'm disappointed in him; I thought he loved my sister."

"I'm trying to stay out of it. He was always nice to me. I find it best to stay out of adult's business," Paul said as he looked at April through the corner of his eyes.

"Well, don't expect me to be impartial. He hurt my sister."

"I can understand that, anyway, he showed me a nice jeep. I'm going to look a few more places before I make a decision."

"Good, are you going walking this evening?"

"No, I think I'll stay in tonight and spend some adult time bonding with you," Paul chuckled.

"Sounds good to me! You know I love our alone time. The kids are asleep and the kitchen is clean. Let's start by taking a shower together."

"Okay, let's get this party started," Paul flirted with April as he danced around the kitchen. He chased his wife through the livingroom, diningroom, kitchen, hall and up the stairs. Upon reaching the top, they tip toed down the hall to avoid waking the children. April and Paul undressed each other and ran into the shower giggling like two children.

Reggie is a devoted father and husband. He and his wife Carol have a good marriage and three children; two boys and a girl. Reggie is determined to raise his children in a two parent household. As a mailman, he arrives home first from work and relieves the babysitter. He starts dinner and helps the children with their homework. Carol, a nurse works different shifts at the hospital; she finishes cooking dinner when needed and gets the children ready for bed. Reggie is proud of his relationship with his children, because he grew up without a father; he died when he was ten years old. Being an only child, Reggie was very close to his father and he misses him, even to this day.

Reggie and Carol are celebrating their twelfth anniversary. A new diningroom set is the surprise gift he has bought for his wife, and he has asked Wayne to help him take the old one to a second hand furniture store.

"Thanks for your help Wayne, I really appreciate it," he said with gratitude.

"You're welcome, I'm glad I could be of some help to you. You've been there for me through thick and thin and moving furniture is a little thing. You, Carol and the kids mean the world to me; you're family."

"You're family too man."

"Did I tell you that Lori's brother in law came to my job a couple of days ago to look at a car?" Wayne asked.

"No, you didn't; what did he have to say about Lori? Is she almost ready to have the baby?"

"No, Paul said she lost the baby not long after we broke up."

"Really! And she didn't even tell you. Man that's cold! I know she's angry, but she should have made sure that you were notified."

"Yeah, I was surprised and hurt by the news. I thought I was going to be a father soon," Wayne said sadly.

"I'm sorry to hear that."

"Yeah, I was sorry to hear it too. I guess Lori is really through with me. I was hoping the baby would bring us closer together. Now, I just don't know. When I tried to talk to her, she didn't want any parts of me, and when I heard things from her perspective it sounded pretty bad. I don't know if we'll be able to get beyond it."

"Don't wait too long for her forgiveness man, you may have to cut your losses and move on. The world is full of beautiful women and I'm sure there's one out there for you," Reggie cheerfully said.

"I guess you're right. I still love her, but I can't make her forgive me. I know my stuff was weak. She was devastated that I cheated on her, and now she's lost the baby, and I wasn't there to help her through it. Damn," Wayne said regretfully.

"It was her decision not yours. It was beyond your control. She wouldn't give you a chance to make up and save your marriage, so you couldn't be there for her."

"Yeah, I guess I should just give up. If it's meant to be, then it will happen," Wayne relented.

"You're right, you can't force it."

"I know I didn't give my marriage a chance. I had the wrong attitude. I know I wouldn't make the same mistakes twice, but she won't even talk to me,"

"Let it go Wayne, let it go."

"Hi Reggie, how are you doing man," Wayne said as he entered the foyer of Reggie's house. He showed Wayne into the family room, where his family sat watching TV.

"Hi Wayne," Carol said. "How are you doing?"

"I'm fine, and you?"

"I'm doing good," she responded.

"We've just finished eating and the food is still hot, let me fix you a plate," Carol suggested.

"Thanks, but I don't want to inconvenience you."

"You're family Wayne, as long as we have it, you have it. Sit right where you are and I'll fix you a plate," she said as she headed towards the kitchen.

"So, what have you been doing with yourself, I haven't heard from you all week?" Reggie asked.

"Nothing much, I've been going to work and coming home," Wayne said sadly.

"You should get out and socialize man."

"I'm not up to it."

"Making yourself miserable won't change a thing. Life is too short," Reggie said.

"Wayne would you like to eat in here or in the kitchen?" Carol asked.

"I'll eat in the kitchen," Wayne answered.

"Come on man, I'll sit in there and keep you company while you eat," Reggie volunteered.

"Okay, thanks man." Wayne sat down and ate greedily. "This stir fry is good. Who cooked dinner tonight?"

"Carol made it. I only cook basic stuff, like baked chicken or hamburgers, easy stuff."

"Your wife sure can cook. You're lucky Reg, your wife is pretty even after three kids and she can cook," Wayne said

"Yeah, I know, Carol is an intelligent and sensitive woman."

"Hold on to her man, there aren't many left like her."

"I know, there weren't many like her available when I married her. The women I met couldn't hold a candle to her; I just got lucky when I met Carol."

"You're right about that," Wayne said as he cleaned his plate and sat back in his chair looking full.

"Do you want some more food?"

"No thanks, I'm full. I'll have a little more juice though."

Reggie refilled Wayne's glass and rejoined him at the table. "Did Shelly let you test that baby yet?"

"Yeah, that's what I came by to tell you about."

"That little girl must be a few months old by now, who does she look like?"

"She doesn't look like me or Shelly, she obviously looks like her father," Wayne said with a smirk.

"Did you get the DNA test results yet?" Reggie inquired anxiously.

"Yeah, now I know why she fought so hard to keep me from getting the test."

"Well, what were the results?"

"It's not mine, just like I said," Wayne said triumphantly.

"No shit! She knew it wasn't yours all that time! That's why she didn't want the DNA test. She's rotten man."

"I knew it wasn't mine, I don't think she knows who the father is."

"That's the way it is when you're sleeping around. I guess she'll have a line of guys taking DNA tests. That's sad man!" Reggie said as he shook his head in disgust.

"I'm just thankful it wasn't mine. I want children, but not with her."

"So, what did she have to say when you got the results?" Reggie asked curiously.

"She tried to cry and say she was sorry. She claimed she didn't know it wasn't mine."

"If you believe that, then I'll sell you the Brooklyn Bridge," Reggie teased.

"I know, she knew exactly what she was doing. I wonder if she was harassing those other guys like she was harassing me?"

"I doubt it. She was determined to make that baby yours; she didn't have time to harass the other guys. That's a damn shame man, all of that for nothing." Reggie lamented.

"I'm just glad to get her hands out of my pockets."

"That's true."

"It's too bad Lori didn't hang around long enough to learn the truth; that Shelly's baby wasn't mine," Wayne lamented.

"That is too bad, maybe you could have overcome the infidelity, but she was pregnant and blaming you; Lori couldn't take that."

"Yeah, she made everything ten times worse than it was," Wayne said regretfully.

"You're right about that, but life goes on. It's time for you to try dating now and then, don't just sit around feeling bad; that's not good for you and it won't change anything," Reggie advised.

"I know man, I'm going to start dating," Wayne said solemnly. "I'd better get ready to go."

"Okay, stop by anytime."

"I will," he said as he walked back towards the family room. "Carol, the dinner was delicious, thanks a lot."

"You're welcome, take care of yourself and come back soon," Carol responded.

Reggie walks Wayne to the door and returns to the family room to watch TV with his family.

"Reggie, I'm concerned about Wayne. He looks like he has lost some weight. He's truly in mourning for his wife," Carol said.

"I know, I'm concerned about him too. I just don't know what else I can do for him other than listen to his problems."

"Maybe we can help him to get back on the bike and keep riding," Carol suggested.

"What are you talking about?"

"You know what people say, if you fall off of a bike, get back on and keep riding," Carol revealed.

"So, what does that have to do with Wayne?" Reggie asked.

"Wayne lost his woman, so maybe another woman can help him to heal. There's a really cute nurse on my floor that I think Wayne might like. I can set them up with a date," Carol offered.

"Wayne won't want to go out with her; he's still pining over Lori."

"Let's invite both of them to dinner, if they like each other, then they can go out; if they don't then they don't have to."

"Do you think it will help?"

"At least it will give him something else to think about," Carol said.

"It's up to you, I guess it can't hurt," Reggie said.

"Okay, I'll set it up for two weeks from Saturday at 7:00 PM. You invite Wayne."

"Thanks Baby," Reggie said as he kissed his wife on her cheek. "You're so thoughtful"

"I think I'm going to start looking for a condo to buy," Lori said "I have saved some money and I think I'm ready to get my own place."

"You don't have to rush. I enjoy having you here. You're good company, and you're a lot of help around the house. I know your Dad enjoys having you here, so just take your time," Leeanna urged Lori.

"I appreciate that; it does make me feel better, but you and Dad need your privacy, besides, I'm looking for something close to you and Dad. I'll visit often, I promise."

"You just remember what I said, this is your home too," Leeanna reassured her daughter.

Frank sat on his throne listening to Lee and Lori talking in the kitchen. He was happy to hear Lori say that she was looking for a place to live. She should have had a place by now. Lori should go back home and work out her problems with her husband, but no; she has to let her false pride destroy her marriage. She thinks she's going to find someone better out there, she's sadly mistaken. I'll have to tell Lee it's time for Lori to go so she can stop encouraging her to stay. I need my privacy. I want things to return to normal around here. Lee isn't thinking about me, she's busy trying to play mother to a grown woman. I can't have a private conversation with my wife unless it's in the bedroom at night. She should have saved enough for her own place by now, Frank thought.

"Lee, I want you to tell Lori that it's time for her to go home to her husband or to get her own place, I need my privacy," Frank ordered.

"Frank, Lori is our daughter. We're supposed to stand by her," Leeanna responded.

"We have stood by her, but it's been eight months. She works everyday, she should get a place of her own," Frank stated.

"I don't think she's quite ready yet. Give her a little more time," Leeanna pleaded.

"No, I want my privacy! I work hard everyday; I should be able to come home to a little peace and quiet. If you don't tell her, then I will. It's up to you," Frank said firmly.

"Okay, I'll tell her, but in my own time."

"I mean what I say, don't fight me on this Lee. I've been very nice about the whole thing, but enough is enough."

Leeanna didn't respond. This is my house too, she thought. I won't let Frank throw our daughter out of her home.

Frank sat in the livingroom watching the six o'clock news. Lee and Lori were cleaning the kitchen. It wasn't a familiar sound. It was the sound of women giggling and chatting. This wasn't a soothing sound that lulled him to sleep; this was an annoying sound that kept him awake. He could hear them chatting about who lost weight, gained weight, who had a new car, an old car, who could cook or who couldn't cook. He learned to tune out the specifics. Tonight he was listening to hear when Lori was leaving. He'd told Lee to tell her she had to leave two weeks ago. He was expecting her to be gone by now. Frank shifted in his chair, he felt uncomfortable in his pants.

"You know Mom; I think I'm going to get a new car. My car is almost four years old and I think I could use a change. I'd like a Honda CRV in a bronze color," Lori announced.

"Yes, they're nice and they're good for the snow. I like the silver one too," Leeanna agreed.

"The silver one is my second choice. I think I'll go look at some tomorrow," Lori said.

Frank jumped up out of his chair and quickly walked into the kitchen. He looked at Lee and Lori with contempt. "Why are you two in here talking about buying cars? Do you have the money to buy a new car Lori?" Frank asked.

"Yes, I'm thinking about it," Lori answered.

"Oh, you are, are you? And when do you plan on getting a place to live? You can't stay here forever," he said in anger.

Lori looked hurt by her father's outburst. "I know that Dad."

"Don't you think we're entitled to some privacy? We've raised you and educated you so that you could take care of yourself."

"Dad I thought you wanted me to stay here. I...I didn't know you wanted me to leave," Lori said as her eyes filled with tears.

"Yes, I think you've over stayed your welcome. Get yourself a place as soon as possible."

"I will be out of here this week," Lori assured her father. She walked out of the kitchen and ran up the steps to her room and closed the door.

Leeanna was speechless. She couldn't believe the scene she had just witnessed. She glared at Frank in disbelief. Her fury finally found a voice. "Frank, I can't believe what you just did to our daughter. How could you hurt her like that? How could you make her feel like she's all alone, that we don't care about her?"

"I don't want to hear that shit Lee, I told you to tell her two weeks ago. I warned you that if you didn't tell her, then I would."

"This is my home too, if I want my daughter to stay here until she's ready to face the world, then that's my business. How dare you speak for me? I'll never forgive you for this," Leeanna shouted, as she continued to glare at him.

"What do you mean, you won't forgive me? This is my damn house! I make the rules in here; I say who can live here and who can't! Lori is a thirty-six years old professional woman. She can take care of herself. I'm not going to spend the rest of my life catering to a grown woman that chooses not to forgive her husband. If she wants to be so independent, then let her do it in her own house, not mine." Frank asserted.

"I cook for you, I clean for you, I wash your clothes for you, I do everything for you and you don't even have the decency to say please or thank you, but yet I can't say that our daughter can stay in this house? Well, you start taking care of yourself, because I'm not waiting on you anymore," Leeanna shouted, as she turned to leave the kitchen. "Fuck you Frank."

Frank reached over and grabbed Lee and shoved her against the wall. He grabbed her shoulders and shook her like a rag doll. "I'm getting sick of you disrespecting me in my own house. I'm not going to take that from you; do you understand me Lee?"

"Get off of me Frank! I said get off of me," she shouted as she struggled for her freedom from his grip. His nails tore into her skin as she ripped her arm free. His hand went up to her throat as he tried to restrict her movement. Leeanna reached towards the stove, grabbing the handle of the frying pan. She swung the weapon quickly and forcefully, landing a blow against the front side of Frank's head. He immediately released his grip and put up both of his hands to shield his head from a second blow.

His eyes widened in disbelief. The blood started to flow freely from the wound on the side of his forehead, above his brow. Leeanna screamed, when she saw the blood spurting out of the gash and realized what she'd done. Frank took a dish towel from the sink and staggered backwards to a chair near the table.

"Are you alright Frank?" she asked while searching his face with her eyes.

"You hit me, you tried to hurt me!" He answered softly, as he tried to stop the blood that was soaking the towel.

Leeanna ran to the foot of the stairs and called for Lori. She tried to yell above the sound of the music coming from Lori's room. No response. Leeanna ran upstairs out of breath and pushed Lori's room door open, "Lori, come to the kitchen quick, there's been an accident!"

Lee turned and ran back down the stairs with Lori following behind her.

"What's wrong? What happened?" Lori asked as her eyes surveyed the scene in the kitchen. There were drops of blood on the floor, a frying pan lay near by. Frank sat with his head leaning forward, holding a towel to his forehead, which was quickly becoming saturated with his blood.

"Are you alright Dad? Let me see." She slowly lifted the towel, which revealed a deep gash that required stitches. "I think we'd better get you to the hospital. Mom get Dad's shoes. We have to get him out of here. He's losing too much blood!" Lori ordered.
Leeanna ran to get Frank's shoes from the livingroom and returned; placing them on his feet. She ran to get her purse and shoes from the bedroom and joined Lori to take Frank to the hospital.

Lori and Leeanna sat in the waiting room of Chestnut Hill Hospital's Emergency Room. Lori felt bewildered by this incident. She couldn't imagine how her father cut his head like that. Leeanna felt guilty and ashamed. I could have killed Frank, she thought. I didn't mean for this to happen. What must Lori think of me assaulting her father with a frying pan? This seems surreal; like a bad dream. The Amos family has never had violence among family members, Leeanna thought.

"Mom, what happened between you and Dad? Did you hit him with that frying pan?"

"Yes, I'm afraid I did. I didn't mean to hit him, it all happened so quickly," Leeanna lamented.

"Why, why did you hit him? I hope it wasn't because of me. Tell me it wasn't because of me," Lori begged.

"No, it wasn't because of you; it was because he manhandled me. I'm sick of him grabbing on me every time he gets angry. He doesn't know if he wants to be my husband or my father."

"That was taking it too far, don't you think? I mean, Dad is in there getting stitches in his face. He'll have a scar for the rest of his life."

"He left me no alternative. He grabbed me one time too many and I grabbed the first thing I could get my hands on, and let him have it. Maybe this will teach him to keep his hands to himself," Leeanna said defensively.

"Well, I'm sure you've achieved that, but how will it look; Dad going to school with stitches in his face?" Lori asked sarcastically.

"I'm sorry it had to come to this, but he asked for it. Go and ask the nurse if we can see your father?" Leeanna ordered her daughter.

"Okay." She walks up to the desk, "Can we go in the back to see my father, Frank Amos?" Lori returns to her seat after hearing the nurse's response.

"Mom, they said only one of us could go in the back to see Dad. You go back, you're his wife."

"No, you go, I don't think he's too anxious to see me right now."

"Maybe you're right, I'll go." Lori goes through the double doors to her father's room. He was sitting on the side of the bed with a big bandage on the side of his head. He looked so old and pitiful. He's such a proud man, Lori thought as she looked at her father gazing into space, looking lost. "Are you okay Dad? How do you feel?"

"I'm alright. They just put eight stitches in my forehead."

"Are they finished with you yet?"

"Yes, I'm waiting for a prescription for pain. I have a terrible headache."

"How long do the stitches have to stay in?"

"The doctor said five or six days. He'll give me an appointment to come here to get them out, or I can go to my own doctor. Where's your mother?"

"She's waiting in the waiting room. I hope this didn't happen because of me."

"No, don't worry about it. Let's go, I'll pick up the prescriptions from the desk on our way out," Frank told his daughter. He didn't look at Lee or talk to her on the way to the drugstore to get the prescriptions for pain, nor when they arrived home. He went upstairs and prepared for bed. He went to sleep in his home office on the pull out sofa after taking two pain pills.

Leeanna went upstairs when she thought Frank was asleep. She was surprised to find him asleep in his office. She felt remorse for injuring her husband. Leeanna slept little during the night, she was worried about Frank. She awakened to check on him several times and found him sleeping soundly each time. His handsome bronze face was marred by the large white bandage that extended into his mixed gray hair. His Indian nose had a red bruise on it. Frank looked like he'd been in combat, and in fact he had.

Lori went to see her sister the following day. April was standing at the stove cooking her family's dinner wearing blue jeans and a navy sweatshirt that hid her slim figure and contrasted with her pale skin. She had her mother's complexion and her father's Indian facial features. Her long black hair was held back with a red bow. This outfit gave her a very youthful appearance. Paul was picking up the children from their swimming lessons on his way home from work.

"April, I just had to come and tell you about your mother and father," Lori said excitedly.

"What about them? What are they up to now?"

"Mom hit Dad in the face with a frying pan."

"She did what!"

"She hit him in the face with a frying pan."

"I don't believe it. Mom did that? Did she hurt him? Of course she hurt him. Is Dad okay?" April asked with concern.

"He had to get eight stitches in his forehead," Lori reported.

"Really, why would she do something like that? Is she going crazy or what?" April asked in disbelief.

"She said he was bullying her and she grabbed the first thing she could get her hands on, and hit him with it."

"Dad needs to learn to keep his hands to himself. I knew someone would get hurt sooner or later if they kept carrying on like they've been, but I thought it would be Mom," April said

"I'm glad it wasn't Mom, but I love them both. I don't want either of them to get hurt." Lori said sadly.

"I feel the same way. They're too old to start fighting after all of these years. They're old enough to know better. They're grandparents for goodness sakes," said April while shaking her head in disgust.

"You're right about that."

"What were they fighting about?"

"I think it was because Dad wants me to move and Mom wants me to stay. We've spent a lot of time together since I've been home. I guess Mom likes the company."

"Yes, and Dad is probably jealous. He wants her all to himself. Well, Lori I guess it's time for you to move. He probably wants his privacy," April surmised.

"Yes, I know. I'll get an apartment in one of those complexes near Mom and Dad's house. I don't want to cause any problems."

"I think that would be best. You can get a six months lease if you want and buy a condo after that, then you'll have the time to look around to find what you really want," April suggested.

"Yes, you're right, I'll move by the end of the week," Lori promised.

"That's for the best. They're older and they need their space."

Lori returned home to find Frank in his office and Leeanna eating at the kitchen table alone. Lori got a plate and joined her mother at the table. Leeanna looked worried and she didn't have much to say, despite Lori's prodding.

Leeanna felt introspective. She was shocked at her own rage. She knew Frank was under a great deal of stress and it contributed to his outbursts, but she didn't understand where her violence came from. It frightened her. It surprised her. The swiftness, the force with which she swung the frying pan could have proved deadly. She could have killed Frank! The reality of her actions made her feel depressed. Every time she saw that bandage on Frank's forehead, she felt like a stranger to herself. When she closed her eyes, she could still see Frank's look of horror in his eyes and his hands rising to ward off a second blow; a second blow. Frank was expecting the violence of a second blow!

I can't believe that Lee wanted to hurt me. I wasn't trying to hurt her. I was just trying to restrain her. She deliberately picked up that frying pan and hit me with it. Now, I'm lying here with eight stitches in my face and I'm getting a black eye. How is that going to look in school? I'll have to lie and say I was in a car accident, or I fell. Of course everyone will be suspicious. They'll think I'm lying. They'll tell jokes about my injuries behind my back for the next few years. They'll be thrilled to see me with this injury. How could she do it after I've loved her and supported her for almost forty years? How could she disrespect me like that? If I knocked her on her ass, then I would be the bad guy, and believe me, I have felt like it, but I use control, Frank thought.

I thought Lee was finished changing life, but she obviously hasn't. The old Lee would never have hit me the way she did. She didn't respect me as her husband, which hurt me deeply. That's what it comes down to, a lack of respect. I can't go to work looking like this. I'll have to call out for a couple of weeks. Frank looked at the mirror opposite the hideaway bed, I look like a victim. I look like I've been attacked.

I'm sure Lee realizes what she's done. She has left lunch for me everyday and she's been preparing my favorite meals. I know she's sorry. I have been losing my temper with Lee lately. I guess I brought some of this on myself. I did grab her by the throat; maybe she was scared that I would hurt her. I would never hurt her. I shouldn't grab her like that. I always feel bad after I grab Lee, but sometimes she makes me so angry, until I lose control of my temper. I need to control my temper. Lee is a good woman and a good wife, I shouldn't treat her like that. She deserves better, but when I tell her I want Lori out of the house, then I mean what I say. It's not for her to challenge my decisions. Lori will stay as long as she can live free and spend her money shopping for clothes to throw around the house. If she buys a new car, then she won't have the money to get her own place. No, I mean what I say, Lori has to go.

April was the family mediator; trying to keep the peace in the family. Her parents have had their differences over the years, but they were always verbal. She didn't know what to make of her parents allowing their disagreements to become physical. She knew her father's temper could get out of hand sometimes, but he usually made a lot of noise with no actions. Her mother usually ignored him, staying calm and talking softly to him until he calmed down. She was always the even tempered one. She was surprised that her mother had become violent, taking matters into her own hands.

When April arrived at her parents' home she found Leeanna preparing Frank's dinner tray.

"Hi Mom, how are you doing today?" April greeted her mother.

"I'm just fine April, how are you?"

"I'm okay. I thought I'd stop by to check on you and Dad. How is he?"

"He's doing better. He still isn't speaking to me unless he has to. He won't ask for food unless I offer it to him. He's sulking. I think he's very angry with me," Leeanna surmised.

"I can understand that. No one likes to get hurt."

"That's true."

"Maybe you should talk to him. At first, he may be resistant, but he'll come around before too long," April suggested.

"I hope so; this silence is driving me crazy. I'm sorry for what happened, but he should be sorry too, after all, he started it."

"I'm sure he is sorry Mom, you know Dad is very proud. Just give him some time. I'm sure he's even embarrassed for Lori and I to know that you hit him with a frying pan."

"I'm embarrassed as well, it is embarrassing for your grown children to know that you're fighting and acting like children."

"I'm going upstairs to visit Dad for a few moments. Has he been out of that room yet?"

"If he has, then it's been during the day while I'm at work. When I come home, I can see that he's been in the kitchen and has eaten his lunch, but he never comes down while I'm home." April goes upstairs to see her father.

"Hi Dad, are you feeling any better? April asked.

"Yes, I'm beginning to feel better."

"Good! Did they take the stitches out yet?"

"Yes, they did, in fact they took them out this morning," Frank responded.

"Good. When can you take the bandage off?"

"In a few days," Frank answered.

"Mom is getting ready to bring your dinner tray upstairs. Do you think you might feel better if you came downstairs to eat?" April inquired.

"No, I don't. I feel better where I am," Frank responded.

"Okay Dad, you know what's best for you. I'm going to get ready to go home to my family. I hope you continue to feel better, and think about going downstairs. Goodbye."

"Mom, Dad's waiting for his dinner. I'm going home now. Just give him some time, he'll come around.

Where's Lori? Isn't she usually home for dinner?"
April asked.

"Yes, she is, but she's moving tomorrow, so she
has a lot of little things to get done. She had to find
movers on short notice, and she had to go to the storage
company. She has to pay them off and notify them of
her moving date and time. I'm going to take the day off
work tomorrow to help her. It's too much for her to do
by herself. I wish she would go back to Wayne and give
her marriage another try, but she doesn't even want to
discuss it. She's so hard headed. She doesn't realize
how lonely she's going to be without Wayne, because
she's been here with us," Leeanna predicted.

"I know, she'll have to learn for herself. Tell her
I said Hi, and I'll talk to her tomorrow. I'll talk to you
soon Mom."

"Okay April," Leeanna said as she started up the
steps with Frank's dinner tray. "I love you."

"I love you too Mom," April said as she left the
house through the back door.

"How are your parents doing," April, Paul asked
as he cleared the dishes from the dinner table.

"They're not speaking yet, but other than that,
they're fine."

"I can't believe your mother hit your father with
a frying pan. They're always so prim and proper. I
don't believe they are over there fighting," Paul chuckled.

"I know, sometimes older people don't have enough patience to deal with each other. They love each other, they'll work it out."

"I hope so. I guess you never stop negotiating your relationship, even after thirty-eight years. I hope you don't hit me with a frying pan when I'm old and gray," Paul laughed.

"No, I'm going to hit you with a big pot. What do you think of that?" April asked as she started to wash the dishes. "Why don't you go for your walk, I'll do these dishes alone, so we can get to bed early tonight."

"Okay, I won't be long, I'm tired too. Do you want anything from the store while I'm out?" Paul inquired.

"Bring back some milk, bread, and something sweet," April requested.

"Whatever your little heart desires," Paul flirted. He kissed her lightly on the lips and went upstairs to change into his sweatsuit

Paul walked down the street at a brisk pace. The sky was cloudy, and rain was predicted for tonight. He could feel the moisture in the air. He loved to feel his blood rushing through his veins and the wind on his face. He felt alive! Walking always cleansed his soul. It was an addiction he knew, he couldn't stop walking if he wanted to; it was a part of him. Walking enabled him to continue to perform the sedentary cerebral work of

180 CARLA DIANE ELLIS

an accountant. It increased his virility. The down low
sexual activities added spice and intrigue to an otherwise ordinary life. He loved April and they had a passionate sex life, but that was only a part of his sexual
desires. April was the only female he had ever loved
and she had given him two wonderful children, but he
still yearned for the caress of a male. The sex was different from the softness of sex with a woman. The hard
firm body of a male excited him. He felt like the Greek
Gods, abandoning all inhibitions; like phantoms in the
night giving and receiving pleasures.

"He walked past the mini mall and crossed the
street to enter the park. The bench was empty. He sat
there excited by the possibilities. A man entered the
park, walking at a fast pace. He sat on the bench near
Paul and looked him up and down. Paul slowly and
provocatively walked behind the big oak tree. The man
followed. He slammed Paul against the tree and kissed
him abrasively in the mouth, forcing his tongue down
Paul's throat. He spun Paul around, slamming his face
against the tree bark, pulling his sweat pants down to
his ankles. Paul breathed deeply, enjoying the take
charge, aggressive behavior of his lover. Paul received
him with great anticipation. He enjoyed being a bottom
as well as a top! The sex was exhilarating!

Paul went into the mini mall to buy the milk,
bread and ice cream. He rushed home to his wife. He
was still stimulated by his encounter with the stranger
and he was excited by the possibility of sex with April.
The contrast always left him satisfied.
"I'm home Sweetheart," Paul announced.

"I'm up here in the bedroom."

Paul rushed to the shower, returning to the bed holding the baby oil in his hand. "How about a massage," he asked his wife with a smile on his face.

"Anything for you," April responded with a smile; returning his sexual anticipation.

CHAPTER 11

Lori's new apartment was located in an apartment complex in Cheltenham Township, not far from Mt. Airy. She rented a two bedroom apartment, because she had so many clothes and other possessions from the house. It was nice to have her own space again, away from her parents and their madness. Lori was glad to have her privacy, no matter how old you are, you are still a child in your parents' house. She was ready to move on with her life. Wayne was her past and she had rented out their house, which paid the mortgage and left a little money for repairs. She kept all of their furniture, so she didn't see a need to rush the divorce. She wasn't ready to deal with Wayne and his infidelity yet. She just wanted to enjoy her life; that would be enough for now.

I need the love of a good man. I haven't had sex in so long; I'm ready to jump the bones of the first man that walks through that door. Lori stood at the window of her new apartment looking down at the young men that were playing basketball on a court. They were stripped down to nothing but shorts, with the sun reflecting off of their firm sweaty bodies. The sixpacks of their abdomens and their broad shoulders made Lori horny. She closed the blinds and continued to unpack her belongings. I like the scenery around here, she thought as she smiled to herself.

Lori hated the thought of dating all over again, looking for Mr. Right. I thought all of that was behind me, but here I am faced with the same dilemma again. It took years to find Wayne. Most men can't handle a woman like me. I'm too assertive for them, too independent. I'm my own person, and Wayne understood that. We were perfect for each other in so many ways. Why did he have to ruin everything by sleeping with that Ho? They deserve each other. Now, here I am alone again. Oh well, it's not as if I didn't do it before, but still, it would be nice to have a man around the house. She walked back to the window and peeped through the closed blinds. She smiled as she thought; it looks like I have some interesting neighbors!

T.J. sat on the hideaway bed lacing his sneakers. His hair was still wet from the shower he'd taken earlier. He walked to the small kitchen and opened the refrigerator, removing the almost empty carton of orange juice. He shook his head in disgust. His roommate had once again drank all of the juice and replaced the carton in the refrigerator. He poured Frosted Flakes into a bowl and was grateful to have enough milk for his cereal. He sat on the sofa eating and staring mindlessly at the TV. Things weren't going well between him and his roommate, but he couldn't afford to lose his share of the rent and he refused to go back to his mother's house. He couldn't live like that again.

He was tired of his mother's drinking. After drinking beer, wine, whiskey or whatever she could get her hands on, she'd start an argument; cursing, yelling and throwing things at him, telling him that she wished she had flushed him down the toilet; at those moments, he wished Big Mama had flushed her down the toilet, then neither of them would be here going through this craziness. She and her boyfriend started drinking as soon as they woke up, and they drank until late at night when, they fell asleep wherever they were sitting. When she wasn't arguing and fighting with her boyfriend, then she was arguing and fighting with T.J. His older brother left home three years before T.J., leaving him without someone to share his pain.

Growing up in Logan, a section of North Philadelphia wasn't easy. Decaying homes and empty lots were a breeding ground for the crime and gangs that were everywhere. His mother and father raised him and his brother in a three bedroom house with a front porch. Both of his parents were alcoholics, drinking all day and fighting all night. His father stopped drinking seven years ago, and tried to get his wife to stop too. She refused to join him in his sobriety, so he packed his bags and left; leaving his sons to suffer under their mother's drunken reign. T.J. tried to stay home long enough to finish community college, but it became more difficult to tolerate her behavior as he became older.

T.J. secured a job at a temp agency in Mt. Airy and began looking for a roommate. Placing an ad on the community board at school brought a number of interested students. He found an apartment and selected the only person that had enough money for the security deposit. He lacked the money to return to school, but he was working full time to save. After paying his share of the bills, there was little left to put away. He had a small bank account and he made deposits weekly. He participated in activities that didn't require much money.

T.J. had a couple of girls he talked to and dated from time to time, but nothing serious. He played basketball, almost daily and he enjoyed skating. He had an out going personality and a pleasant smile, which won him many friends. T.J. placed his bowl in the sink and ran water in it, because the basement apartments had an ant problem. He picked up his basketball and headed out the door to join his boys on the court.

Lori parked her car in her reserved parking space. She went to the trunk of her car to retrieve the last of the boxes from her storage space. When she reached into the trunk to pull out a box she could smell the aroma of a sweaty man. She turned and looked into the handsome face of one of the regular basketball players. She felt vulnerable. He looked young and delicious.

"Why don't you let me help you with those boxes? You are too pretty to strain that beautiful body."

"Well, I don't know you. I could use some help and I would appreciate it, but we are strangers," Lori said.

"Let me fix that. I'm Timothy Davis Jr., my friends call me T.J.. I live in the back of the complex with my roommate. Now, we're not strangers, we're neighbors."

"I'm Lori, as you can see, I'm just moving in."

"Let me welcome you to the neighborhood."

"Thanks, I really do appreciate your help," she said as T.J. lifted the box and followed her into the apartment. Lori had most things in place, so her apartment was starting to look like home.

"You have a nice apartment and your things fit in here perfectly."

"Thanks, it was nice of you to help me. You're obviously a gentleman. Can I offer you something cold to drink? I have juice, water or beer, which would you prefer?"

"I'll take a beer. You know, you can become dehydrated shooting that ball," T.J. said as he stood in the middle of the livingroom floor feeling awkward.

"I've seen you play, you're pretty good." Lori left T.J. standing as she walked to the refrigerator to retrieve a beer for him.

"Thanks, I get my share of lay ups," he said modestly as they stood drinking the beers.

"Come and have a seat on the sofa. Are you a student or do you work?"

"Yes and no, I was taking classes at a junior college, but now I'm trying to get into a real college. I work for a temp agency."

"Junior colleges are real colleges, they just offer two years degrees, and then you can go to a four year college for the last two years; if you want a bachelor's degree." Lori informed him.

"I think I'd just like to go to a four year college, then I won't have to worry if they will accept all of my credits. I'm working to save money for books and things. What kind of work do you do?"

"I'm a fourth grade teacher."

"You don't look like a teacher. I wish I had a teacher like you," he said as he looked her up and down with admiration.

"I guess that's a compliment. Thank you."

"Look, you are fine. Could you and I get together sometime, maybe take in a movie, or go to a club or something?"

"Are you old enough to get in a club?" Lori asked sarcastically.

"Yeah, I look young, but I'm a man. I ain't no boy, besides, age is just a number. How old are you?" T.J. asked defensively. "Maybe twenty-seven…..twenty-eight?"

"That's good enough. Let's just say, I'm older than you."

"So what, like I said, age is just a number. I like you. I don't care how old you are. We can kick it sometimes, right?"

"I don't know, I've never dated a younger guy. Have you ever dated an older woman?" she laughed.

"Sure, I've dated lots of girls older than me. It's no big thing. Come on, let me take you to the movies tomorrow night. Please!"

"Okay, since you're so nice and helpful, we can go to the movies. What time?

"Good, I'll pick you up at 7:30PM. Okay?"

"Okay." She stood up to walk him to the door. T.J. stood and handed her the empty beer can. After closing the door, Lori took a deep breath and let it out slowly through her mouth. What am I getting myself into? He's too young. I'm about thirteen years older than him, she thought. Oh well, I guess a movie won't hurt, it's just a movie.

Lori pulled a fitted tee shirt over her Guess jeans. She laced her matching blue Nike sneakers. She combed her hair away from her face to make her look younger. The doorbell rang promptly at 7:25 PM. Lori rushed to the door, stopping momentarily to compose herself. She opened the door with a fixed smile on her face. T.J. was quite handsome in his Fubu gear. The monotone gray, complimented his mahogany skin.

"Hi, don't you look handsome," Lori said pleasantly.

"Thanks," T.J. said accepting the compliment with a broad smile that revealed a perfect set of white teeth. "You look good in those Guess jeans, and blue is definitely your color."

"Thank you," She reached for her sweater and said "Let's go."

They settled for an action movie with a leading Black actor. As they were returning to T.J.'s 1994 green Nissan, they walked pass an arcade.

"Let's go inside and see how competitive you are," T.J. suggested.

"I can play games with the best. I've always been competitive. Let's go, I'll teach you a thing or two."

"I'm sure you can teach me a lot of things," he whispered in her ear.

Lori smiled as she felt his hot breath on her ear and neck. They played games for a couple of hours.

"I have to go. I have one million things to do tomorrow," Lori said.

"I'm sorry to hear that. I hoped we could have a late breakfast together," T.J. flirted.

"Now aren't you full of yourself," Lori laughed.

When they arrived at her apartment door, they stood awkwardly looking into each others eyes as T.J. held Lori's hands. She attempted to give him a peck on his lips, but he wrapped his arms around her and pulled her to him. His tongue darted in and out of her mouth. When he paused to take a breath, she broke away and opened the door to her apartment with her key. She took T.J.'s hand and led him into her apartment. They embraced each other frantically; while Lori closed the door with her foot .They fell back on the sofa enjoying their foreplay, before going into the bedroom to get better acquainted.

"Would you like some eggs and grits with your coffee T.J.?" Lori asked.

"Whatever you feel like making Baby," he answered as he lay in bed with his arms wrapped around her. "What I really would like for breakfast is you. You feel so good, I'd like seconds."

"I thought you'd never ask." Lori cooed as she rolled on top of him.

T.J. left after taking a shower about noon. Lori spent the afternoon smiling. Sex with T.J. gave her more energy to finish putting her belongings away. He has the right equipment, but he needs an owner's manual to make the best use of it, she giggled to herself. I'll have to give this young boy some lessons. I like him; he's young, but manly. He knows how to open doors for a lady, and I like the way he places his hand in the small of my back to lead me through doorways. He's so cute, and he tries to please. He makes me feel young.

T.J. came to visit Lori the following weekend with his Play Station II and four games. They ordered pizza and played games well into the night. T.J.'s laughter filled a lonely space for Lori. He really is a nice guy, she thought. She laughed as she beat him, she laughed as he beat her. Their play continued into the bedroom.

"You really are good people, Lori. You're down to earth and I like that. I'm going to take you to meet some of my friends," T.J. announced.

"I don't know about that. They'll look at me and think I'm your mother," Lori responded.

"You don't look like my mother, you look good. I'm not worried about what other people think. Can you skate?"

"Yes, I can skate, although I haven't skated in quite some time," she answered.

"You know skating is something you never forget. I love to skate. I want you to go to the skating rink with me Saturday night. Will you go?"

"I don't know. Are your friends going to be there?"

"Some of them. They're cool. You'll like them."

"I don't know if I'd be comfortable being the older lady in your life with your young friends."

"My friends aren't all young; I have friends in all age groups. I wouldn't put you in the position of feeling out of place. You'll fit right in."

"Are you sure I won't be the oldest one there?"

"I wouldn't lie to you."

I don't own any skates, can I rent them there?"

"Sure, but if you like skating, we'll work on getting you a pair of your own," T.J. promised.

"We'll see."

Lori and T.J. arrived at the rink at 9:00PM. The rink was half full with adults from twenty to seventy years of age. The music was hot; it varied from rock to hip hop. The older skaters were very youthful, moving with the flexibility of persons twenty years younger. At the snack bar T.J. introduced me to a number of people, they were all very friendly. I did receive some stares from some young girls that were jealous of the attention T.J. was showing me. I felt proud to be with him. He's an expert skater and everyone was in awe of him as he flipped, split and danced to the music all over the rink. He attracted crowds when he put down his thing. He looked adorable, but I couldn't keep up with him. His energetic movements on the floor made me want to take him right there on the floor of the rink in front of everyone, but I waited until I got him on my livingroom floor!

T.J. looked forward to spending time with Lori. She definitely is a classy lady. He smiled to himself as he lay on the couch waiting for 8:00 PM to arrive. He was tired after working at a bank all day. He needed to get a little rest before going over Lori's, he knew they would make love and he wanted to be in shape, so he could maintain his reputation as a good lover, he thought. She's not like these young girls out here that are just looking for a brother to spend all of his cash on them. Lori usually pays her own way when we go out and she always pays when we order food in. She says she doesn't want me to spend my money on her, because she knows I'm trying to save my money to go back to college. She says she doesn't want me to think that she's trying to keep me from getting an education. Now, that's my kind of woman! She's not trying to use a brother up.

I just love the feel of her body; it's so warm and soft. She's always ready for sex; we have sex almost every time we're together. I love that about her, because I can never get enough pussy. She's the kind of woman a brother could settle down with. She loves sex as much as I do. She makes me feel like the king of the world. Lori says she's just getting over a bad marriage, that man must be crazy to let a beautiful woman like that go! His loss is my gain. I can feel the envy of other men when I'm out with her. I know they're jealous, because they can't take their eyes off of her. I don't mind, because I know I'm the one that will be going home with her; we'll be mixing sweat, so they can look all they want. I'm the man in her life, and I make sure that I leave her satisfied. It's good to have sex with a female that knows what she's doing for a change; those young girls don't know nothing. She's even taught me a thing or two. I can't wait to lay between those beautiful soft thighs, he thought as he massaged his penis. The young girls in the hood are always trying to make a baby, and the uppity girls in Mt. Airy are always trying to empty your pockets. They want a brother to spend, spend, and spend.

April has lunch with Lori at her school. They sat at Lori's table in the back of her classroom. Lori ordered pizza and salad to share with her younger sister. April brought a large soda and two slices of pound cake for dessert.

"You must meet him April, he is so adorable," Lori said playfully.

"I'm sure he is. What are you doing, robbing the cradle?" April questioned Lori.

"He's over twenty-one and that makes him an adult, just like me." She giggled

"Well, in that case, I'm glad he's not sixteen. I don't think I want to meet your toy boy. Keep him in the closet, and be careful not to hurt his feelings. Tell him up front what kind of relationship you want before he falls in love with you."

"What's love got to do with it?" Lori laughed. "Seriously, I don't want to hurt him. He's a sweet person, so open and honest; just as cute as he can be."

"How is the sex, is it worth it?"

"He's a novice, but I'm teaching him a few tricks. He's well endowed, but he's not quite sure what to do with it. The sex is good because I've been without it for so long."

"Well, I know he won't be around too long, only until you can replace him, right?"

"You've got that right," Lori chuckled. "He makes me feel like I'm twenty-three again. His energy and zest for life is contagious. When I finish with him, the next young girl he gets won't let him go, because he'll know how to keep her happy," Lori laughed.

"That's good, at least he will have learned some skills," she chuckled. "I'm sure you could use some laughter after all that you've been through. He's put a smile back on your face!" April said as she rose to place her trash in the bin.

Lori walked April to the schoolyard and picked up her students, and took them to the library. While her class watched a film, Lori thought about T.J.. She liked him a lot and she enjoyed having sex with him, but a friendship is all she could offer T.J.. We're like playmates; as long as he doesn't try to get serious, then we can keep on playing. He makes me feel beautiful and alive and in control.

Frank sat at the table with Lee eating his dinner. They smiled and chattered about events of the day. Lee told Frank about the demands of Dr. Phillips and Frank shared his frustrations with the teachers and union at his school. Frank retired to the livingroom. His shoes were in front of the sofa; his pants were stretched across the sofa with the creases in tact. His jacket and tie were hung on the back of the livingroom chair. Frank sat on his throne.

Lee and I didn't talk for several weeks after the incident. I was very hurt that Lee would actually try to hurt me. Lee apologized for hitting me and I apologized for grabbing her. We both promised to talk our problems out and not to become physical with each other. Lee's a good woman and I love her. She asked me not to have more than two drinks, because she felt that my drinking caused some of our problems. I don't think so, but she may be right; I agreed. We're trying to be intimate more frequently, even if it's just cuddling, that seems to make Lee happy.

Everyone at school wanted to know about my scar, but I told them that I was in a car accident and cut my forehead on the windshield. That seemed to satisfy them. Frank watched the six o'clock news. He could hear the familiar sound of Lee cleaning the kitchen. Boy, it's good to have my house back. I'm sure Lori is happier too in her new apartment. I know Lee and I are happy to be back to our routine. We raised our kids and we are entitled to a life of our own. Lee entered the livingroom and approached Frank.

"Honey, would you like some dessert?

"Yes Baby, could you bring me a slice of pie and some tea, please.

"Okay." Lee placed the pie and tea on the table beside Frank's chair.

"Thank you Lee, this looks good," he said, while placing his hand over hers.

"You're welcome Frank, I'm going upstairs to lay down and watch television.

"Okay, I'll be up a little later, Frank said.

Carol opened the front door for Wayne. "Hi Wayne," she said as she hugged him. "How are you doing?"

"I'm okay, I'm hungry and ready to eat some of your good cooking," he said as he walked to the livingroom.

"Hey man," Reggie greeted his friend.

"Hi Reggie, what's going on?" Wayne said returning the greeting.

"Just waiting for you man, so I can get some of this food my wife made," Reggie laughingly said.

"Wayne, let me introduce you to my friend, Annie. She's having dinner with us tonight".

Wayne is caught off guard, he didn't expect to be ambushed at Reggie's house. While maintaining a smile, Wayne greeted Carol's friend. "Hi Annie, nice meeting you."

"Wayne and Reggie have been friends since grade school," Carol informed her guest.

"That's wonderful, to have a friend for all of those years. Good friends are hard to come by," Annie responded.

"Annie works at the hospital with me, she's a nurse on my floor," Carol informed Wayne.

"That's nice. Nursing is an important career. Do you enjoy it?" Wayne asked, while trying to hide his disappointment with Carol for arranging this meeting. He thought Annie was pretty, but a little petite for his taste.

"Yes, I enjoy it very much," Annie answers nervously.

"How long have you been into nursing?" Wayne asked.

"Ten years; what kind of work do you do?"

"I sell cars, all kinds. If we don't have it, then we can get it for you."

"Spoken like a true car salesman," Reggie laughed.

"Let's go to the diningroom, the food is ready," Carol announced. She led the procession into the diningroom and invited them to have a seat on her new diningroom chairs. Wayne laughed, ate, drank and talked away the evening. Annie seemed to like Wayne, and he appeared to enjoy her conversation, but at the end of the evening, Wayne bid them all farewell.

"I had a wonderful time, and the food was delicious as usual. Thanks for your hospitality. Annie, it's been nice meeting you, and I hope to see you again," Wayne said as he left the house. Annie seemed disappointed that Wayne didn't ask for her phone number. She thought Wayne was quite handsome and intelligent.

"Reggie, what do you think Wayne thought of Annie?" Carol asked him as they put the dishes into the dishwasher.

"I don't know, because Wayne will talk to anyone, so it's hard to tell."

"Annie liked Wayne, so if he asks for her phone number, I'm going to leave it in this drawer in the kitchen," Carol informed her husband.

"I don't like playing cupid with my friends. Wayne meets plenty women on his job. I don't think he needs our help to find a girlfriend."

"He looked so sad, and I wanted to see him smile again, so if nothing else; he enjoyed the evening," Carol replied.

"That's true, he did enjoy himself, but I'm not going to pressure him about Annie. If he's interested in her, he'll tell me."

"Okay Honey, I tried!"

"That you did, and we all enjoyed the dinner and had a good time; now try to make your man smile," Reggie teased, as he put his arms around her waist and drew her close to him.

"That should be easy," Carol responded as she kissed her husband.

T.J. sat in the hotel business office at the computer trying to concentrate on imputing some figures. Thoughts of Lori disrupted his thinking frequently. He kept making mistakes and had to erase them and do them over. I think I am falling in love with her. She's so pretty and she's a good lover, maybe I like her so much because she's a teacher. I always had a thing for teachers. My first love was my second grade teacher Mrs. Taylor. She noticed my neglect, and was very kind to me. When I'd arrive at school late and unfed, she'd make sure I had breakfast in the morning; sending me to the lunchroom to eat even though I was late for school, and she kept a washcloth, soap and a comb, so I could wash my dirty face and hands and comb my hair. She didn't punish me when I came to school without my homework; she seemed to understand that my brother and I were on our own. All of that changed when my maternal grandmother visited our house and found no food in the refrigerator; my parents' had sold the food stamps to buy some alcohol. She packed our clothes and took us to live with her. She took good care of my brother and me. We had home cooked meals everyday, our clothes were clean and our hair was cut every two weeks. She took us to church on Sundays, and taught us how to pray.

Big Mama helped us with our homework everyday and made sure we got to school on time. She's the reason I did so well in school. She taught us to set goals in life. She's the reason my brother is a paralegal and she's the reason I'm working to save money to go back to college. Big Mama died after five years and we had to go back to live with our drunken parents. At first, they tried to do better, but after a couple of months; it was back to the same old shit! At least Big Mama took care of us until we were big enough to take care of ourselves. My brother and I bagged groceries at the local supermarket to get money to buy food and clothes for ourselves. Thank God for Big Mama! Big Mama is the reason I don't hate women, she taught us that women could be loving and caring people.

Lori cooked T.J. breakfast. Last night they had played video games and ordered sandwiches and fries delivered to the apartment. As usual, they ended up in bed, having sex. T.J. confessed his growing feelings for Lori, which made her feel uncomfortable. They sat on the sofa watching cartoons while eating corned beef hash and eggs with coffee.

"T.J. I think we need to talk," Lori said cautiously.

"About what?" he asked inquisitively.

"About us."

"What about us? I don't know about you, but I dig you."

"I like you too T.J., but that's all there is. I'm not in love with you and I don't want you to love me. I'm just looking for friendship."

"I thought we had something going on. I thought we had more than that."

"I think you're a wonderful guy and I like you a lot, but I'm just getting over a difficult marriage, and I'm not ready for anything serious."

"I think you have to take love where and when you find it." T.J. said solemnly.

"If you're looking for love, then you have to look somewhere else."

"I'm sorry to hear that, but if friendship is all you want, then I guess I have to respect that."

"Good, I'm glad you understand," Lori responded. "I don't want you to get serious about me." T.J.'s eyes betrayed his pain, as he placed his plate in the sink. He put on his sweats and left with only a goodbye. He looked like he was hurt by her decision, but better now than later, she thought. Lori felt stronger after dating T.J.. She felt more confident and in control. She felt ready to date a man her own age. T.J. filled many lonely days and nights for her. She didn't see or hear from him for two weeks. She missed him!

Lori sat on the sofa in her livingroom marking spelling tests as she watched television. This was a weekly ritual. The ringing of the doorbell startled her. Who could that be at 11:00 PM, she thought as she walked to the door to peep through the peep hole. T.J. stood at the door looking quite sad. She cautiously opened the door. He fell into her arms smelling of alcohol. "I missed you so much," he blurted out.

"I missed you too," She responded as she walked him to the couch.

"You didn't miss me, you don't want to be my woman. You don't love me."

"I did miss you and I like you very much."
He wrapped his arms around her, kissing her repeatedly; long passionate kisses. Lori returned his passion, leading him into her bedroom.

Lori and T.J. laid in the bed wrapped in each other's arms. She really did care about T.J., but once they'd finished having sex or playing games, there was nothing else for them to talk about.
"T.J. you're a wonderful man and I enjoy having sex with you, but it's time for us to go our separate ways. We enjoyed each other, it was fun, but we have to let it go before someone gets hurt."
"If that's the way you feel about it then so be it."
"I'll have to ask you not to drop by my place without calling. That's unfair to both of us."
T.J. dressed and left the apartment. Lori felt sad for his inability to accept the relationship for what it is. She felt guilty that his immaturity made it difficult for him.

Lori and Sandy taught at the same school for the past six years. They both taught fourth grade, and they shared materials and lesson plans. Their classrooms were side by side, and they often visited each other during the day. They were supportive of each other professionally and personally. They shared their joys and sorrows. Sandy was happy for Lori when she met and married Wayne. She gave her three pair of pants with the elastic waists when she was pregnant and she sympathized with her during her separation and the loss of her baby. Lori and Sandy sometimes shopped for clothes, but now Lori was on a budget and couldn't shop very often. Sandy knew Lori had been seeing T.J. and they had broken up. She felt a new man in her life might lift her spirits, so she called her cousin to go on a blind date with her. Lori was reluctant at first, but after a little prodding she gave in and agreed to the date.

Lori sat at the table in the corner of the Italian restaurant. She snacked on the sourdough roll and bread sticks that sat on the table. She was waiting for her blind date. Sandy insisted that her cousin was the perfect guy for me, she thought; I'll see if that's true. A man walked towards her with a broad smile on his face. He appeared to be 5'8, and very thin, but cute. He looked like Sandy with freckles on his face.

"Hello, are you Lori?" he asked.

"Yes, and I guess you're Michael. You favor your cousin."

"Lots of people tell us that."

"Have a seat and join me in eating this bread, it's delicious," Lori said in a friendly manner.

"No thanks, I'll wait for my food. Have you been waiting long?"

"I've been here about fifteen minutes," she responded.

"I'm sorry, I was in a meeting that lasted longer than I anticipated," Michael said apologetically. The waiter brought the menus. After perusing them, they made their selections.

"I'll have the linguine in a clam sauce, with a salad," Michael ordered

"I'll have the same,'"" Lori agreed, "and would you like a white wine?"

"Sure, the house white wine would be fine," Michael confirmed.

He's too thin for me, Lori thought, I like my men with a little meat on their bones. His eyes are too close together too. They talked about various movie stars, the latest CD's and the weather. He shared some of his experiences as a financial planner. He made predictions of the economy in the states and the world market. He's pleasant and he can hold an intelligent conversation, Lori thought. The waiter brought the check and gave it to Michael. He reviewed the charges.

"Why don't we go Dutch, I mean it is a first date?" Michael suggested.

"If that's the way you feel about it," Lori responded. She counted out her half of the check and tip; placing it on the table. She rose from the table and shook Michael's hand. "It's been nice meeting you," she said and walked away from the table.

"Wait, I'd like to see you again," Michael said.

I kept walking. He's pompous and cheap! If his cousin thinks he's the perfect man for me, then how does she see me? After that, I avoided his cousin at work.

T.J. missed Lori, but he wouldn't allow himself to call her. He'd hoped their relationship would grow into something permanent; he thought she felt the same way. She was always so responsive; she couldn't keep her hands off of him. When they sat watching TV, she always laid in his arms or across his lap. They laughed all of the time. They liked a lot of the same things, but all she wanted is a friendship; and he felt he had enough friends. He went to the kitchen and scraped the uneaten spaghetti down the garbage disposal. He didn't have much of an appetite. He removed a beer from the refrigerator. He drank that beer and then another. He thought they got along good, he thought they could live together.

You never know with these older women, they'll make you think they're in love with you and then they just drop you. You never know what they want, he thought. You never know what they're looking for. I didn't ask her to be my wife, I just wanted more of what we had going. Friends; I don't need her to be my friend, I have plenty of friends. To hell with her! I don't need her. You can't depend on women. She didn't give us a chance. He picked up the phone and called Shantel, a girl he'd been talking to before he met Lori. Shantel was a twenty year old student he'd met at Community College. T.J. asked her to meet him at a local club. He found her to be nice, but immature. All during the evening he kept finding his thoughts drifting back to Lori. Shantel had long pretty hair and curves in all the right places, but she seemed shallow in comparison to Lori. After spending several hours talking to Shantel and many beers later, T.J. started home. As he neared Lori's apartment, a longing for her rose up in him forcing him to park beside her car. He could see the light in her livingroom. Maybe she misses me as much as I miss her, he thought as he climbed the stairs to her apartment.

Once again Lori took T.J. into her arms and into her bed, but she knew that this was the last time. She'd have to sever all ties to be kind to him. She would no longer take his calls or answer the door when he rang her bell. That's the kindest way; I have to be strong for both of us. She found herself longing for Wayne. She still loved him, but she knew she could never forgive him for deceiving her. She felt lonely, but she had faith that she would meet someone to love, to trust, to respect.

CHAPTER 12

Lori knew she had to learn to be alone. It wouldn't be easy meeting someone she was compatible with, and blind dates weren't an option. She would refused to go, she didn't care who suggested it. She'd simply have to find something else to do with her time. She began to spend time with her niece and nephew. She took them to matinees. She had sleepovers with them. Lori and Ashley baked cookies and Lori and Anthony went to a basketball game at a local high school. She enjoyed spending time with them. She even took them to the zoo. Paul and April were thrilled to have time alone. Lori knew she was lonely when she started to miss the children when they went out with their parents. She decided to take a class at a nearby college; at least she could interact with adults.

Lori selected a computer class that met twice a week. She wanted to familiarize herself with computers; after all they are the technology of the future. She wanted to use computers in her classroom. The room where the class was held was very large. It had two rows of computers and there was an area with chairs with writing arms in front of the blackboard. Her classmates were a diverse group of people of varying ages and nationalities. The teacher was a middle aged unattractive female, with a loud annoying voice. The students were assigned to work in pairs, because there was only one computer for two students.

Lori's partner was Bradford Carter, a forty-eight years old businessman. He was a tall, well built man with flawless skin and mixed gray hair. He was a talkative and friendly person. He was very detail oriented and he kept excellent notes. Bradford was committed to mastering the computer. Initially their conversations centered on classroom assignments. Bradford was very helpful, often explaining assignments to Lori, occasionally she explained assignments to him.

Bradford had a lovely old house in Elkins Park, a suburb of Philadelphia. He and his late wife collected antiques, and artifacts from around the world, which were displayed throughout the house. Custom draperies framed the windows and matching bedspreads covered

212 CARLA DIANE ELLIS

the beds. The house was kept neat and clean by Jenny, the cleaning woman that came twice a week. She cooked meals for him and left them in the freezer. She'd worked for his family for many years.

Bradford's father was a well known undertaker in the city of Philadelphia. He grew up in East Oak Lane in a large house that was both a funeral parlor and their family home. He lived in a house that was filled with death and the smell of formaldehyde. As a child, he and his two sisters often played in the showrooms that housed the corpses, crawling under the caskets and hiding behind floral displays. Bradford and his sisters hid things inside the coffins under the bodies, like report cards, retainers, one orthopedic shoe; they were never seen again.

They weren't allowed in the embalming room, because of the chemicals. Bradford walked through the funeral parlor everyday to get upstairs to his family's living quarters, and he had no fear of death; until death began to claim the lives of those he loved. First, his mother died when he was thirty years old, and his father followed her one year later. His older sister died suddenly four years after his father, but the death that hurt him the most was the death of his wife, Audrey.

Bradford and Audrey met in high school. From the first day she walked into his classroom, he knew she was the one for him. They were lovers the last two years of high school; they attended the same college and married immediately following graduation. They spent all of their time together. Audrey helped him to establish their business and they worked the store together; making it a success. They had one daughter and she played in the back of the store while they worked. When Audrey became ill with breast cancer, he prayed that her life would be spared. He couldn't imagine life without her. He went into a deep depression when she died; everything reminded him of her. Their daughter became his reason for living, trying to be there for her. Work became his solace.

He has been a widower for three years and has had to fight off many of Audrey's friends. Several of them made a big play for him, cooking him food, inviting him to various affairs; one of them even showed up at his house unannounced wearing nothing but a raincoat. Of course, he sent her on her way. She was definitely not his kind of woman. Audrey was an equal partner in his life. She wasn't the kind of woman that would demean herself by going to a man's house naked. She knew she had much more to offer. Audrey was a proud independent woman. She sexually stimulated him with her mind. They took two to three vacations a year; traveling the world. He took for granted they would spend the rest of their lives together. He was not prepared to lose her to death so soon. She was not a woman that was easily replaced.

As Lori and Bradford became more comfortable communicating with each other, they began to share information of a more personal nature. Lori told him that she was separated from her husband and he told her that he was a widower. Bradford told her he had a twenty-two year old daughter in her last year of college. He explained that his daughter delayed college a year to stay with her mother, who was dying from breast cancer. He owned a sportswear store in Old City Philadelphia. He felt the computer could help him keep a handle on store inventory and ordering merchandise. He had professionals to handle his books, but merchandising was the area he wanted to master. Lori shared her frustration with the slow progress of some of her students that needed a more individualized approach to learning. She wanted to use the computer for independent classwork and possibly homework assignments for students with access to a computer after school.

Bradford invited Lori to lunch several times. They went to dinner near the school after collaborating over homework in the library. Lori invited him to an Italian restaurant after class one evening.

"What do you feel like eating?" Lori asked Bradford.

"I'd like some Ravioli," he answered.

"That sounds good. I'll get the same, with a salad on the side. I love Italian food," Lori added.

"So do I," Bradford agreed. "I make a mean spaghetti sauce, why don't you come to my house for dinner next Friday and I'll make you the best spaghetti dinner you've ever tasted?"

"I'm not a great cook, but I can make a good spaghetti sauce too. It's my Mama's sauce," she said while laughing.

"That's great, you come to my house for spaghetti this Friday, and I'll come to your house for spaghetti next Friday, and we'll see who makes the best sauce," Bradford challenged Lori.

"Okay, but I know mine is better than yours," Lori joked.

"That remains to be seen. It's a date then for Friday?" he asked.

"It's a date," Lori agreed.

After the spaghetti challenge, they began to gradually spend more and more time together. Before Lori knew what was happening, she and Bradford's friendship had evolved into a relationship. One minute they were talking about a classroom assignment and the next minute they were locked in an embrace. When Bradford came to Lori's house for the spaghetti dinner, he brought a bottle of red wine and some Italian garlic bread sticks. They sat on the sofa after dinner sipping wine and listening to music.

"I'm stuffed, your spaghetti was delicious. I'll concede, it was better than mine," Bradford said.

"Do you really think so?" Lori asked.

"Yes, I know it was better than mine. Tell your Mama I said she wins," he laughed.

"How gallant of you," she smiled with pride. "My mother will like hearing that. She makes it better than I do. One day you'll have to taste her sauce," Lori said. Her eyes were sparkling as the light reflected off her pupils. Bradford reached over and kissed her. At first, she was surprised, their friendship was going well. She didn't expect it, but before she knew it she was returning his kiss. He waited two weeks before trying to seduce her. She had thought about this moment long before it happened. She didn't know how she would respond. When the moment of truth arrived, Lori returned his overtures.

He was a patient and tender lover His lovemaking was different from any she had ever experienced. The foreplay made her feel like the most beautiful woman on earth. It lasted forever. The foreplay was the climax to the sexual act.

Bradford found Lori to be a beautiful and intelligent woman. She had an outgoing personality. She's a dedicated teacher, trying to find new ways of meeting her student's needs. He was surprised by the attraction he felt for her. He'd dated several women since Audrey's death, but Lori was the first one to touch his heart. She made him laugh. Lori was her own woman, she met the world on her terms. She reminded him of a younger version of his wife. He didn't know when it all started, but he found himself infatuated with her. He enjoyed her so much; he wanted to be with her all of the time. He knew he was getting to be an old man, but Lori made him feel young again. She made him want to start life anew. He hadn't felt like this in years, even with Audrey. The romance had faded from their marriage, but it was replaced by a warm solid love. They had a forever marriage and they knew that death was the only thing that would separate them.

I feel butterflies in my stomach when Lori's around me. When I'm not with her, I feel like something is missing. I know she's much younger than I am, but she seems to enjoy my company too. I don't know if she feels the same way about me, that I feel about her, but that's alright because I'm thoroughly enjoying her, and that's worth her weight in gold! Whatever she sees in me, I just hope and pray that she keeps on seeing it, Bradford thought.

Lori knew that Bradford was a father figure to her. He made her feel secure. He easily swayed her opinions. He manipulated her decisions and made her think it was her idea. Bradford was overly protective of Lori. He would drive her to work and pick her up after work. He was very kind and loving, but she began to feel that she was losing her freedom. His love was stifling. She felt caged in!

Bradford began to spend every night in Lori's apartment. At first, he stayed two nights a week, then four nights a week, then every night! He left personal items like his toothbrush and toiletries in her bathroom, and then it was socks and underwear in her dresser drawers. Lori noticed that Bradford had taken over a section of her closet; she couldn't understand why he was trying to move into her apartment when he had a beautiful empty house. It didn't make sense to her because he didn't live very far away. She didn't invite him to move in with her, he took too much for granted.

"Bradford, why are your clothes occupying space in my closet?" Lori asked in an annoyed tone.

"Just for convenience sake, do you want me to move them? I will, if that's what you want," Bradford offered. "I'm over here so much; I thought it made sense to keep some clothes here."

Lori enjoyed Bradford's company, but constantly being together was overwhelming. He's a good companion in many ways; he's handsome, intelligent and very interesting. He tells great stories about his travels. He's been to Europe, Australia, Egypt, and many islands. He has lovely artifacts around his house with a story to tell for each of them. He's a generous man. He appeared at the door with a dozen red roses and a diamond bracelet. She was very impressed, but she told him she couldn't accept such an expensive gift. He said he enjoyed doing nice things for his woman, and if he was worried about the cost, then he wouldn't have purchased it. Lori returned the bracelet to him, telling him that if they were still together in one year, she would accept it. Bradford was hurt; he viewed her rejection of the bracelet as a rejection of him. She still wouldn't accept it. She didn't want to sell her soul to the devil, she thought. He's already too possessive!

One day, after Bradford picked her up from school, Lori decided to go out alone.

"I'm going shopping. I want to pick up a few things," Lori told Bradford.

"Okay Baby, where do you want to go? I'll take you."

"I don't want you to take me. I want to go alone," Lori asserted.

"I thought you liked spending time together," he said.

"I do, but not all of the time. I like some time to myself too," Lori responded.

"But it's dangerous out there. I'd feel better if I drove you. I'll wait in the car," he conceded.

"No, I want to go by myself!"

"Why? Are you sure you're going shopping, or maybe you have something else in mind" he said suspiciously.

"Yes, I'm sure I'm going shopping; I've gone shopping all of my adult life on my own, and I don't see any reason to stop now," Lori protested. She grabbed her purse and walked out of the apartment. Damn, I'm leaving my apartment to get away from him, she thought. The class is over and he's still in my life!

Lori felt like she was suffocating. She walked through the mall, wandering aimlessly. She stopped in a store and bought a pair of sneakers. She couldn't believe she was out of the house by herself. She and Bradford had been together for three months. It was three months too long. She wasn't in love with him, she liked him, but there was no love. How did I let this man move into my apartment and into my life? Lori returned home with her new sneakers and a new attitude. It had taken her three hours to buy one pair of sneakers. She was becoming too dependent on Bradford. She knew she'd have to have a talk with him. When she arrived home Bradford was sitting on the sofa looking perturbed.

"I have to talk to you Bradford, this is not working out," she blurted out to him. "This relationship isn't working for me!

"What do you mean, it's not working out? We've been getting along just fine, until now."

"You may feel that way, but I don't feel that way. I'm not the type of woman you're looking for."

"You're what I want Lori. Don't try to tell me what I want."

"I think you're a wonderful man, but I think you're too old for me; you're suffocating me," she said as she stood in front of him, trying to make eye contact. He sat looking at the floor. "I have to run out of my apartment to get away from you, to have a moment to myself."

"You didn't have to leave, all you had to do is tell me you wanted me to go."

"I don't know how you ended up living in my apartment in the first place. You spent a few nights here, and then you started leaving your clothes here. The next thing I knew, you were living here. You have an empty house of your own."

"You wanted me to stay."

"Did I ask you to stay?"

"You didn't ask me to leave," Bradford said.

Well, I'm asking you to go now. Pack your things and leave my apartment, please!" Lori demanded.

"Oh, all of a sudden, you want me to go, you must have someone else. Just say it Lori, you have someone else," he accused her.

"How could I have someone else, you never give me a moment to myself," Lori complained.

"Why didn't you say something before, why wait until now?" He asked with a puzzled expression on his face.

"Because, I'm sick of it; I want my space back, I want my life back. I'm getting over a difficult marriage and I'm not ready for this type of relationship. I need my space!" she said firmly.

"But I think I'm falling in love with you, what am I suppose to do?"

"I don't know. I've never told you that I love you. I don't love you, I like you."

"I know you don't love me now, but I hoped you would grow to love me. Maybe if you gave it some time," Bradford suggested with pleading eyes.

"That will never happen. I can't love you, I like you. I think you're a nice person, but I can't make myself love you. I'm still in love with my husband, so I couldn't possibly love you! Please leave; just pack your things and leave. This relationship is moving too fast for me."

"If you're sure that's what you want, because once I leave, I'm not coming back," Bradford threatened.

"Please don't come back!" Lori responded. She got two trash bags from the kitchen and began throwing his belongings into them.

"I think you're making a mistake, Lori."

"I don't, this is the first thing I've done in the past three months that makes sense!" she said as she continued to fill the bags, and placing them at the door. Bradford finally got up from the sofa, looking upset.

"You're not the only woman in the world, there are plenty of women looking for a good man, but you wouldn't know that; you've never had a good man!" He walked to the door and picked up his bags and turned to Lori and said. "Don't ever call me or contact me again."

He slammed the door as he left. Who does she think she is? Someone has made this girl think she's special; her kind comes a dime a dozen. She's cute, but she's not as cute as she thinks! He thought to himself, she's the kind that will end up alone.

April came to visit Lori the next day. Lori had called her the night before crying.
"Hi Lori, I thought I'd stop by to see how you're doing."
"I'm glad you did. How are Paul and the kids doing?" Lori asked as she hugged her sister. "Come on into the kitchen and I'll see what I have to offer you."
"I know you single women don't cook or shop for food," April teased.
"You've got that right," Lori responded with a smile. "I have some hotdogs, bran muffins or leftover Chinese food."
"I'll take a bran muffin and some hot tea."
"I can do that," Lori answered. She put a cup of water in the microwave and placeed the pack of bran muffins in the center of the table. She removed the hot water from the microwave and gave it to her sister with a teabag and a spoon. She put the sugar bowl in front of April. "Girl, I am so glad to get Bradford out of my apartment. He was driving me crazy. He was suffocating me."
"You thought he was wonderful, before. What happened to change your mind?"

"He treated me like a doll. He drove me everywhere; he drove me to work, he drove me home from
work, he drove me shopping, it was too much." Lori
confided to April.

"You liked his companionship, remember?"

"I thought I did, but I was just lonely. Don't get
me wrong, he's a nice guy, but he's a little old for me."
Lori revealed.

"These things happen when you run from one
relationship to the next, without giving yourself breath-
ing room. Don't start another relationship, Lori; you're
not free of your marriage yet. Maybe you need to take
some time to get to know yourself and what you want
out of a relationship. Stop going for the quick fixes,
they'll always end up this way." April advised her sister.

"What way? What do you mean?"

"You'll end up with someone you don't know or
want. You'll end up with a stranger."

"I guess you're right, that's exactly what I
ended up with a stranger. I thought he wasn't going to
leave. I never told him he could move in here. He just
kept leaving his things at my place and the next thing I
knew; he was living in my apartment, while his house
was empty." He has a beautiful house of his own!

"Really, maybe he was lonely; you did say he is
a widower."

"Yes, I know he is lonely and so am I, but I
didn't want a permanent situation with him," Lori confessed. "I felt we could meet each others needs until
something better came along."

"You should have stopped him when he started
leaving his clothes over here," April advised.

"I know, but I didn't want to hurt his feelings. I think he's looking for a wife."

"You're probably right, were you interested in becoming his wife?" April said while laughing.

"Absolutely not! I just wanted to be friends."

"You're right; he was looking for a wife. Now that he's gone, don't be so quick to jump into another relationship."

"Believe me, I won't. I was sick of him," Lori said with a sigh of relief.

April finished her muffin and tea. "I have to go and pick the kids up from their swimming lessons."

"I'm going to clean up my apartment. I'm so glad to have it to myself again," she said as she walked April to the door. "I'm learning April, these people out here are crazy."

"You've got that right," April responded as she left the apartment laughing.

Lori realized that she couldn't allow herself to fall victim to male domination; It had to be her choice. She had allowed Bradford to dictate the relationship. She wanted a friendship and he wanted a mate. He was treating her like a child. She had to wrestle her power away from him. She promised herself, that she would never allow that to happen again. She reveled in being her own person. She celebrated with activities for one. She went shopping at the mall and bought herself several new outfits for work. She treated herself to a delicious dinner and jazz show in Center City at Zanzibar Blue, and then she went to a late night movie. Lori returned home exhausted after 1:00 AM. She felt free, she felt emancipated.

Wayne thought she was cute. She had a great smile and she seemed to be hanging onto his every word. She was helping her cousin to look for a car. She'd flirted with him the whole time she was there. Her cousin bought a used car with her sanction. She gave Wayne her business card, before she left the dealership. Wayne called her that night. She sounded like she expected his call.

"Hello Tammy, this is Wayne Jackson from the car dealership. Yes, I was looking at your card and I thought I'd like to get to know you better. Maybe we can get together for a movie and drinks on Friday. Yes, Great! I'll pick you up at 9:00 PM. Until then…

Tammy removed her sneakers, jeans and fitted tee shirt. She curled her long legs under her hips as she tried to get comfortable. She perused the daily paper while sipping a cup of coffee and snacking on a Danish pastry. She'd had a busy day shopping for food, picking up clothes from the cleaners and accompanying her cousin to buy a car. She'd tried to get out of going with her cousin at the last minute, but her cousin insisted that a promise was a promise; so she went. Now, she was happy that she'd gone with her cousin. She spotted him right away. He was cute. Patty spotted him too. She walked right up to him and asked him to help her to find a car. She tried to flirt with him, but he only had eyes for me. I thought he was a doll. I just love hand-some men with bald heads.

I switched my ass around that lot, and batted my eyes at him as much as I could, without being too obvi-ous. He picked right up on it too. That's the benefit of having five brothers, I can communicate with men eas-ily, she laughed to herself. Patty didn't stand a chance, even though she's the one that bought the car. I was be-ing unusually forward when I gave him my card and told him to call me, but I could feel the chemistry be-tween us, she thought. As soon as I got home this eve-ning he called and invited me out for drinks and a movie.

Wayne seems like a confident and intelligent man; he spoke very well. I hope he won't become in-timidated by me; many men are. It will be nice to be in the company of a charming man again. I just hope he isn't like the loser I just divorced. They're all nice when you first meet them. Jimmy pretended to be the ideal man. He had his own insurance business and was doing quite well. He pretended he didn't mind me having my own business; saying he liked independent women, but after we were married, he decided he wanted to start a family immediately. He wanted me barefoot and preg-nant. I assured him that I wanted a child too, but not until I got my business on solid ground. No, he didn't want to hear that. He became abusive; trying to intimi-date me. We argued when I had to work late or bring work home. When he worked late or brought work home it was a different story. He actually had the nerve to slap me across my face. It took everything I had to keep from using that 22 that my brother gave me on his ass, but he wasn't worth me going to jail. I know my brothers would have killed him if they knew he had slapped me, so I didn't tell them, because he wasn't worth them going to jail either.

I'll just date and not get serious with anyone. I don't plan on answering to anyone about anything anytime in the near future. Jimmy just made it harder for the next man that enters my life. My first husband wasn't a bad guy. We were both too young and didn't know what we were doing. Dean was a Mama's boy that loved women. He could romance the underwear off of an elephant. I caught him cheating on me over and over again. Those big pretty brown eyes could fill with tears on demand. I'd forgive him and he'd swear to be faithful until the next time; it would last for about a couple of months. Finally I set him free after two years of marriage. I loved him, but I couldn't take him screwing everything that wiggled walking down the street.

I wonder what kind of man Wayne is? Is he a woman beater, a womanizer, a gambler, a drinker, a lazy ass or maybe I'll be lucky and he'll be a nice guy. I could use a nice guy about now. God knows I've had my share of losers.

Wayne arrived at Tammy's house at 9:10PM. He didn't want to appear to be too anxious. She opened the door looking more beautiful than the first time he saw her. She was wearing a long red dress that showed her voluptuous body. She was tall like Lori and her hair was curly like Lori's. She was ready when he arrived at her townhouse. They were catching an 11:00 PM movie, so they went to a club for drinks before the show.

"I was pleased to hear from you Wayne," Tammy said with a tempting smile on her face.

"I have to get to know you, you're very beautiful."

"Do you have any children?" Tammy inquired.

"No, I don't, but I am married. I'm separated from my wife," Wayne confessed.

"Thank you for being honest, I appreciate that. I've been married twice and my second divorce was finalized two months ago. I just can't seem to get it right," Tammy confessed with a smile, as she searches his face for acceptance.

"Do you have any children?"

"No, I don't, I would like to have a child sometime in the future," she admitted.

"So would I, in fact I'd like to have three children," Wayne added. The waiter came and Wayne ordered two white wines. "Do you get out often?"

"No, I really haven't dated since my divorce. It's a little scary getting back out here in the dating scene."

"I feel the same way; I haven't dated since my separation. It's hard."

"I don't think I'm ready for a serious relationship, and I guess you feel the same way; I'd like to date and have a little fun," she stated.

"That's great, because that's all I'm looking for, nothing serious," he confessed. "What kind of work do you do?"

"I'm a tax accountant, and I work for myself. I primarily service small businesses."

"That's right, I have your card. That sounds interesting. It must be great to work for yourself," Wayne said as he probed to find out more about her.

"It is a lot of responsibility; you have to depend on yourself."

"What kinds of activities do you enjoy?" Wayne asked.

"I'm a Sixer's fan. I love basketball and football, I love to travel, I enjoy long walks, movies and plays. How about you, what do you enjoy?"

"I enjoy everything you just mentioned. It sounds like we have a lot in common. You don't find too many women that love sports." Wayne responded.

"I had no choice, I grew up the only girl with five brothers, so I've always been a Tomboy," Tammy laughed.

"Five brothers, man, I'll have to treat you right or your five brothers will come gunning for me," he joked. "I guess we'd better go if we want to be on time for the movie." He paid the waiter and they left the club feeling very optimistic.

Wayne took Tammy home after the movie. She invited him to dinner the following Friday at a restaurant in Chestnut Hill. The service was good and the food was better. She invited him in for a nightcap. Wayne spent the night. He left early the next morning to go home and get ready for work. He worked Saturdays and so did she. He called her Sunday and told her how much he enjoyed her company. He invited her out the following Friday. He took her to a restaurant on Delaware Avenue. They ate delicious food and danced to a great reggae band. They talked and laughed and perspired. He took her home and spent the night. He left the next morning. Wayne thought Tammy was a wonderful woman and he enjoyed her company. He didn't feel any pressure from her; they were both looking for the same thing, a little companionship and a little sex.

Tammy planned a weekend getaway to the shore for the two of them. Wayne took the time off work because he felt he needed a break. They rode bikes in the morning, and ate breakfast on the boardwalk. They laid on the beach in the afternoons and they had seafood dinners in the evening and walked the boardwalk. They had a wonderful time. They went to the casino and Wayne won $300, he gave Tammy half. Tammy was a successful business woman and she always paid her share for their dates. If she invited him out, she would pay and if he invited her out, he would pay. It was a hassle free relationship. She was a confident woman and Wayne enjoyed women that could think for themselves.

Tammy had a good sense of humor, often making him laugh. They enjoyed talking about sports; she was very knowledgeable about the teams and their players. They went to several basketball games together, and enjoyed screaming and shouting for their team. Reggie invited Wayne and Tammy to his house for dinner and a video. Wayne accepted, but Tammy was a little nervous about meeting Wayne's best friend and his wife. Reggie's wife Carol was anxious to meet the woman in Wayne's life.

Wayne and Tammy arrived at Reggie's house. Carol answered the door and invited them into the livingroom, where Reggie sat waiting. Carol sized up Tammy. She wanted to see what this woman had that her friend didn't have. She immediately noticed that she looked a little like Lori. She was tall like Lori and she had Lori's curly hair. Wayne introduced Tammy to Carol and Reggie.

"This is my friend Tammy, and this is my best friend Reggie, we've been friends since I was eight years old; this is his lovely wife and also my friend Carol," Wayne said proudly.

"That's wonderful; it's hard to keep friends for so many years. Wayne speaks of you both often," Tammy responded.

"Thank you, he speaks highly of you," Reggie said. Tammy is beautiful, she sounds intelligent and she has a nice body, Wayne did well for himself, Reggie thought, although she looks a lot like Lori. I hope he likes her for herself and not because she reminds him of his wife.

Carol was happy to see their friend smiling again. She showed them to the diningroom, which looked beautiful after Carol added her woman's touch to the room.

"This is a lovely diningroom and the table looks very pretty," Tammy complimented Carol.

"Thank you,' Carol responded. She served shrimp scampi with a white wine sauce, and a garden salad. They ate and enjoyed conversation throughout the meal. They retired to the livingroom for coffee and Wayne's favorite coconut layer cake. Carol thought Tammy was pretty, but she appeared to be more comfortable talking to Reggie than she was talking to her. She found her to be a little standoffish; detached. She was familiar with all of the football teams and players, but she showed no interest in cooking or children. They were able to talk a little about clothes, although Carol was sure that Tammy didn't look for bargains when she shopped. Her outfit cost more than Carol made in a week. Reggie was fascinated by Tammy. He thought she was a breath of fresh air. Wayne was very talkative and he really seemed to enjoy Tammy's company. Wayne and Tammy left to spend the night at Tammy's townhouse.

Tammy enjoyed the company of men. She was the only girl in her family. Growing up with her Dad and five brothers; she was just one of the boys. She played basketball and football with her brothers and she watched sports with her Dad and her brothers. She didn't enjoy helping her mother cook and clean. She helped her mother, but so did her brothers. She refused to allow her parents to delegate the household chores to her unless her brothers helped too.

I enjoyed meeting and talking to Reggie. He is a really nice guy. Carol on the other hand is too prissy for me. I knew that Carol was sizing me up, but I didn't care. I wasn't trying to impress her, Reggie is his friend. When Wayne told me Carol is a nurse, I knew what to expect from her. Women that take on the traditional female roles are always hard on women that don't. They try to force you to fit the mold. She was a good hostess, and the food was fine, but she wasn't going to sit me in the kitchen to help her clean up while the guys were laying back having all of the fun. I had a drink with the guys and talked about football. We had a stimulating conversation, Tammy thought.

I enjoy Wayne's companionship. He knows how to treat a lady. He isn't cheap and he knows how to open doors. Wayne dresses well and he looks good in his clothes. Wayne is a good lover and he's not demanding or too clingy. We date once or twice a week, which leaves me plenty of time for my business and my social life. I like to pay my own way when we go out, because I don't want a man to think that he owns me or that I owe him something. Wayne respects my space and I respect his. Wayne can hang around as long as things are going well, but he'll have to go if things start to sour. For now, things are going great and this could be a long term relationship.

Carol embraced her femininity. She loved being female; being a woman. She felt that women had their role to play in life, and men had their role. She loved pretty things, she loved floral scents, she loved make up, she loved different hair dos, she loved children; her children and she loved men; her man, Reggie. Carol thought Tammy had a feminine appearance, but not a feminine presence. She had the presence of a man. She gave Carol short answers to her questions, but when Reggie asked her about sports, she talked extensively. Carol felt that Wayne was attracted to aggressive women and that's why he had so many problems with them.

CHAPTER 13

Leeanna sat in the livingroom with her feet elevated. It was finally over. Today was her last day working for Dr. Phillips. Yes, she'd finally retired after working twenty years for Dr. Phillips. He'd generously set up a small pension plan for the women in his office. She'd reduced her spending, and now she could be satisfied with the monthly check she would receive. She wore a smile of self satisfaction. Dr. Phillips gave her a plague that said, "Job Well Done."

Now, after almost forty years of marriage, Frank and I can retire and spend the rest of our lives enjoying each other. Where have the years gone? It seems like only yesterday when she was a young bride, preparing for her wedding. She thought about her father, taking her to the lake and pointing at the swans swimming across. While still pointing at the swans her Dad said, "Those birds have accomplished what humans have great difficulty accomplishing. They select a mate and remain committed for life. Humans stand before God and man, and promise to do the same, but very few keep their promise. We expect our mates to be perfect, and if they aren't, then we throw them away and search for another. Before you walk down the aisle and swear before God to stay married, make sure you truly look at your chosen person for who he really is; not who you want him to be. Make sure you love him enough to mate for life. Look beyond his physical traits, look into his soul. Be sure that you love his spirit. Be sure that you love his essence. Over the years, everything else about him will change, except his spirit and his essence. Although he may have faults, you must remember that you have faults too, and you are coming to this union as two imperfect beings that God has created.

A tear rolled down her cheek as she thought of her dead father. He was a good man, and a good father. Frank is a good man too. I still love his spirit and his essence; he is a good husband and the father of my children, and we have been committed for almost forty years. My father would be proud. We are swimming with swans, she thought, as a smile broke through the tears. My father would say, "Job Well Done." Now that I no longer have a job, I can start getting this house ready for sale. We've seen some lovely condos. We'll live here part of the year and we'll find a place in Florida to live the other part of the year. Maybe we'll travel for six to eight weeks a year. Frank is a good man, and he's cut back on his drinking. We've had our ups and downs, but we've always gotten back on track. Frank is retiring next month and we'll start to enjoy our lives; the time we have left.

Leeanna rose from the sofa and went into the kitchen to prepare dinner. She looked at the chicken breast she had left in the refrigerator to thaw. She started to prepare the chicken, washing and seasoning it. Then, she had an idea. She and Frank could go out to dinner to celebrate her retirement. She wrapped the chicken and put it back into the refrigerator. She went upstairs and took one of her unworn special occasion outfits from the closet. She went into her secret lingerie drawer and removed pretty underwear to wear under her outfit. She made herself beautiful and went downstairs and sat on the sofa to wait for Frank. Frank entered the house and called out for his wife. He was surprised to find her sitting on the sofa in a new outfit.

"Hi Frank, today I retired after twenty years with Dr. Phillips."

"That's right, I'm sorry I forgot." Frank said. He noticed that he didn't smell any food cooking. "It's going to be great, having you home again."

"Yes, thank you. I'm looking forward to staying home too," she replied.

"I can hardly wait for my retirement next month."

"It will be wonderful. I remember when I thought going to work was something special, now I think staying home is something special," Leeanna laughed.

"I agree with you. It will be nice to live life without all of the stress associated with work. We'll be able to spend our time doing whatever we want to do," Frank said with a smile as he removed his jacket and shoes.

"I can't wait until we go to Florida and look for our apartment," Leeanna said cheerfully. "You know they call Florida the playground for senior citizens. I could use some play in my life. I'm in the process of closing everything out at school. I've been ignoring the union, they can't aggravate me any longer. I won't let them; they'll be someone else's problem now. I'm looking forward to coming out." Frank looked at his wife and saw happiness in her eyes. "Would you like to go out to dinner to celebrate your retirement?"

"Yes I would, that would be lovely. Let's go to the restaurant in Chestnut Hill that April told us about," Leeanna said happily. They left the house making plans for the future.

After returning from dinner, Frank sat in the livingroom in his recliner with his shoes and pants off. He found himself dozing off to sleep. He gathered his clothes and went upstairs. Upon entering the bedroom, he saw Lee laying on top of the quilt in a beautiful nightgown. Her hair was combed and she was still wearing makeup. Frank smiled at Lee and walked over to her side of the bed. He took her into his arms and kissed her.

"You look beautiful Baby. Stand up and let me see you in that lovely nightgown." Lee returned his smile as she stood up and pranced across the room like a run way model; spinning with her hands on her hips.

"You like it Frank?" she asked her husband.

"I love it Lee, I love you." He took her hand and pulled her close to him, kissing her over and over again.

Lori sat in her apartment grading math tests. Her students were making good progress in math, so she was in a good mood. She had spent the last three days waiting for a phone call. She'd met a fine guy when she and her friend Marie went to the club Saturday night. He approached her in the club and offered to buy her a drink. He was a handsome man with a bald head and wire frame glasses. He said he was an executive for IBM, and he often had to travel for his job. He appeared to be a little shy, blushing whenever she complimented him. He was insistent that he found her attractive and he wanted her telephone number. He promised to call the next day, and she believed him. The telephone rang; it was him.

Trent entered his apartment and dropped his briefcase on the floor beside the door. He removed his suit jacket and tie and threw them over the back of a chair in the livingroom. He wiped his brow with the sleeve of his shirt, as he walked to the refrigerator. He was hot and thirsty. He had a long hard day at the office and he was overwhelmed by the volume of work that crossed his desk. Trent removed a cold bottle of water from the refrigerator and returned to the livingroom and sprawled across the sofa.

He was bored with his job as a supervisor at the IRS. He was sick and tired of being tied to a desk all day, everyday. He resented the confrontations with people that cheated on their taxes. He tired of their cat and mouse games. He wished he could travel the world, and if not, then at least the states. After drinking the water he went to his bedroom, stripped and took a cool shower. He laid across his bed and took a nap.

He stood in front of the mirror brushing his mustache with a small brush. He then used the brush to shape his eyebrows. He stepped back from the full length mirror and assessed his appearance. "You're looking good boy." He said to himself and headed out the door to a club. Trent went out to clubs a couple of times a week. He enjoyed the music and he preferred the company of people he didn't know. He could reinvent himself to be anyone he wanted to be.

He had always lived a boring life; even when he was a small boy. His mother kept him in the house studying all of the time, while the neighborhood children were outside playing and having fun. His father was out of the house a lot, so his mother kept him in to keep her company. She didn't talk to him very much; she just didn't want to be alone. He had to listen to her talking to her friends on the telephone. She was happy and jovial on the telephone; laughing and talking loud, but when she hung up the receiver, she withdrew into herself. She became quiet and sullen.

Trent was a nerd in school. Most of his classmates teased him or ignored him. He tried to fit in with them, but the clothes that his mother bought him labeled him a nerd. He dressed like he was going to church everyday. He tried to tell his mother that his clothes made him different from the other children, but she wouldn't listen. She said her son was going to be somebody one day and she didn't want him looking like everybody else. That sealed his fate; he didn't have any friends. The only children he was allowed to play with were the children of his parents' friends. They were nerds too. Angela often visited his home with her mother when they were small, and that's when the crush began. He was in love with her all through school. She was very pretty with wavy hair that framed her face. She played with him when they were little, but she completely ignored him in high school. He could only dream about her because she never looked his way. He looked for Angela in every girl he met, and when he found her he married her.

    The marriage lasted less than a year. One day his wife just packed her clothes and left, saying she wasn't ready for marriage. It broke his heart. After that, Trent refused to take women seriously. He loved them and left them. He felt that women liked to play too many games, so he was going to play their game, but by his rules. He felt that women usually had preconceived ideas of what a man should be, and he didn't think they would accept him for himself, so he reinvented himself to meet their expectations. He thought most women were bored with a man that goes to work and wants to come home to a peaceful life. They prefer men that run around cheating on them, taking their money, and mistreating them, at least he didn't take their money, and he was good to them while he was in their company.

Lori sat in her livingroom waiting for Trent to arrive. She knew she was looking good in her black fitted dress and black stiletto heels. Nothing looks more elegant than basic black, she thought. He arrived fifteen minutes late, apologizing for his tardiness. He took her to a seafood restaurant and bar. The ambiance was perfect for an intimate dinner. The crab cakes with bell pepper sauce were delicious. Lori and Trent talked endlessly about their lives, never running out of things to say. They found that they had a lot in common. Trent went to Morgan College with a friend of Lori's and his aunt lived three doors away from her cousins. They both grew up in Mt. Airy.

She found Trent to be very intelligent and charismatic. After numerous glasses of white wine, she felt a closeness to him. Trent took her home and they had a pleasant goodnight kiss at the door. Lori wanted to take things slow. Three days later she called him to thank him for a lovely evening, and he invited her to his apartment for a home cooked meal on Friday night. She accepted.

Lori arrived at Trent's apartment on Lincoln Drive in an upscale apartment building with a doorman. She took a bottle of white wine, to share as a gift. His apartment was a typical bachelor pad. He had black leather and black lacquer furnishings. He had some interesting Black art hanging on his walls. He cooked baked chicken, baked white potatoes and a salad. Not very creative, but the food was edible. The chicken was a little dry, but everything else was okay. This guy has potential, Lori thought.

After dinner, they sat on the sofa and drank the rest of the white wine. Trent put on some jazz, turned the lights down low and they talked for a couple of hours. Trent excused himself, went into the bedroom and reappeared wearing black silk pajamas. He smelled sooo good. He looked sooo good. He changed the music to Luther Vandross. Lori removed her shoes and laid back in his arms thinking, he smells sooo good. They made passionate love on satin sheets all night long.

She walked through the apartment cleaning up and picking up tossed clothes. She wore a smile on her face. Trent is so together, she thought. I can't let him see this mess. Lori hummed as she cleaned the bathroom. She sprayed air freshener throughout the apartment. She was going to make Trent spaghetti dinner tomorrow night. She wanted to make a good impression, he impressed the hell out of me, she thought. Luther sang me right out of my clothes, and Trent was a tender, and considerate lover.

Trent arrived at Lori's at 8:00 PM. He was casually dressed in black jeans and a red tee shirt, with black loafers. Lori poured him a glass of red wine. He sipped the wine and she placed the garlic bread into the oven. She joined him on the sofa. This guy definitely has potential, she thought. She sat there on the sofa mesmerized by his smile; she remembered the bread in the oven. She hurried to the kitchen and removed the bread from the oven. It was slightly burned. She took the butter knife and scraped the black from the edges of the bread.

"Did something burn in there?" Trent called from the livingroom.

"Just the edges of the garlic bread are a little dark," Lori answered. "You can come back now, the food is ready."

"Everything looks delicious."

"This is my Mama's spaghetti," Lori said.

"It's very good, you'll have to give me the recipe," Trent complimented Lori.

"Okay, just let me know when you're ready for it," Lori consented.

After eating, Lori washed the dishes, while Trent watched her, talked and sipped a glass of wine. As Lori walked past him to go into the livingroom, he took her hand and pulled her to him; she feigned resistance with laughter. He took her into his arms, kissing her while leading her to the bedroom. They made love over and over.

Lori was awakened by Trent's movements as he dressed to leave.

"Where are you going in the middle of the night?" she asked him.

"I'm sorry, but I have to go. I have something to do in the morning," he apologized.

"Okay."

"I had a great time and dinner was a real treat. I'll give you a call," Trent said, as he let himself out of the apartment.

Trent raced home to change clothes for work. He had an early meeting with his boss. He enjoyed sex with Lori, but she was an aggressive lover. I prefer taking the lead, he thought. She's a beautiful woman, a high maintenance woman. Her closets are bulging with clothes, and she carries designer handbags that cost several hundred dollars. She's the kind of woman that likes to sink her fangs into you and take control of your life. She's okay for a date now and then, but nothing serious. Trent removed his contact lenses and put on his frames to rest his eyes. He prepared his clothes for work. He pressed his answering machine to listen to the messages of several women that had called the night before. He showered and dressed quickly to attend the meeting with his superiors.

She waited to hear from him all week, afraid to go out, for fear of missing his call. He didn't call. Lori spent many nights replaying their evening together, trying to figure out what went wrong. She couldn't think of anything. The second week she called him and got his answering machine. The third week went by without contact. She felt depressed. Finally he called. She was lying in bed watching television when the phone rang. He greeted her and talked as if he'd just left her house. She felt awkward at first, but she didn't want to appear foolish. He told her how much he missed her. He said, he really wanted to see her and he wanted to come over to her house. He said everything she wanted to hear two or three weeks ago. She reluctantly agreed.

She jumped out of bed and into the shower. She ran around the apartment picking up clothes and dusting furniture. She sprayed the entire apartment with vanilla air freshener. She brushed her wet hair back and put a bow on it. She put on black stretch pants and a short purple shirt. She'd just finished running around the apartment when the bell rang. She took a deep breath to slow her rapidly beating heart. She closed her eyes momentarily, then she opened the door. He looked sooo good, he smelled sooo good.

"Hi there, you look so good!" he said as he took her into his arms. "I've missed you so much," he said as he kissed her tenderly. They sat on the sofa embracing, and Lori had a few questions she wanted answered, but she didn't want to ruin the mood. This man is definitely a hunk, she thought.

"Would you like a drink," she offered.

"I have what I want right here in my arms; all I want is you," he said as he looked into her eyes and kissed her passionately. They made love twice before drifting off to sleep in her bed. At 5:30 AM, he shook her softly and kissed her on her cheeks. "I had a wonderful evening with you, but I have to leave to get ready for work." Lori had to go to work too. As he closed the door of the apartment, Lori experienced a feeling of emptiness; she felt used, but satisfied. She waited for his call. A week passed with no phone call from Trent. Lori called him and left a message.

Trent laid in his bed listening to his telephone messages. Lori's message was one of four. She sounded a little annoyed with him for not calling her. He enjoyed Lori sexually, but he found it necessary to distance himself from her to avoid getting too emotionally involved. He'd decided long ago not to entrust his heart to any woman. They were too callous and uncaring, when they didn't get what they wanted, and they would break your heart without thinking about it twice. She's just angry because she's not getting what she wants, he thought. I told her I wasn't looking for a relationship, but her kind never listens to what you tell them. They think they can manipulate you into doing what they want you to do. She'll get over it. Trent got out of bed and headed for the shower. He was meeting an old buddy at the club tonight. We'll have a good fun laughing about old times. Maybe I can talk him into going to the Bahamas with me next month. There's always lots of pretty girls there, he thought as he smiled to himself.

Lori went to visit April She was home sick with a cold. Lori brought her some fruit.

"What have you been doing with yourself lately?" April asked as they sat at the kitchen table drinking grape juice.

"Well, I met this good looking guy. He went to college with a friend of mine. He's a real hunk," Lori bragged. Her face was illuminated when she spoke of him.

"Tell me about him, he seems to have made a strong impression on you," April said while watching Lori blush. "What does he do for a living?"

"He's an IBM executive, and he graduated from Morgan College."

"That's nice, has he ever been married?"

"I don't think so; I know he told me he didn't have any children."

"How old is he?"

"He's thirty-nine Years old, and he's a real gentleman. He took me to a nice seafood restaurant. He even cooked dinner for me," Lori answered excitedly. "I met him a couple of months ago, but I didn't want to say anything until I got to know him a little better."

"Can he cook?"

"Yes, he cooks very well, but there's something about him that puzzles me," Lori confessed.

"What would that be?"

"When I see him, we have great chemistry. We make love and then I don't hear from him for a couple of weeks,"

"What do you mean; you don't hear from him for a couple of weeks?"

"He'll say he's going to call and then he doesn't call for a couple of weeks."

"Sounds like this guy is as slippery as an eel. You need to be careful with him, be careful," April warned her sister.

"Yes I am. I think he works a lot and he doesn't have much time," Lori said as if she didn't really believe it herself.

"Men have time for the things that are important to them. If he isn't making time for you, it's because you aren't high enough on his list of priorities. He's probably a lady's man, or he's married," April theorized.

Lori was annoyed at April's perception of Trent. She doesn't even know him, so she's just guessing, Lori thought. "Well, enough about me and my love life. How are you feeling?" Lori asked, changing the subject.

"I think I'm developing allergies," April said.

"What would make you think that?" Lori inquired.

"I keep coming down with these cold like symptoms. Paul thinks I'm getting sick too often, so he made me go to the doctor's office. He gave me some antibiotics, and I have to take them for ten days."

"Are they helping?" Lori asked with concern.

"I don't know, I haven't finished taking them yet," April responded.

"Make sure you take all of them, because they won't work unless you do."

"Yes, I'm going to take them all."

"And make sure you eat before taking them. They can mess with your stomach if you don't." Lori warned April.

"Yes I usually eat before I take them, and I've been drinking lots of juice and lemon tea," April reassured her sister.

"That's good; you have to take care of yourself! Have you talked to Mom?" Lori asked April.

"Yes, I talked to her last night. It sounds like she and Dad are getting along much better. She's waiting for Dad to retire so they can go to Florida to look for an apartment. They want to spend half of their time here and the other half there," April explained.

"What are they going to do with the house?"

"I don't know; I guess they'll sell it." April answered.

"I'd hate to see them sell our family home; it holds so many memories for me. Growing up, holiday celebrations, it's our roots," Lori reminisced.

"That's what it is to our whole family, but it is also an asset to them. They'll need that money to make their retirement more secure," April reminded Lori.

"I didn't think of it like that. You're right." Lori said sadly.

"After all, we're grown. We have to let go and make some new memories. They can't afford to leave the house empty for half of the year. Those houses have gone up in value. They can get at least $175,000 for it," April guessed.

"Do you think it's worth as much as that?" Lori asked in a surprised manner.

"Oh yes, maybe more. That will be a nice nest egg for them, and it will make Florida more affordable. That's the place for senior citizens, they'll have a ball."

"That's true, they've worked hard all of their lives; they deserve it. Then Dad can have Mom all to himself when they're in Florida," Lori surmised.

"I keep telling you, Dad hates to share her. He wants all of her attention for himself," April laughed.

"I know, and after all of these years," Lori giggled. "Now he'll have her to himself."

"I guess that's what happens when you get older."

"Yes, you get ridiculous," Lori joked. She felt pleased that her parents were getting along. She loved them both. "I'll go to see them soon."

"Good, you should," April agreed. "I'm going to go back upstairs to bed, this medicine makes me sleepy. Call me, and don't be a stranger."

Trent called Lori two weeks after their last sexual encounter. "Hi Sweetheart, how are you doing?" Trent greeted Lori.

"I'm fine, how are you?" she returned the greeting.

"Just working too hard; I never have any time for myself. I'm stressed out," Trent added.

"Sorry to hear that," Lori said nonchalantly.

"Listen, I have some time, and I was wondering if we could get together for a drink?" he asked.

"I have to work tomorrow, and I won't want to get up if I go out drinking with you," she responded.

"Then, why don't I come over to your place? I missed you and I really want to see you."

"You do, do you?" Lori asked sarcastically.

"Yes I do. I've been dreaming about you."

"Oh really, I've been right here."

"I know, I've just been so busy; this job is destroying my social life. It's not good to just work all of the time. I have to make myself find the time for some pleasures in life. In fact, I'm just leaving work now and I'd like to come over to your place to see you. Please don't disappoint me," he begged.

"I don't know Trent, I feel like I'm being used. You come over here, telling me how much you miss me, and we have sex; then I don't hear from you for weeks. Nobody works that much."

"I'm focused on my career right now, and I'm not in the position to make a commitment to anyone at this point in my life. That's why I have a hard time maintaining relationships; please be patient, things will get better," Trent lied.

"I can understand that, but you could call," Lori reasoned.

"I know, my bad. If I'd talk to you, then I'd want to see you; it just makes it harder. I feel like we're two mature adults enjoying each other's company."

"Well, at least I have a better understanding of where you're coming from."

"I'm not trying to hurt anyone. I really do want to see you. You're so beautiful and warm," he whispered into the phone.

"Okay, you can come over for a little while, but I have to go to work in the morning."

He was wearing a navy blue suit with a multi-colored tie. He's so handsome, she thought. He makes me weak in the knees. She invited him to have a seat on the sofa. She poured him a glass of white wine while he removed his wire framed glasses and placed them on the coffee table. The fatigue showed on his face as he wiped his eyes with his hand. He sipped his wine as he continued to complain about the demands of his job and his inability to maintain relationships, because of his lack of free time. He looks like a lost puppy, tired and dejected, she thought. He sat on the sofa and started to nod off to sleep. He smelled sooo good. She sat drinking her wine and admiring his flawless skin. This one is for me, she thought. She shook him awake and led him into her bedroom. They made love and she fell asleep in his arms.

Lori was awakened to the smell of bacon and eggs cooking in the kitchen. She put on her robe and went into the kitchen to find Trent finishing up breakfast. They sat to the table and ate breakfast from one plate. They drank coffee while showering and getting dressed. Trent gave Lori a lingering kiss and said, "I'll call you over the weekend."

"Okay, I'll look forward to your call," she said through rosy cheeks. She went to work feeling radiant. She felt like the sun was shining just for her.

Lori spent the weekend cleaning her apartment and grading her student's papers. She was in a happy mood, humming and singing as she went about her chores. As she lay in bed on Sunday night sadness enveloped her as the same old question came to mind. Why didn't he call? The anger grew within her, taking over her body. I knew he was lying, he's always lying, she thought as she began to cry. How could he treat me this way? What have I done to deserve his betrayal? Since he's not calling me, then I'm going to call him and give him a piece of my mind. She dialed his number, knowing that he probably wouldn't answer the telephone. She listened to his pleasant generic message. It only made her angrier.

"Hello Trent, You may or may not be at home listening to this message, but it doesn't matter, as long as you hear what I have to say. I thought you were a mature, sincere adult, but you've proven that you're not. You're a wolf in sheep's clothing. You pretend to want a relationship, but you really just want to take advantage of people that do. What you're looking for can be found in any red light district. For a small fee, there are women that will give you what you're looking for without much effort or deception; just a little cash. Do not dial my number ever again. Do not come to my house ever again. I don't have time for scum like you. I'm looking for a real man, and you don't qualify."

She hung up the telephone and smiled to herself. That feels a little better, she thought. I really cared for him; I made excuses to myself for him. He's the loser, he had a good woman interested in him, and he blew it. This is the last time that I'll sit around waiting for a man to call me. She laid her head on her pillow and wept. It was cleansing. She hadn't cried over a man since she and Wayne separated. At least Wayne is my husband, why am I allowing this nut case to arouse these feelings of helplessness in me? I'll have to leave him alone. He's a liar and I think April is right; he is as slippery as an eel. I'm probably just one of many, she thought.

Trent returned home from his vacation in the Bahamas. He had a great time over there. Beautiful women were everywhere you looked. They were all pleasant and ready to have a good time. He got a few phone numbers of women that liked to party. He turned on his answering machine and listened to his messages as he emptied out his suitcase. He'd been away for ten glorious days in the sun, and he wasn't looking forward to going back to his stressful job at the IRS. He had too many years there to just walk away, so that meant he had to tolerate at least five more years of this aggravation. At least the vacation relieved some of the stress and he was feeling pretty good now. Lori's message was the fifth one on the machine. He could hear the anger in her voice, so he stopped what he was doing and listened. When she finished, he shut the machine off. He didn't want to hear anything else that might ruin his happy mood.

Who does that girl think she is? She enjoyed it as much as I did. I didn't force her to do anything she didn't want to do. She was always ready and willing, in fact sometimes I felt like she was seducing me. She's mad because I'm not over her house at her beck and call; trying to play boyfriend and girlfriend, that's not my game. A man can never win at that game, that's a woman's game. I'd hoped she'd be good for a few more dates, but I guess it's time to move on. There's plenty of pretty woman out in the world looking for a guy like me. Women love men they can't catch, it's a challenge to them. As soon as you let them catch you, then the games began. I want this, I want that, stay home with me, take me out, don't go out with your friends; they are never satisfied. I enjoy my life just the way it is, I won't call her ever again! She doesn't have to worry about that.

Leeanna stood outside of Lori's classroom, as her students filed out in two lines; one for girls and one for boys.

"Hi Mom," Lori said with a surprised expression on her face.

"Hi Lori," Leeanna responded. "I thought I'd surprise you with lunch. Are you free now?"

"Yes, this is my lunch hour; I have to walk my students downstairs to the lunchroom. Go into my classroom and have a seat; I'll be right back."

"Okay, I'll set up our lunch while you're gone. Take your time," Leeanna answered. She went into the classroom and pulled out two hoagies from a bag and placed them on separate pieces of colored construction paper, using them as placemats. She removed a stack of napkins and placed them in the center of the table. From another bag, Leeanna took out a Coke and put it on Lori's placemat, and a gingerale on her placemat. She sat at the table and opened one of the hoagies to see if it had hot peppers on it, Lori loves hot peppers, she thought. Lori entered the classroom with a big smile on her face.

"It's good to see you Mom," she said as she walked towards her mother, giving her a hug and a kiss on the cheek. Leeanna returned the gesture.

"I missed you; you haven't come to see me for a while, so I came to see you."

"I'm glad you did, but I was going to get over to the house soon. How are you doing?" Lori asked.

"I'm fine, how are you? You're looking good," Leeanna quickly responded.

"I feel pretty good. So, how are you enjoying being retired?"

"I'm loving it; I was tired of working. It got to be too much, going to work everyday, and trying to take care of the house and your father."

"I know it, I wish it was me retiring!" Lori joked. "I'm tired too!"

"Girl, you're just getting started," Leeanna laughed as she opened her soda.

"I don't know if I can take it for another twenty years. I'd better look for a rich husband," Lori chuckled. "This hoagie looks nice and fresh mom. Thanks for lunch. You saved me a trip to the store."

"You're welcome; I wanted to spend a little time with you. I miss having you at the house. We used to have a good time when you were home," Leeanna said.

"Yes, it was nice, but you won't be there too much longer yourself. I never thought you and Dad would sell the house. I thought you loved that house too much to sell it."

"I do love that house, but it's too big for your father and me. I'm getting older and it's too much work, trying to keep it clean. Your father and I decided to sell it and move to Florida for part of the year."

"Why Florida? Why not just buy a smaller house here?" Lori asked.

"Well, I thought about that, but it'll be nice to have the warmer weather and avoid the harsh winters. You know lots of couples retire to Florida. They have all kinds of activities for senior citizens."

"I know they do, I'm just being selfish. I'll miss you and Dad and our family home," Lori confessed.

"I know you will Baby, but it will give you and your sister some place to go. You'll be able to visit us any time you want."

"I know," Lori responded, as she picked some of the onions off of her hoagie. "How is Dad acting these days? Is he keeping his hands to himself?" Lori asked as she looked at her mother's face to see her reaction to her question.

"I think he learned his lesson. He knows that I'm not going to take it anymore."

"Do you think you'll be okay in Florida with him by yourself?" Lori asked cautiously, she didn't want to offend her mother.

"I'll be fine; I'm not scared of Frank. He was stressed out when he was working; he's much more relaxed now. He's looking forward to the change. You know, we've been together a long time, I can handle Frank," Leeanna reassured her daughter.

"I hope so Mom. Just remember, you can always come to stay with me. I don't want you feeling like you have to take any of Dad's stuff. You can stay with me. All you have to do is call me and I'll have a plane ticket waiting for you at the desk," Lori offered.

"That won't be necessary Lori; we're going to enjoy our later years."

"If you say so Mom," Lori replied.

"How is your social life? Are you dating?"

"Not much, every now and then," Lori answered with a smile.

"Are you still seeing that older guy?"

"No, we broke up; he was too possessive. I don't need a man trying to own me and dictate my life."

"So, who are you seeing?" Leeanna inquired.

"Just some guy, nothing serious."

"I hope that you will find someone to take care of you. Your sister has a good husband to take care of her and I want the same thing for you," Leeanna admitted.

"I know you do Mom, but don't worry, I can take care of myself. I don't need a man to take care of me."

"Every woman needs a man to take care of her Lori. Whether you admit it or not, we all need a man to protect and care for us." The bell rings ending the lunch period. "Lori, you go and get your students, I'll clear away the lunch." Leeanna rises and walks over to Lori and hugs and kisses her again, before throwing the remains from lunch into the trash.

"Thanks Mom, I enjoyed the food and your company. I'll call you."

"Do you need any money Lori? Are your bills paid up to date?" Leeanna asked.

"No, I don't need anything. I'm trying to live within my budget." She responded with a laugh. "I'm fine, and I'll talk to you soon. I love you," Lori said as she left to retrieve her students from the yard.

Leeanna smiled sadly as she watched her oldest daughter leave the room. I hope she finds someone to love and understand her, she thought. She's a good girl and some man will be lucky to find her.

April was sick again; her glands were swollen and very painful. She finished the second prescription of antibiotics and now she had the same symptoms again. Paul took her to the doctor's for some blood tests. She'd have to wait for the results before the doctor would prescribe anything else.

April sat at the dinner table eating with Paul, Ashley, and Anthony. April cooked dinner despite feeling ill. She wanted to function as normal as possible. She sat down as much as she could while she cooked.

"April the stir fry and linguine was delicious. You take the children into the family room and relax while I clean the kitchen," Paul volunteered.

"Thanks Paul, I wanted to play some Dominos with the children. It helps Anthony with math." April took the children with her, while Paul cleaned the kitchen and put the food away.

"Honey, I'll give the children their baths now, and then you can read them a story while I take a walk," Paul said.

"Sounds like a good plan to me," she said, as she sat with her feet elevated, sipping hot tea.

"The kids are ready for their stories now. They have selected some Dr. Seuss books. I'm going for a walk and I'll return soon. Do you need anything while I'm out?"

"No, we just went shopping last weekend. I don't need anything," April said.

Paul walked briskly down the street near the mini mall. The evening was a little chilly. He wore two sweat shirts. He crossed the street and entered the blackness of the park. Paul saw two men sitting on the park bench, one on each end. Paul sat in the middle of the bench. He enjoyed the variations of his adventures. They'd have a threesome, if everyone agreed. The two men were very pleasant looking; displaying open mouth smiles. They took turns caressing each other with their eyes. The first tall slim man walked cautiously behind the oak tree. Paul walked quickly behind him, because he wanted to be in the middle! The third short muscular built man slowly walked behind Paul. Paul smiled to himself, because he knew tonight would be a stellar night; tonight he would give as well as receive pleasure. They would have a standing pyramid, and he'd experience the euphoria of being a top and a bottom at the same time!

As Paul hurried home, he reflected on the excitement of the evening. The crisp air only contributed to his stimulated state of mind. He felt invigorated. The day was ending much better than it had started. He and his partner had a disagreement, because he was trying to put a difficult client off on Paul. He was sick of his partner trying to use him, so he stood up to him, and told him, no. Paul had meeting after meeting scheduled, and he was late picking up the children from their swimming lessons. Tonight was a perfect ending to a harried day. The sex was great! I'll sleep soundly tonight, he thought.

"Sweetheart, I'm home," he shouted as he entered the house. "I'm going to take a shower."

"Did you have a good walk?" April inquired.

"Oh yes, perfect, a perfect walk.

Lori was alarmed that her period was late. She was six weeks late. How could this happen? If I'm pregnant, then it's Trent's baby. I haven't seen him since he cooked me breakfast. He hasn't called in all of this time. Leave it to me to find a loser that looks like a winner. If I'm pregnant, then I'm going to have the baby. "I can't ask God to forgive me twice for taking a baby's life ," she said aloud to herself. I had a hard time forgiving myself. I can't do it again. Mom and Dad will just have to deal with it. I'll be another statistic; a single Black mother. I'll wait a couple of months before I shock my family with this news. Wayne has his child and now I'll have mine. Me, a mother, she thought as she smiled to herself.

Lori waited for Trent to call; six weeks had already passed. We were so close and intimate the last time we were together. He cooked me breakfast for God's sake! We took a shower together. I thought we had crossed a milestone and we were going to a higher level; then nothing. I called him after three weeks and left a message; nothing. I'm not going to call him again, he knows where I am. Let him walk out of my life, just like he walked in. I don't need him. I can do this on my own!

Lori picked April up from her home for a lunch date. She wanted to have an uninterrupted conversation with her sister. April entered the car with a smile on her face.

"To what do I owe this invitation?" April teased Lori.

"Can't I invite my one and only sister to lunch?" Lori responded while laughing.

"I guess so."

"Let's go to Alexander's in Abington, their food is always delicious," Lori suggested.

"Okay, I love their crab cakes. I haven't been there for lunch in a while, but their breakfast is always good," April agreed.

They sat drinking herbal tea to wash down their crab cakes. "I have something to tell you, I'm pregnant," Lori blurted out.

"Oh no Lori, by who? Who are you pregnant by," April asked in a surprised tone.

"Trent,"

"The slippery eel, the elusive man?" April asked with disappointment.

"What are you going to do?"

"Nothing, I'm not going to do anything. I can't bare the guilt of another abortion. My biological clock is ticking and this may be my last opportunity to have a baby," Lori explained.

"That's true, but can you handle a baby on your own? You know you won't get any help from him," April warned Lori.

"I'll have to, because I'm keeping it," Lori said adamantly.

"Are you keeping this baby because you want the baby or Trent?"

"I don't want Trent, I was attracted to Trent, but he plays too many games for me. I had enough of games with my husband. I'm thirty-eight years old, and I'm having this baby!" Lori stated.

"What about Mom and Dad, they don't even know Trent? How do you think they'll take the news that you're pregnant and you aren't even with the father?"

"I don't care; I have to live my life, just like they're living their lives. I may never get pregnant again, and spend the rest of my life regretting getting an abortion. No, that's out of the question. They'll just have to adjust to having a single mom in the family," Lori defended her position.

"Well, you have to do what will make you happy. If you're happy about this pregnancy, then so am I. I'll do whatever I can to help you," April reassured Lori.

"Thank you April, it looks like you're going to become an aunt after all."

"How do you think Trent will handle being a father?"

"I don't know, I don't think I'm going to tell him."

"You're not going to tell him? Why not? Don't you think he'll make a good father?"

"No, I don't. This baby is for me, not Trent. Just think of him as a sperm donor."

"What if he finds out?" April asked with concern.

"He won't, and if he does, I'll just say it's my husband's baby. He won't know the difference, besides; I haven't seen or heard from him in three months. He's not interested in me or a baby. No, this baby will be mine."

"I'll help you, you know I'll be there for you and your baby," April pledged as she held her sister's hand.

"Thank you April, I'm so lucky to have a sister like you. I just hope that one day I will meet a wonderful man like Paul. You two have the perfect marriage."

"I wouldn't say that, but we do have a good relationship; maybe it's because we were friends first. Our relationship isn't just about the children, we're still best friends," April declared.

"You're lucky, it's not easy to find that," Lori said with envy. "How did you make out with the blood tests, did the doctor say that you have allergies?"

"No, he didn't say what it is; he said he had to take some more tests, and I have to wait for the results before he will give me any more medicine," April revealed.

"I guess he needs to know what he's treating you for, before he'll know what medicines you'll need."

"I guess you're right. I'm just tired of feeling sick."

"Try to be patient April, the doctor will find the problem soon," Lori reassured her sister.

"You're right, I'll try to be patient."

CHAPTER 14

April and Paul sat in the doctor's office. Dr. Turner sat at his desk with a somber expression on his face. "I'm afraid the results of the tests I gave you are not very good. I'm afraid your tests revealed that you are HIV positive," the doctor stated.

"What did you say? Repeat it."

"April, you are HIV positive."

"That's impossible; you need to check your results again!" April demanded.

"I ran the tests twice, because I didn't think you were in a high risk group," he said.

"No, I'm not, I'm a thirty-five years old married woman, and I've had one sexual partner for the past eleven years. I haven't exchanged bodily fluids with anyone but my husband," April said incredulously.

"I think we need to test you too Paul," Dr. Turner said.

"There must be some kind of mistake here," Paul said anxiously.

"If you think so, I'll be glad to run the tests again on April, but I want to test you too Paul. I'll make an appointment for you when the results come in, until then, try not to worry," Dr. Turner urged them.

"How can I not worry when you've told me something like this?" April said with concern.

"We're double checking, so don't worry. I'll see you next week."

"I can't believe Dr Turner, he needs to get another lab; something is obviously wrong," April said to Paul as they drove home.

Paul drove home in silence, with all kinds of thoughts racing through his head. God, please don't let this be true. Please God, please!

Paul walked at a brisk pace. He needed to walk to clear his head. Dr. Turner's news hit him like a ton of bricks. Could it be true? Could April really be HIV positive? She hasn't had sex with anyone but me. I know she's been a loving and faithful wife. I've betrayed her! I've been betraying her for years. If April's HIV positive, then I must be positive as well. Could this be happening to us? I'll never forgive myself, if April is HIV positive because of me. We have two children to raise. What will become of them? I want to live to raise my children. I want to see them graduate from school. I want to teach my son to be a man. I want to walk my daughter down the aisle at her wedding. I want to see my grandchildren. I want to live! I want April to live! Tears ran down his face as he picked up his pace and began to run. He ran past the mini mall and the park. God please don't let it be true!

April sat in the bed looking at TV. She was unable to follow the program, because her mind kept drifting back to the meeting in Dr. Turner's office. The tests results had to be a mistake. Paul and I are a married couple. Dr. Turner has been our doctor for years and he knows how close we are. How could he possibly believe those results? He should have known right away that those results were wrong. When he said that I am HIV positive, my heart dropped to the pit of my stomach. It was scary!

"Paul, you're back early. How was your walk?" April inquired.

"It was okay, I guess I just wasn't in the mood to walk tonight," Paul answered with a defeated expression.

"Why, what's wrong Honey?"

"I'm still worried about what Dr. Turner said today," Paul answered.

"Why are you worried? I'm not," she lied. "It has to be wrong, it's that simple," April reassured him.

"I just couldn't take it, if it were true; that's all," Paul said in a frightened manner.

"It couldn't possibly be true," April said.

"I have to tell you something, but I want you to know that I love you more than any other person in this world," Paul stated sadly.

"What are you talking about Paul? What do you have to tell me?" she questioned him anxiously.

"I've been unfaithful to you. I'm sorry, I'm very, very sorry!"

"You what! With whom?"

"Not with a woman."

"Who is it?" April asked in shock.

"It's….it's, I've been having sex with men," he confessed.

"With men! I thought you were no longer interested in men. I thought that was a one time thing in college. You lied to me!" April shouted at Paul as she began to cry.

"No, I didn't lie to you." He said as he tried to hug April. She pushed his hands off of her as she looked him in the face. He lowered his head as he said, "At the time it was true; I fell in love with you and I didn't need anyone else. I love you! I started having attractions towards men several years ago." He continued. "I didn't know what to do, I was confused." He sat on the side of the bed with tears running down his cheeks.

"Oh, so you started sleeping with men behind my back? Paul, how could you deceive me? How could you jeopardize our marriage, our children, our lives?" April cried.

"I'm sorry, I've never had sex with another woman; you're the only woman I've ever loved or made love to." He sat on the side of the bed trying to appeal to April. "I discovered that I am bisexual. I didn't want to start a relationship with a man; I felt it would take away from our marriage, so I started Living on the Down Low. I had casual sex with men like myself; men that had relationships that they wanted to protect. I always used condoms! I thought it was safe. I never dreamed it could put our health at risk," he confessed.

"I can't believe you betrayed me! I thought we were best friends, I trusted you," April cried.

"I know April, I've lived with the guilt of my infidelity. I even convinced myself that because I was having sex with men, it wasn't so bad."

"Paul, infidelity is infidelity, whether it's with a man or a woman. It's the same thing, and today the dangers are the same," April retaliated.

"I know April," he said as he dropped his head into his hands and sobbed.

"This can't be happening to us. Does this mean that you think I am HIV positive? Is that the reason you are telling me this now?" April asked with fear.

"I don't know; I pray to God it's not true, but there is a possibility that it could be true. I could have it as well," he said as he threw his arms around April and cried on her shoulder.

April sat there on the bed in shock. She couldn't believe Paul's revelation. It's surreal! This isn't happening to me, to my family, April thought.

"What are we going to do April? What are we going to do?" Paul sobbed.

April was speechless….. "We'll have to wait for the test results and pray to God that your behavior hasn't brought this wrath upon our family," she responded with disgust.

April called out sick from her job as a counselor. How could I go to work and listen to the problems of others when my life is falling apart? I'm glad Paul went to work, because I don't want to look at him right now. He cried himself to sleep last night. This morning he made breakfast and took the kids to school. I refused to get out of this bed or leave this room. Paul has broken my heart. I can't believe he put me in jeopardy, for that matter, put himself in jeopardy; and what about Ashley and Anthony? What is to become of my poor children?

April and Paul sat stoically in Dr. Turner's office. He looked very alarmed. He shuffled the papers on his desk several times. He left the room and returned, avoiding eye contact with them. He sat at his desk with his fingers intertwined looking at his hands. Finally he spoke, "Paul your tests revealed that you are a carrier of the Aids virus." He paused to compose himself before continuing," April your tests show that you are HIV positive; you have the Aids virus.

April and Paul both began to cry. Dr. Turner continued, "Before we get ahead of ourselves, I would like to explain what these results mean. Both of you have been exposed to someone with the Aids virus. It is very contagious. It is passed on through the bodily fluids of an infected person. Paul, you have the virus in your body and you are a carrier. You don't have the disease yet, but you can develop it and you can pass it on to others. April, you have been exposed to someone with the HIV virus, and you can develop full blown Aids. At this point, we don't have a cure for Aids, however, there is a great deal of research taking place as we speak; and a cure could be found at any time. Please try to remain hopeful. I don't know which of you infected the other; only the two of you would know that. I'd like to suggest that you try to be supportive of each other. You've had a good marriage for all of these years, and you'll need each other more now than ever before. Remember, a cure could be found tomorrow."

"I am the one that strayed outside of my marriage. April is a loving and faithful wife. I should be the one with the Aids virus. April doesn't deserve this! She's the most caring considerate and loyal person I know. I'm not important, April is the important person here; what can be done to help her?" Paul asked.

"I can give you some information that I have, and you can secure the most current information from the internet. There are some experimental drugs being used today in an effort to prevent patients from developing full blown Aids. I've prepared this folder of information for you. Take it home and read it and discuss it among yourselves. Come back to me and we'll plan a course of action. I like for my patients to be well informed of their options."

April recalled saying thank you, and leaving Dr. Turner's office. She was in shock, and she didn't have anything to say on her way home. Paul kept pulling the car over to cry, saying he was blinded by his tears. He kept repeating, "I'm so sorry April, I'm so sorry!"

Paul read all of the literature that the doctor gave them. He went on the internet and downloaded information. He felt helpless. He couldn't undo the harm he'd caused his wife. Paul worked all day, came home and cooked dinner, washed the dishes, washed the clothes and helped the children with their homework. He missed his wife; he missed his best friend.

April wasn't herself. She felt her life was out of control. She had no future. She thought she was going to die. She felt depressed, and she found it difficult to get out of bed. April had fits of crying and she lost her appetite; refusing to eat most of the time. She lost ten pounds in a short period of time. She was heartbroken, she was scared! She had a difficult time looking at Paul, she couldn't believe his betrayal. April loved Paul, but it pained her to look at him and realize that she didn't know him at all. When she looked at her poor children, her eyes filled with tears, poor Ashley and poor Anthony she thought.

Paul was concerned about April's mental status He'd never seen her in this state. Many days he came home from work to find her still in the bed, unwashed. He tried to talk to his wife, to encourage her to try to have hope. She ignored him and wouldn't respond. Paul called Lori. "Hi Lori, April is sick and she needs your help. Please come over and talk to her; she's depressed. Thanks."

Paul opened the door for Lori on his way out to take the children to the movies. He wanted to give Lori and April some time alone. "Please help her Lori," he said with tears in his eyes. Lori was puzzled by his demeanor. What's going on here, she thought. She went up the steps of her sister's home to her bedroom. When she opened the door, she saw April sitting up in bed looking terrible. Her hair was uncombed, she'd lost weight and she smelled as if she needed a shower.

"Hi Sweetheart, how are you feeling today?" Lori asked with concern. "You're not looking very well. Do you want to tell me about it? Talk to me Baby, I'm here for you."

"Oh Lori, I'm so glad to see you. I don't know what I'm going to do. I'm so glad that you came!" April said with a surprised expression on her face.

"Of course I came, I'm here for you. Why didn't you call me if you were this sick? Let's get you out of bed and into the shower, you'll feel better." Lori pulled the covers back and grabbed April's arms to help her out of bed. "Come on; let's get you out of that bed." She took her sister to the bathroom and put her in the shower. She changed the sheets while April was in the shower, and raised the windows to allow some fresh air to circulate around the room. Lori gave April a set of clean pajamas to put on, and she combed her hair. She fluffed the pillows and sat April up in the bed. Lori went down to the kitchen and cooked April some eggs, grits, toast and tea. She brought the tray up to the bedroom and encouraged her sister to eat. They sat propped on pillows watching TV, laughing and talking. April ate most of her food, and Lori removed the tray, asking

April, "Now, doesn't that feel better?" She returned to the bedroom to have a heart to heart talk with her little sister. Although April acted like the older sister most of the times; every now and then, Lori had an opportunity to be the big sister.

"Okay little sister; let's talk about what's going on here."

"Did Paul talk to you?" April asked.

"No, he didn't, does this have something to do with him? What is it?" Lori asked.

"You know that I've been sick for some time now with swollen glands and upper respiratory infections, right?"

"Yes, I know."

"You know the doctor ran tests to find out why I kept getting sick."

"Yes, I know."

"Well, I got the results from the tests back."

"And...and, what?" Lori asked impatiently.

"The tests showed...." April stops in mid sentence and buries her face in the pillow and cries uncontrollably. Lori pats her on the back with a puzzled expression on her face.

"Get it out, cry as much as you need to," Lori says. She is perplexed. She can't imagine what could be so upsetting, but she knows it's not going to be good news.

April sits up and wipes her eyes and face with the tissues on the bed. "Lori, the tests say that I'm HIV positive." She stares at Lori to watch her reaction.

Lori's expression is one of shock and horror. "How can you be HIV positive, how is that possible? It has to be a mistake."

"Paul is bisexual…. He's been having casual sex with a number of men; obviously one of them was HIV positive. He gave it to Paul and Paul gave it to me."

Lori felt sick, she wanted to vomit. Thoughts raced through her mind; Paul bisexual, April HIV positive, Paul HIV. Paul cheating on April with men? It was a lot to absorb at once. April, April, April, I must remain calm for April. No wonder she's depressed, she thought to herself.

"The doctor said you're HIV positive? Is that what he said?" Lori inquired with tears in her eyes.

"Yes, that's what Dr. Turner said."

"What about Paul? Is he HIV positive as well?"

"Paul is a carrier, he can pass it on to others, but he hasn't developed the disease yet; he doesn't have any symptoms."

"He gave it to you, but he doesn't have it; now isn't that a kick in the behind?" Lori said with contempt.

"I feel the same way," April lamented.

"How is Paul taking the news?"

"He feels terrible, but it's too little too late! I don't even want to look at him," April confessed.

"I can understand that, and I don't blame you! I still can't believe Paul cheated on you! He pretended to love you so much; you two were inseparable. I just don't believe it!"

"It breaks my heart to know that he cheated on me. I don't care if it was a woman or a man; he was still unfaithful."

"I always thought Paul was the perfect husband, the perfect man. I wanted a husband just like him," Lori said in disbelief.

"I guess this shows that no one is perfect, not even Paul. I always thanked God for sending Paul to me. He was such a good husband, father and friend. I trusted him completely. Maybe I expected too much," April said softly.

"I can't believe that Paul is bisexual. I've heard of Black men that consider themselves heterosexual, but have sex with other men! They call it Living on the Down Low. Did you know he was attracted to men?"

"I knew in college, he had a short relationship with a guy, but that was over before we started dating," April admitted.

"Really, so you aren't totally shocked about his bisexuality, you're hurt by his betrayal?"

"Yes, I guess that's it. I'm hurt by his betrayal and the HIV he has given me!"

"I'm hurt too; I loved him like a brother. I've always been grateful that he was such a good mate to you." Lori said.

"Yes, he has been that. We did everything together. He always cooked, washed clothes, cleaned the house, bathed the kids; we did it all together," April said, "He was acting!"

"I just never would think that he is bisexual. It seems so unfair for you to be HIV positive; you weren't unfaithful, he was."

"I know, but what can I do; I'll get Aids and die!"

"Don't say that! They have new drugs that they are experimenting with on patients. I've heard of people being HIV positive for ten, twenty years. Look at that basketball star, he's been HIV positive for years and he doesn't have Aids. He and his wife even had a baby that doesn't have the virus," Lori encouraged April.

"That's true, that's true," April admitted. "Lori promise me that if something happens to me, you'll take care of my children. If I get too sick to care for them or if I die, you'll raise Ashley and Anthony; you'll be their mother. Promise me!" April pleaded.

"I promise, I'll raise them, but I don't think I'll have to do that; I think you'll be here to raise them yourself."

"Do you really think so?"

"Yes, I know you will."

"Really, do you really believe that Lori?" April asked her sister, grasping for hope.

"Yes, I believe it, I wouldn't say it if I didn't believe it," Lori reassured April.

"Thank you Lori, I love you!"

"I love you too!" Lori said as the tears ran down her cheeks.

"Now, you get up out of that bed, you're not going to die; Get up and live April! We have to fight this thing. We have to fight for Ashley, and Anthony, who will need their Mommy; and for my baby, who will need her aunty!" Lori teased. Lori helped April out of bed and into a sweatsuit. They went downstairs to the kitchen, and sat eating cookies and drinking tea.

"Lori, I want Paul out of this house."

"Are you sure? If Paul leaves, who is going to help you to take care of the children and the house?" Lori asked April.

"I don't know, but we'll make it some how," April responded.

"But you need as much normalcy as possible for the children," Lori reasoned.

"He doesn't deserve to enjoy these children, to have them loving and admiring him as if he were worthy. No. I want him out of here. I won't allow him to sit around here watching me fight for my life," April said with rage in her tone.

"I don't blame you! You want him out of here, then, I'll get him out," Lori the protector said. "We'll take care of you. He has money, let him hire a housekeeper."

Paul returned home from the movies with the children. April and Lori were still drinking tea in the kitchen. The children ran to their mother to tell her about the movie they saw. Paul greeted them and went into the family room. He was relieved to see April up and dressed. Lori left April and the children and followed Paul into the family room. She shut the door.

"Paul, why didn't you tell me why April is depressed?" Lori asked him. Paul looked down at the floor. He felt too embarrassed to look Lori in the face.

"I didn't know what to say," Paul responded.

"How about telling the truth," Lori dared him.

"I was too ashamed to tell you," he confessed.

"You should be ashamed, do you realize what you've done?" she shouted while pointing her finger in his face.

"Yes, yes, I do, but I can't undo it. I wish I could, but I can't. I would give my life, if I could undo it" Paul said tearfully.

"If that were true, you would have killed yourself before screwing those men and then coming home and having sex with my sister."

"It's the truth whether you believe me or not."

"I don't believe you for one second. If that were true, we wouldn't be having this conversation. You don't love anyone but yourself. You've been lying and deceiving all of us; pretending to be a model husband, while Living on the Down Low. Isn't that what you call it?" she asked sarcastically. " No wonder your father and brother don't want anything to do with you."

"I deserve that," he said looking hurt.

"April wants you to move out of this house to-day!"

"But, who will take care of her and the children? They need me," Paul protested.

"I think you've done enough damage to April and these children, don't you? You can afford to hire a housekeeper to care for them. April doesn't want you here, so get out!"

I want to help April, I want to care for her," Paul cried.

"I don't believe a word of what you're saying Paul. You obviously are a greedy man, trying to satisfy all of your varied sexual needs, but you lacked the fore-sight to see you were headed for a collision course; with your wife and children paying the price for your self-ishness," Lori scolded him.

"You're right Lori; I can't deny anything you've said. I was Living on the Down Low, and I thought no one would get hurt. I thought I was protecting my wife and children by having casual relationships and using condoms. I guess nothing is one hundred percent," Paul said acknowledging his guilt.

"You've learned the hard way. I just hope it doesn't cost you and April your lives. I hope your children aren't orphaned by your desire to have sex with everyone and anyone, because you were Living on the Down Low, or were you just being Low Down?" Lori said in anger.

"I deserve that, but I do love my wife more than life, and I love my children as well. I just don't know what to do," Paul said helplessly.

"April wants you to leave, now!" Lori shouted in his face.

"It just hurts so much when she doesn't look at me. I love her so much! I miss our love, I miss our trust!"

"Well Paul, you betrayed her trust; the more trust you have for a person, the more it hurts when they betray you! I know this from experience, I felt betrayed by Wayne when he impregnated that women! I've felt that pain. It takes time to realize that we are all imperfect," Lori stated.

"I know you're right Lori. I'll wait for her forgiveness. I'll wait forever, if necessary," Paul pledged. I'll go and pack my bags and I'll hire a housekeeper, but I'm going to come by to check on April and my children," Paul pledged as he left the room with tears streaming down his face.

Paul loved April and his children and he knew that he had to respect her feelings and give her some space. She had every right to hate him, but he wouldn't abandon her, no matter what she said. He knew that if she became sick, she would need him, and he would be there for her and their children. He thought he had the best of both worlds, he didn't realize that he was destroying them both. The false sense of security that he felt, because he was using condoms, had faded away. All he felt now, was dread and remorse!

Lori lay in bed trying to go to sleep. She kept thinking about April being HIV positive, and what that could mean. I can't imagine life without April. She could die from Aids. It's unbelievable that Paul is bisexual and he's been cheating on April with strange men. He was always my ideal man; be careful of what you wish for. I can't believe how rotten these men are today. Paul gives April Aids and Wayne gets another woman pregnant; we didn't stand a chance against those two. No wonder April was depressed, he's lucky she didn't kill him! She thought she had a good marriage, and her husband is out in the street banging men. She's very hurt and scared, but she'll have to overcome her pain to fight for her life. She'll have to work at staying healthy, so she can continue to raise her children. How can we tell Mom and Dad that their youngest child has a deadly disease? They think she has developed allergies; we'll have to let them continue to believe that for as long as possible. They deserve to enjoy their lives; they've worked hard for this retirement.

I'm going to have to tell them about this pregnancy sooner or later; you can only hide a pregnancy for so long. They aren't going to like it one bit, but I am a grown woman, and I'll take full responsibility for my child. I'm three months pregnant now and I hope I can hide it from them until they go to Florida. I don't want them changing their plans for me. If April or I need them, they can always come back. I've been wearing those pants with the elastic waists, and my shirts hanging out, and no one seems to have noticed it so far.

I'm not going to be able to wear the bridesmaid's dress for Marie's wedding. I feel bad about that, because she was in my wedding, but she'll understand, we've been friends since grade school. I'll buy a loose dress with her wedding colors and help out at the wedding any way I can. Maybe her younger sister can take my place, she thought.

I wonder where this baby's sorry father is, probably telling some other woman the same lies he told me. I'd better try to get some sleep. She got out of bed and went to the kitchen and heated a cup of milk. She tried to keep her mind from racing. She took several deep breaths and let them out slowly. Lori went back to bed to try to sleep again. She now knew that she not only would have her baby to raise alone, but she might have Ashley and Anthony to raise too, she thought as she tossed and turned.

Leeanna and Frank sat at the table eating dinner. "These shrimps are delicious. Can I have some more of everything?" Frank asked.

"Sure Frank." Lee left her half eaten food to re-fill Frank's plate.

"Thanks Baby." He continued to eat his second helping of food.

"You're welcome Frank," Lee replied. "Our house sold really fast, didn't it.?"

"It certainly did. The second couple that viewed the house bought it, that's luck. I've heard of people trying to sell their houses for as long as a year," Frank said.

"That's not luck Frank; we have a lovely house in good condition. They were smart enough to realize that. They know a good buy when they see one," Lee explained.

"You're right; we've put a lot of money and time into this house over the years."

"We sure did, and we offered it for a good price too. In fact, I began to feel like we could have gotten more money for it," Lee revealed.

"I thought the same thing; I'll bet we could have gotten ten or fifteen thousand dollars more, if we'd asked for it."

"Maybe so; but now we'll never know," she laughed. "I made the reservations for our trip to Florida for next week, so we can go down there and get started on finding a house. I'd like to find something with three bedrooms, so we'll have room for the girls and the grands when they come to visit," Lee said as she cleared the table. Frank sat at the table drinking a glass of wine and talking to Lee while she washed the dishes.

"That would be great, and then they can come down for holidays, so we won't have to come up here in the cold weather."

"They'll come; it will be a little vacation for them. Then you can take the grands fishing," Lee reminded Frank.

"Yes, I can't wait," Frank replied excitedly. "Maybe we can rent out the house in Florida for the six months we're in Philly."

"That's a good idea, let's look into that. Where are we going to live while we're here?"

"I would like to buy a duplex, so that someone would be on the property while we're away," Frank stated.

"That sounds good Frank. I saw a duplex in Chestnut Hill yesterday," Lee said.

"Really, that's a good area. Let's ride up there in the morning and look at it. We would have had a house if that deal hadn't fell through," Frank reminded Lee.

"Maybe it was for the best. That was a single family home and now we're looking at a duplex. I think a duplex is a better idea."

"So do I; let's check it out tomorrow," Frank confirmed.

"Okay, maybe Lori will consider living in the duplex; she could rent the second apartment. That way, she could keep an eye out on the apartment while we're away," Lee suggested.

"That's true, but let's find the duplex first; then we can worry about who's going to live in it. Did you tell the girls about Florida?"

"Yes, both of them are quite excited for us. They thought it was a great idea." Lee responded . Frank smiled with satisfaction. "I'll miss them though," Lee said.

"You know, they're not children anymore, they can take care of themselves. They'll come to visit and they'll call. We've raised them well, they're educated, intelligent women, and they can take care of themselves!"

"You're right; they have each other to depend upon when we aren't here. This is our time to enjoy life and I'm looking forward to it," Lee stated as she tried to convince herself.

"So am I." Frank agreed as he settled into his recliner for the evening. Lee followed Frank into the livingroom and sat down on the sofa.

"Aren't you going to miss our home Frank?"

"Yes, of course I'm going to miss it. This house holds many memories for me. We've been here over thirty years. Why, are you having second thoughts?" Frank asked as he watched her to see her reaction.

"No, it's too late for that, anyway the house is sold. I just know that I'm going to miss it. This house is a part of me, a part of this family. We were young when we came here," Lee reminisced.

"Yes, we were young, and we did what young people do. We raised our children, went into debt, made mistakes and had some small triumphs; all while we were in this house," Frank said.

"You're right; we've lived in this house for over thirty years, it's time to get a house that is suited for us now. It's time to start living for ourselves," she reminded herself.

"What's the alternative, sitting around waiting for our children to call or visit, while we sit here bored, driving each other crazy? No, I think Florida will be an adventure for us. We'll meet new people like ourselves; we'll see new places and do new things. Life will be interesting and exciting. We'll have things to look forward to."

"And we'll grow and change with our experiences. When we come back to Philly it will be spring. The children will be glad to see us and we'll be glad to see them," Lee agreed.

"Sure, and they can visit us when we aren't busy," Frank laughed.

"You can say that again," Lee added.

Lori sat at a table in the reception hall. The wedding was beautiful, she thought. The bride was radiant and she had the most beautiful flowers she'd ever seen. It took Marie forever to find a husband, but it finally happened for her. Blue, yellow and white were a pretty combination of colors for the wedding. The men wore navy tuxes and the bridesmaids wore yellow and blue. Marie asked Lori to be a bridesmaid and she accepted. She had a dress made several months in advance, but now she was pregnant; the fitted waist of the dress no longer fit. Lori told Marie that someone else could wear the dress and she would buy the matching shoes for them. Marie was understanding and she asked her sister to take Lori's place in the wedding. Marie's family was pleased that her sister was in the wedding. Lori bought a loose blue and yellow dress and passed out the programs.

Lori remained at the table waiting for the bridal party to return from taking pictures. She felt a little melancholy as she thought about her own wedding. She was surprised to hear his voice.

"Hi Lori, long time no see."

"Wayne, what are you doing here?" Lori asked. Her voice betrayed her surprise at seeing him.

"The same thing you're doing here; I was invited!" Wayne replied with a big smile on his face. This was the first time he'd seen Lori in months. He was glad he'd decided to come alone.

"You look good, I guess that means you're taking care of yourself," she said trying to mask her nervousness.

"I'm trying, you look good too; as beautiful as ever. Looks like you've put on a little weight, but it looks good on you," Wayne complimented her.

"Thanks Wayne, I'm pregnant," she blurted out. She didn't mean to tell him like that, but she spoke before she thought.

"Really," Wayne said in a disappointed tone. "Congratulations, I'm assuming you're happy about it."

"Yes, I am; I'm not getting any younger, and that old biological clock is ticking," Lori laughed to lighten the mood.

"You haven't aged a day. Do you mind if I join you at this table?"

"No, help yourself."

"Do you plan on marrying the baby's father, or are you living with him?" he asked cautiously.

"No, I'm not living with him and I'm not planning on marrying him; I'm still legally married to you," she laughed.

"Oh."

"So, what did you have a girl or a boy?"

"I don't have any children."

"Did Shelly lose the baby?" Lori inquired.

"Yes, Shelly had a cute little girl, but the baby wasn't mine," Wayne revealed proudly.

"Come on Wayne, don't start that again," Lori laughed. "We're separated, you can tell the truth."

"No, really; I had a DNA test performed on that baby, and the results show that I am not the father of Shelly's baby!"

"Really!"

"Yes, I knew that baby wasn't mine; she was sleeping with three other guys, so I guess one of them is the father."

"I'm sorry to hear that, I know how much you wanted to be a father," Lori said with a pang of guilt.

"That's true, but I didn't want to be the father of Shelly's baby, I wanted to be our baby's father," Wayne said sadly. "I guess it just wasn't meant to be...Enough of that, it's history. Can I get you something to eat or drink?" Wayne asked her.

"That would be nice Wayne." Her heart raced as she watched him walk away from the table. Wayne looks good. I can't believe that slut blamed that baby on him, knowing that he wasn't the father, or at least that he might not be the father. She calls my house harassing me, so I would put him out. I guess she thought he would move in with her. Wayne wasn't a fool, he moved in with his mother. I guess when the DNA test proved he wasn't the father, that's when he started calling me on the phone again, but I wouldn't talk to him. It doesn't change anything, he was still sleeping with her while he was married to me, she thought.

"I hope you like what I put on your plate, and I assumed you aren't drinking alcohol since you're pregnant," Wayne said with a smile.

"Everything looks good, thanks, Wayne," They sat laughing and talking and looking at the bridal party celebrate.

"They look so happy," Lori said remembering their special day.

"Yeah, I hope they don't make the dumb mistakes that I made," Wayne said regretfully. "Would you like to dance?" he asked Lori. It was a good opportunity to hold her in his arms again, he thought.

"That would be nice," she answered while blushing. After the reception Wayne drove her home. They sat in the car and talked.

"I hope I'm not going to get shot by your boyfriend for sitting out here talking to you," Wayne said with a coy smile.

"No, you don't have to worry about that."

"How do you know? He could be in there looking out of your window at us right now," Wayne laughed.

"No one is waiting for me, I'm not seeing anyone," Lori revealed.

"What about the baby's father? Did he run out on you when he found out you were pregnant?" he asked in a concerned manner.

"No, he didn't."

"Is he still around?"

"No, we only dated for a short time; after we broke up, I found out I was pregnant. I felt like my biological clock was ticking, so I decided to keep the baby," Lori explained.

"I can understand that. Is he happy about the baby?"

"He doesn't know about the baby; we weren't together, so I saw no reason to tell him."

"Don't you think he has a right to know?"

"Maybe he does, but I decided not to tell him. I can raise this baby by myself," she asserted.

"Well, if you need anything, anything at all, just give me a call. If this is what you want, then go for it; you've always had your own mind."

"Yes, I really thought about it before reaching a decision."

"How do your parents feel about the baby?" Wayne probed. "Are they happy to have another grandchild on the way?"

"I haven't told them yet,"

"Why not?"

"You know how my parents are, they'll have a fit. I've been postponing it. How do I tell them that I'm pregnant by a man they have never met? I'll have to pick the right moment."

"I think your mother will take it a lot better than your father."

"You're right about that, but I'm a grown woman and they'll have to accept my decision."

"That's true, but your father will probably hunt that guy down for abandoning his daughter. You know, Frank don't play!" Wayne laughed. "If I can help you in any way, just let me know."

"I will Wayne, thanks a lot for understanding." Lori smiled as she walked to her apartment. It was nice seeing Wayne again, she thought.

Reggie opened the door of his house for Wayne. "Hi Wayne, you look like you're feeling pretty good today; you're smiling from ear to ear," Reggie said as he walked towards the family room.

"Reg, I saw Lori yesterday at the wedding," Wayne said excitedly.

"Oh, so that's why you're smiling?" Reggie teased.

"Yeah, I sat at the table with her, and we talked."

"That's great man, I told you to go to that wedding. Women are sentimental and weddings always bring their emotions to the surface. I knew she would talk to you!" Reggie said with a broad smile.

"She looked beautiful, but she was pregnant," Wayne said while watching Reggie for his reaction.

"Oh, who is she pregnant by?"

"She's pregnant by some guy she used to date for a short while, she said she didn't tell him, because they had already broken up by the time she found out she was pregnant."

"How pregnant is she?"

"I don't know, maybe three or four months."

"Is she seeing anyone else?"

"I don't think so, she said she isn't," Wayne replied. "I told her about Shelly and the DNA test."

"What did she say?"

"She didn't say anything, but I know she was taking it all in."

"Yeah, that Shelly broke up your marriage for nothing. She thought you would come running to her and her three kids if your wife was out of the picture."

"Never man, never; I hate that girl. I'll never forgive her for what she took me through, and what she did to my marriage," Wayne said with remorse.

"I don't blame you! You want a beer man?"

"Yeah, I'll have one. So, do you think I can get back with Lori?"

"Do you want her back? She is carrying someone else's child," Reggie asked while looking Wayne in the eye to gage his true feelings. "It takes a big man to raise another man's baby."

"Yeah, I think I could do it, especially after what I took her through. She is my wife, and I'm not even worried about this other guy. He doesn't know that she's pregnant. Lori doesn't deserve to be treated that way; she has a good heart man. You know, some of these men out here are real dogs."

"Well, if you want her back, this is the perfect opportunity. Every woman wants a father for her baby," Reggie advised.

Wayne laughed out loud, "I'll be her baby's father, if she will forgive me and take me back. I'll be glad to be her baby's daddy; no one has to know that it isn't my sperm. I want a family like yours Reggie."

"You're right, go for it little brother. What do you have to lose? She is still your wife....but what about Tammy? You two have been getting along pretty good, haven't you?"

"What about her? Tammy is a special lady, and I really do care about her, but I don't know if anything will ever come of this relationship. She's just getting over her second divorce. If I can't have Lori, then Tammy is the next best thing. We get along great and we have a lot in common. We don't argue, like I did with Lori, but then again, we've never lived together. I have a special feeling for Lori, I love her with all of my heart," Wayne said with tears in his eyes.

April opens the door of her house smiling. "Hello Lori, good to see the two of you!"

"Me and my baby are doing fine, Little Sister, How are you feeling?"

"Much better, thanks. Come on into the kitchen, I'm making some soup and a sandwich. Are you two hungry?" she laughed.

"I'll have a little soup," Lori accepted. "But first I want you to sit down with me. I have some wonderful news to tell you."

"What is it?" April asked inquisitively.

"Today on the news, I heard them say that American scientist have isolated a protein that can stop HIV from developing into full blown Aids. Isn't that wonderful news?'

"Really, you heard that today?"

"Yes, today," Lori said happily.

"That is wonderful news, but I don't know if it would help me. I think it may help the people that haven't developed any symptoms," April said pessimistically.

"Try to remain optimistic April. I know it isn't easy, but you never know what discoveries they will make next. Try to keep your mind and body healthy,"

Lori encouraged her sister. "How is the housekeeper working out?"

"She's doing a good job, but it will take the children time to adjust to her," April replied.

"Has Paul visited the children yet, I know they miss him."

"He called and asked if he could come by, but I told him that I'm not ready to see him, and I don't know when I will be ready; if ever. I told him that I would have the housekeeper bring the children to visit him."

"What did he say to that?"

"He was okay with it, he really doesn't have a choice," April answered adamantly.

"Guess who I ran into at Marie's wedding?"

"Who?"

"Wayne."

"Wayne, what was he doing there?"

"Marie invited him; I guess because she was in our wedding," Lori answered.

"So, how is he? How did it go?"

"We talked," Lori said while blushing.

"Did he notice that you're pregnant?" April inquired anxiously.

"Now you know he did, he knows every inch of this body," Lori laughed.

"So, what did he say?"

"What could he say, I don't have anything to hide, after all; we are separated. I came right out and told him I was pregnant. I didn't mean to tell him that way, but it just came out of my mouth before I realized what I was saying."

"You could have told him more gently, he is still your husband. Well, he can't say anything, because he got that girl pregnant while you two were together," April said sarcastically.

"The baby isn't his. He had a DNA test done and the baby isn't his," Lori informed her sister.

"The baby isn't his?" April asked anxiously.

"No it isn't his; he's always denied that he was the father of that baby, but I didn't believe him. He was sleeping with her."

"That shameless husband stealer lied. That's terrible. Poor Wayne bit off more than he could chew with that one," April chuckled.

"He sure did, but she had some nerve calling my house telling me all of her lies,"

"That's the way some women are, they can't stand to think you're happy,"

"Did you and Wayne get a chance to talk?" April probed. She knew Lori still loved her husband and she preferred Wayne to the men Lori had dated since their separation.

"We talked a little; he said he would call me."

"That's good; you need to clear some things up. If he asks, would you go out with him?"

"I might, but that doesn't mean anything, don't forget, I am carrying another man's child," Lori reminded April.

"That's true, but if he still loves you, than that won't matter. It's not as if Trent is still around. He doesn't even know about the baby, and I'm sure he doesn't want to know. When Wayne calls, give him a chance; I think he's learned his lesson," April suggested.

"I'll think about it," Lori laughed. She became more serious, "It takes more than love to make a marriage work. Wayne and I loved each other, and we had a good sex life, but that didn't stop him from sleeping with Shelly; and it didn't stop Paul from cheating on you. You know April, I don't know if I still believe in marriage. Mom and Dad have been married for forty years and they have struggled through every one of those years; it's not realistic, not today."

"I don't know about that Lori, I think it works for some people, you just have to have the right two people that are willing to be monogamous and committed for life, like swans!

Wayne called Lori and invited her out to dinner. They sat in the restaurant looking at the menus. They were both a little nervous. Wayne ordered the fried shrimp with fries and cold slaw and Lori ordered the same. They laughed and teased each other all during dinner. Wayne drove Lori home and she invited him inside for some herbal tea. She turned on the TV to the video channel and they sat sipping tea and watching videos; commenting on the performances and singers. The tension between them was building.

"Lori, you look very beautiful tonight. The pregnancy agrees with you."

"Thank you Wayne, you look quite handsome yourself," Lori returned the compliment.

"You know I still love you; I know I've made mistakes, but I didn't know what marriage was about."

"I don't know about this Wayne, things are more complicated now," Lori said.

"Lori, let me show you the kind of man that I can be. Let me be your baby's father and your husband again. Baby, I love you, and only you," Wayne begged.

"I don't feel that I would be enough for you, I wasn't before."

"I know that you're enough woman for me, I made a horrible mistake, and I would never stray from this marriage again. If you'll only give me another chance, I know I could make you happy, Lori please!"

"Wayne, I believe you still love me, and I still have feelings for you, but that doesn't mean that we are ready to jump back into a marriage. You cheated on me with Shelly and who knows how many other women, so you obviously weren't happy in our marriage," Lori said as she sat across from him rubbing her hands together.

"I didn't understand the commitment of marriage. Those other women didn't mean anything to me, I just didn't know how to say no," Wayne confessed.

"That may be true Wayne, but you hurt me terribly. If you really loved me, it would have been easy for you to say no to them."

"I've always loved you Lori, even when I didn't show it," Wayne said softly, as he dropped his head.

"I wasn't exactly the perfect wife myself," Lori confessed. "I wasn't ready to be the kind of wife I should have been. I'm … not ready to rush back into this marriage and I don't think you are either Wayne,"

Lori said sadly. She could see Wayne's shoulders slump as he sat on the sofa. He was silent for a while.

"Well, can we at least be friends? I failed you before and I want an opportunity to prove to you that I am a better man. I want to be there for you; you'll need someone to help you through this pregnancy," he said with pleading eyes as the sweat began to form on his forehead.

"I guess we can be friends Wayne, but I don't want to give you any false hopes. I can't promise you that I will ever want to give our marriage another try," she warned him.

A smile crossed Wayne's face. "Let's just take one step at a time. I don't want to rush you into anything you don't want. I want you to learn to trust me again at your own pace," he said with a smile. "You loved me before and I think you can love me again. I'm really not such a bad guy!" He reached for her and kissed her lightly on her lips.

"I know you're not such a bad guy Wayne," she repeated as she smiled at him.

"Your baby needs a father and I would hate to see your child grow up without a father like I did. We should at least try to make this marriage work for the child's sake!" Wayne pleaded.

"I know you're right Wayne, but do you think you could really accept another man's child as your own?" she asked him as she looked into his eyes.

"I love you and your baby is a part of you, so I know I can love your child; our child!" Wayne promised.

"You have to build trust Wayne, and I'm willing to take things slow; we can start off by dating again, and if things work out, we'll give our marriage another try," Lori compromised.

"That's all I ask, Wayne said, as he took Lori into his arms and kissed her tenderly.

Paul walked briskly towards the park. It was a pleasant star filled night, with a slight cool breeze, that relieved the humidity of the day. Paul was scantily dressed in track shorts and a tank top, because of the heat. His heart began to race as he came closer to the park. These sexual encounters still excited him, even though he was now aware of the dangers involved. He'd found an apartment in a high rise, three blocks away from the home he'd shared with his family. He enjoyed the neighborhood and he wanted to be close to April and the children. He talked to them everyday and he took the children for a few hours several days a week. He still picked them up from their activities and he took them to the library to help them with their homework when needed.

April was back to work and for the present, her health was good. Her specialist had her on medications, to try to prevent flair ups of symptoms. Gradually, her rage had diminished to a manageable anger, and she was able to talk to him on the telephone daily. She now, allowed him to come into the house, when he came to pick up Ashley and Anthony. Paul still missed the friendship and intimacies he shared with April, and he knew they were probably gone forever. He knew she was the love of his life, and he didn't know if he could ever love another woman. It quieted his guilt to continue to pay the housekeeper and the household bills.

Since their separation, he'd developed several relationships with men on the DL, like himself. On occasion, he visited the Center City DL gym to workout and socialize, but he still preferred the anonymity of the park. Paul entered the darkness of the park and sat under the light on the bench. He was alone. He relaxed, thinking about Clyde, one of his new friends. He was a high school Chemistry teacher, married with three children. He was developing a trust for Clyde's discretion, and he allowed him to visit for sex once every couple of weeks. He looked like a football player, not your typical DL man. Paul enjoyed his bulk and his aggressive lovemaking.

A stranger entered the park and slowly walked towards him. Paul's heart raced with anticipation. The tall slender man approached the bench and sat at the opposite end. Paul looked him up and down and stared into his eyes. They made a connection. They flirted silently. Paul slowly walked behind the big oak tree. The slim figure quickly followed.

AUTHOR

CARLA DIANE ELLIS, a Philadelphia, Pennsylvania area
resident and educator is the mother of two sons. A
novelist, she enjoys creative activities, music, plays and
reading.

Please contact me on my website and let me know what
you thought about the book and it's characters!
Website - Author Carla Diane Ellis . Com

CARLA DIANE ELLIS BRINGS A REFRESHING
TONE TO THE VOICE OF FICTION! LOOK
FOR HER NEW NOVEL
"IT'S TIME TO LET YOU GO" TO BE
RELEASED IN 2005.